MISSING ME

GIRL, MISSING

Winner Richard and Judy Best Kids' Books 2007 12+
Winner of the Red House Children's Book Award 2007 12+
Winner of the Manchester Children's Book Award 2008
Winner of the Bolton Children's Book Award 2007
Winner of the Grampian Children's Book Award 2008
Winner of the John Lewis Solihull Book Award 2008
Winner of the Lewisham Children's Book Award
Winner of the 2008 Sakura Medal

SIX STEPS TO A GIRL

Winner of the Manchester Children's Book Award 2009

BLOOD TIES

Overall winner of the Red House Children's Book Award 2009
Winner of the Leeds Book Award 2009 age 11–14 category
Winner of the Spellbinding Award 2009
Winner of the Lancashire Children's Book Award 2009
Winner of the Portsmouth Book Award 2009 (Longer Novel section)
Winner of the Staffordshire Children's Book Award 2009
Winner of the Southern Schools Book Award 2010
Winner of the RED Book Award 2010
Winner of the Warwickshire Secondary Book Award 2010
Winner of the Grampian Children's Book Award 2010
Winner of the North East Teenage Book Award 2010

THE MEDUSA PROJECT: THE SET-UP

Winner of the North East Book Award 2010
Winner of the Portsmouth Book Award 2010
Winner of the Yorkshire Coast Book Award 2010

SOPHIE McKENZIE
MISSING ME

SIMON AND SCHUSTER

ACKNOWLEDGEMENTS:
With thanks to Moira Young, Melanie Edge,
Julie Mackenzie, Gaby Halberstam,
Lou Kuenzler and Lily Kuenzler.

First published in Great Britain in 2012 by Simon
and Schuster UK Ltd, a CBS company

Simon & Schuster UK Ltd
1st Floor, 222 Gray's Inn Road, London WC1X 8HB

www.simonandschuster.co.uk

Simon & Schuster Australia, Sydney

Simon & Schuster India, New Delhi

This book is a work of fiction. Names, characters, places and
incidents are either the product of the author's imagination or
are used fictitiously. Any resemblance to actual people living
or dead, events or locales is entirely coincidental.

A CIP catalogue record for this book is available from the British Library.

HB ISBN: 978-0-85707-726-4
TPB ISBN: 978-0-85707-727-1
E-BOOK ISBN: 978-0-85707-729-5

1 3 5 7 9 10 8 6 4 2

Typeset by Hewer Text UK Ltd, Edinburgh
Printed and bound in Great Britain
by CPI Group (UK) Ltd, Croydon, CR0 4YY

For Elizabeth Hawkins

1

The Announcement

School was finished for the summer holidays. I was free – and on my way to see my sister, Lauren. She had just got back to London after four months away, working in Paris with her law firm. I'd wanted to visit her while she'd been abroad – her boyfriend, Jam, went most weekends – but our mum, Annie, wouldn't let me go. She worries about me . . . about us . . .

I reached Lauren and Jam's flat. As I rang the doorbell, I gazed at my reflection in the brass door-plate. My hair was long, with a thick fringe closely framing my eyes on either side of my face. I liked it that way, though Annie was always nagging me to get it cut.

The door opened. Jam stood there. He and Lauren have been together since I was six so he's like a big brother to me.

'Hey, Mo,' he said with a huge grin. 'How are you?'

'Hi.' I smiled back. 'Good, thanks.' I kept smiling, wishing I could think of something interesting to say to him. I don't know why, because my head's full of stuff that I've seen or heard or been thinking about and I actually feel quite relaxed around Jam. It's just so hard to get the right words out. I mean, I love writing – my biggest dream is to be a journalist – but talking to people can be really hard.

'Lauren's in the bedroom.' Jam was still grinning from ear to ear. 'She'll be down in a sec.'

I wandered into the living room. There was a photo of Dad on the mantelpiece. He died just before I was eight and I'm now fifteen. I used to be able to remember him clearly but now those memories are fading. I'm not sure anymore if the images I see in my mind actually happened, or whether I've just been told about them or imagined them from pictures. Either way, my memories are blurry, just snatches of moments like being on Dad's boat back in America or walking to school holding his hand. When I imagine Dad's face he's always smiling, like in this photo. But I know that can't be the whole truth – nobody smiles all the time.

'Mo?'

I turned round. Lauren was standing near the door, her lower half hidden by the couch. She was smiling, but not a big grin like Jam. More an excited smile, like there was something she couldn't wait to tell me.

I stared at her. Something was different. Something to do with her skin. Lauren's really pretty with bright blue eyes that light up her whole face and she's got long dark hair like me, though hers tumbles down her back in shiny waves while mine is greasy and lank. All that was the same. I frowned. *So what was different?* Was it just that the blue of her top really brought out the colour of her eyes? No, it was much more than that – like she was glowing from the inside.

And then Lauren stepped out from behind the couch and I saw exactly why she looked different. I stared at her belly. It was high and round and big.

2

'You're *pregnant*!' My mouth fell open.

Jam appeared in the doorway. He laughed. So did Lauren. I was still staring at her stomach. In the blue tunic she was wearing it stuck out over her slim legs. I didn't know much about babies but Lauren looked like this one was about to pop out of her.

Still laughing, Lauren held out her arms and I went over and gave her a hug. Her belly felt taut and firm between us.

'I'm thirty-six weeks gone,' she said. 'The baby's due at the end of August.'

Thirty-six weeks? That was, like, nearly eight months . . . which meant Lauren must have been pregnant before she went to Paris . . . pregnant when she said goodbye to me four months ago. I pulled away from her.

'Why didn't you say anything before?' As soon as the words blurted out of me, I wished them back. It wasn't just what I'd said, it was the whiny, angry tone.

Too heavy, Madison.

The smile on Lauren's face faded slightly.

'I couldn't face telling Mum or Annie back then,' she said.

I nodded. I could understand that. Lauren had been adopted as a toddler and brought up away from us – she has two mums and not an easy relationship with either of them. That's one of the reasons we're so close. I could see why Lauren hadn't spoken to her adoptive mother or Annie about being pregnant. They could both be pretty overbearing in their own way. But why hadn't she told me?

Lauren obviously saw the question in my eyes.

3

'As I wasn't telling the others, I didn't want you to have to keep such a big secret,' she said.

'Right.' I couldn't take it all in. My big sister was going to have a baby. Which meant I was going to be an *aunt*. And Lauren and Jam were going to be parents. I glanced over at Jam. He was still beaming that huge smile.

'Isn't it amazing?' he said, putting his arm round Lauren. Then a frown flickered over his forehead. 'Aren't you pleased for us, Mo?'

I gulped again. Apart from Lauren, Jam's the only person I let call me Mo. I'd always taken for granted just how special our three-way relationship was. And now, I realised with a jolt, someone else was going to get right in the way of it.

I stood, awkwardly, chewing on my lip. Lauren was more than a sister to me. When Annie got all anxious and overprotective, Lauren was always there for me, sympathising, with Jam in the background, dependable and funny. Were they going to love this baby more than me? The answer came to me like a slap in the face. Of course they were going to love it more than me. It would be tiny and cute and . . .

'Course I'm pleased.' I forced a smile onto my face. 'D'you know if it's a boy or a girl yet?'

'No,' Jam said. 'We didn't want to know.'

Lauren reached for my hand. 'But you're the first person we've told in either of our families. And . . . and when it's born, we want you to be godmother, Mo.'

'Oh.' I was holding the smile on my face like a mask, but inside I felt like crying. I was being super-selfish, I knew, but

4

I couldn't help it. I'd always been so special to Lauren. And now that was going to change forever. 'OK, sure. I mean, I don't know if I'll be any good as a godmother, but I'll try.'

I could hear how flat and dull my voice sounded and I hated myself for not being more convincingly cheerful. Lauren was staring at me like she knew something was wrong. Knowing Lauren, she was about to ask what it was. But just in the nick of time, the doorbell rang.

2

Discovery

Jam, who was closest to the front door, disappeared along the hallway. We could hear him opening the door, then a familiar voice.

'Darling.' It was Carla, Jam's highly eccentric mother.

'She's early.' Lauren rolled her eyes. 'I'm not telling her before Mum and Annie get here.'

I stared at her, shocked. I'd had no idea she'd invited all the adults over. But Lauren didn't notice. She was too busy disappearing into the kitchen.

Carla swept into the living room. She was dressed in some sort of multicoloured poncho with a long silk scarf wound round her head. A few grey hairs peeked out from under the scarf.

'Madison, darling.' Carla rushed over and air-kissed me.

'Hi,' I said, feeling awkward.

'Where's Lauren?'

'In . . . er, in the bathroom I think.' I looked around at Jam who was hovering in the doorway.

'I'll go and see,' he said, clearly relieved to get away from his mother.

I sat down on the sofa beside Carla who proceeded to tell me that my aura was looking peaky. I let her talk. I was feeling awful. Lauren had sensed I wasn't thrilled about her having a baby. And not being thrilled was just about the meanest thing a sister could be.

Ten long minutes passed during which Carla talked at me non-stop. Then Jam reappeared and she started asking him about his job and whether he was eating healthily. There was no sign of Lauren. At last the doorbell went again and Jam let in Annie. I stood up as she drifted into the room.

'Hi, Annie,' I said.

Annie's eyes filled with tears as she looked at me. I wasn't sure if it was my calling her by her name instead of 'Mum' that was upsetting her, or whether she was remembering the argument we'd had this morning, over tidying my room. We used to get on really well, but recently she'd become totally annoying, always pushing for information on what I'd been doing and who I'd been seeing. Not letting me be.

I started calling her Annie about six months ago. It's mostly like a great big hint to her to treat me like a grown up, though it's also a bit because Lauren does it. You see, although Annie is Lauren's birth mother, Lauren had been calling her adoptive parents 'Mum and Dad' for years before she was reunited with us, her original family.

'Hi, Madison sweetie,' Annie said, her hands fluttering nervously to her face. 'You're here . . . we could have come together, if you'd wanted.'

I looked down at my shoes.

'Where's Lauren?' That was Lydia, Lauren's adoptive mum. She must have arrived without me hearing the bell.

7

Lydia is a lot older than Annie, with a sharp, pointy face and severe grey eyes. I used to be a bit scared of her, but now I like her. At least she doesn't treat me like a baby.

Lydia, Carla and Annie started chatting about what was going on. They clearly had no idea why Lauren had asked them all here together. I don't think they really get on with each other, but they were all making an effort. And then Lauren appeared in the doorway. I saw her first. She gave me a wink, then cleared her throat.

The mums looked up together. Annie gasped. Lydia jumped to her feet.

'What on earth?' Lydia said. Her face was drained of colour.

'I'm having a baby, Mum,' Lauren said defiantly.

And then pandemonium broke out. Everyone seemed to be talking at once.

'Why didn't you tell me?' That was Annie, bursting into tears. 'Oh, sweetie, you're twenty-three, that's *so* young to be doing this.'

'How far gone *are* you?' Lydia demanded. 'What do the doctors say?'

'I have a wonderful arrowroot and blackberry infusion. You should try it – it's a marvellous antenatal drink,' Carla interjected.

Somehow Lauren was managing to answer them all, but the questions kept flying.

'How are you going to manage? Oh, sweetie, having a baby is so challenging.'

'What about your job? Are you going back to it afterwards?'

'Yoga is the best antenatal exercise you could take. And I have some excellent meditation tapes if you'd like them?'

'Enough.' Jam's voice rang out from the doorway. 'That's enough with all the questions.'

Everyone stopped speaking. Jam marched up to Lauren and put his arm round her shoulders. 'I know we're young,' he said, looking round at the women. 'But people a lot younger than us have had babies. We're going to manage fine. We're both going to carry on working and we're both going to look after the baby. My hours as a teacher will fit in really well. Everything's going to be *fine.*'

'Of course, Jam.' Lydia smiled at him. 'Of course, it's wonderful news.'

They all started hugging, then Lauren called her adoptive dad, who was away on business. I glanced at Annie. She was still crying, dabbing at her eyes with a tissue. I slipped outside, saying I needed the loo. I stayed in the bathroom for longer than I meant. I still felt really upset about the baby . . . and really mean to be feeling so upset. At last I took a few deep breaths, came out of the bathroom and went back downstairs. As I neared the living room, I could hear Lauren speaking.

'Yes,' she was saying. 'Everything's fine. I'm swimming every day, I've got the Chelsey Barton pregnancy book, which is *amazing*, and—'

Annie said something I couldn't hear. I moved closer to the door.

'*Yes*,' Lauren said, a note of irritation in her voice. 'I had the tests before I went to Paris. The baby's completely healthy.'

9

'But . . . but Lauren . . .' Annie went on anxiously. 'There might be things . . . problems . . . from your birth father. Things we don't know about.'

I froze. What was she talking about? What didn't we know about Dad?

'I'm sure it's fine,' Lauren said. 'They must have screened the sperm before they gave it to you.'

What?

'But there are lots more things they can check for these days,' Annie said.

'I don't see there's much Lauren can do about that now,' Lydia snapped.

'Exactly, so there's no point worrying about it,' Jam added.

'But I *am* worried,' Annie went on. 'A sperm donor could have had all sorts wrong with him.'

Sperm donor?

'Then there'd be something wrong with me or Madison, wouldn't there?' Lauren muttered.

Madison. *Me?* What did I have to do with a sperm donor? What did Lauren have to do with one?

'Just because we don't have a full medical history for our biological dad doesn't mean Mo or I can't ever have a healthy baby,' Lauren said. 'Honestly, Annie, please can we stop talking about this?'

Annie sniffed. I clutched at the wall beside me. My legs were shaking, my heart hammering. I took another step. I was in the doorway. The others saw me. Annie's hand flew to her mouth. She could see I'd heard.

10

'Oh, Christ,' Carla murmured.

'Mo?' Lauren took a step towards me.

I stared at her, my head still whirling. I couldn't believe it was true. But the look on my sister's face told me that it was. I turned to Annie. 'You lied?' I said. 'About Dad?'

'No.' Annie's mouth trembled. 'He was your father, just . . .' She looked down at the floor.

'Just not biologically.' Lauren stepped forward. 'Mo?'

But I didn't wait to hear the rest. I turned and fled. Along the hall, out the front door and away.

3
The Search

Of course, as soon as I'd got halfway down the street, I wanted to go back. I wanted answers. I didn't understand what I'd heard, just that Sam Purditt wasn't my biological father. But how that was possible I couldn't imagine.

I reached Jam and Lauren's car and stopped running. Yes, I wanted to know more, but I couldn't go back. It was too humiliating. All the people in the room – all the mums plus Lauren – they clearly knew the whole story. About *my* dad. And yet no-one had told me. Why? Was there some terrible secret they thought I wasn't old enough to cope with?

Footsteps sounded along the pavement. I looked up as Jam pounded up to me, then bent over, catching his breath.

'Mo,' he said. 'They are such idiots. I can't believe no-one told you.'

'You knew too?' Tears bubbled behind my eyes. I couldn't bear being left out like this. And I still didn't know what they were all talking about. 'What did they mean? Who was my biological father?'

'I don't know.' Jam frowned. 'I don't know any of the details. I haven't talked about it to anyone since . . . man, it was *years* ago. There was a letter we found, me and Lauren.

Your dad – Sam – he'd written to Lauren before he died, explaining that they used a sperm donor for you and Lauren because Sam couldn't have kids.'

'A sperm donor?' The world felt like it was spinning inside my head. My father was a sperm donor . . . out of a test tube? 'Who was he?'

'I don't know,' Jam said. 'The letter didn't go into details. I . . . I wanted to say something, but it wasn't the right time . . .'

'You wanted to tell me?' My heart was racing.

'Actually, back then I wanted to tell Shelby. There was a letter for her as well.'

'Right . . . thanks.' I turned away. Shelby was my other sister. She died in a fire the year after Dad. 'You're saying you thought Shelby had a right to know, but not me?'

Jam grabbed my arm. 'The letters were for Shelby and Lauren, not you.'

My mouth trembled. So Sam Purditt not only wasn't my biological father, he hadn't even bothered to write me my own letter telling me so.

Jam obviously saw what I was thinking.

'Shelby got a separate letter because her dad was . . . different from yours and Lauren's,' he said.

'Right,' I said.

'And because you were so little,' Jam went on, 'I thought your mum should tell you or something. Please, Mo, you were only eight.'

'OK, but I'm not eight now.'

13

'I know.' Jam sighed. He glanced back towards the apartment. 'Annie's having a total meltdown in there because she knows she should have told you and couldn't face it.'

I nodded. I was used to Annie's meltdowns.

'So will you come back inside?' Jam asked. 'Lauren feels terrible.'

I hesitated a moment. I still wanted answers. Most particularly, I wanted to know who this sperm donor was. But I couldn't face Annie in hysterics right now. And I couldn't face all of them together, feeling sorry for me.

'No,' I said. 'Not right now. I just want to be on my own for a bit.'

Jam nodded. Like Lauren he's good at sensing when it's best not to push me. In fact, he's good at that with everyone – it's one of the things that I imagine makes him a great teacher. 'OK, that's fair enough.' He cleared his throat. 'Hey, Mo, you are pleased for me and Lauren, aren't you? About the baby, I mean?'

I nodded. 'Sure,' I said. 'Course I am.'

Jam went back inside and I trudged away, turning off my phone in case Annie tried to call me. I'd intended to walk around for a bit, but I soon found myself outside a tube station and once I was through the barrier there didn't seem much point doing anything except going home. While Lauren's apartment is close to central London, Annie and I live just ten minutes' walk from Lauren's adoptive parents in north London. Annie chose the house years ago, when Lauren still lived at home, so I could be near to my big sister.

14

How could Lauren have kept such a massive secret from me for so many years? I was used to Annie getting stuff like that wrong. But not Lauren. She'd always been so totally on my side – fierce and loyal and true. And yet she hadn't been honest with me about who our father was. It hurt more than I could bear.

I let myself in and went up to my room. I was sure Annie wouldn't be far behind me and right now I couldn't face the thought of speaking to her. I switched on my phone – missed calls from both Annie and Lauren. I didn't listen to their messages. Instead, I plugged my headphones into my mobile. I needed music. I needed to lose myself in someone else's pain, so I didn't have to think about my own.

I was about to press play when the doorbell rang. I hesitated. I wasn't expecting anyone – and it couldn't be Annie or Lauren. They both had keys. The doorbell sounded again – a long, persistent ring. Sighing, I went downstairs.

Lauren's adoptive brother, Rory, was standing on the doorstep, his friend Marcus beside him. I tugged self-consciously at my hair. It wasn't Rory I was embarrassed to see – we've known each other for years *and* we go to the same school. He's like my cousin or something. We're not close, exactly. But we get on OK.

No, it was Marcus I was shy around. He's the same age as Rory – seventeen – but, like, the most good-looking boy in London. Cool hair, styled with a long fringe today, tall and broad-shouldered, with piercing green eyes. I'd had a crush on him for two years.

'Hey, Madison.' Rory's ruddy cheeks stretched into a smile. 'Are you OK?'

'Sure.' I glanced at Marcus, feeling my face reddening. He was looking bored, stifling a yawn as he leaned against the door frame.

'Mum made me come round, to see if you were here.' Rory rolled his eyes. 'They're all in a panic about you down at Lauren's. Is it true she's pregnant?'

'Yeah.'

Rory rolled his eyes again. 'Is that why you flipped out?'

'No.' My cheeks burned even hotter.

Marcus stifled another yawn. 'If she's OK, can we go?' he said.

Rory looked at me. 'Sure you're all right?'

'Course.' I flicked back my hair in what I hoped was a vaguely sophisticated and confident gesture. Marcus gave no sign that he'd noticed. Then a thought struck me. 'Hey, Rory, d'you know anything . . . about my dad? Stuff that my mum might have told yours, maybe that she didn't want me to know about?'

Rory made a face. 'No. Why?'

I shrugged. 'Never mind.' I started to close the door. Marcus caught my eye and winked. What was he doing? He'd looked so totally bored just a second ago. I smiled uncertainly back.

'Hey, Madison.' Rory's voice almost made me jump.

'What?'

'My mum keeps a bunch of diaries about old stuff,' he said. 'Maybe yours does too.'

The two boys set off along the pavement. In spite of all the turmoil in my head, I couldn't help wishing I'd been a bit cooler around Marcus. He walked with a rolling swagger that managed to convey absolute confidence with a hint of 'don't mess with me' danger.

I shut the door and thought about what Rory had said. Diaries. I couldn't imagine Annie keeping a diary. She had enough trouble keeping track of everyday life to do anything requiring that kind of focus. She didn't even own a computer. Still, it was worth a look.

I raced up to her bedroom, guessing that's where she'd keep something as personal as a diary. Our cleaner had been earlier, so the surfaces were all clear and tidy, but I knew the chaos that would face me as soon as I opened any of the cupboard doors. I tried the bedside table drawer. Sure enough, it was overflowing with tissues and hand creams and manicure kits. No paper at all. Then I opened the wardrobe door. That was crammed with dresses and tops and trousers, most of them half off their hangers. Shoes littered the floor space, plus a pair of my old dolls, three plastic bags, a pottery cup Shelby and I made for her at camp one summer, a box of old lipsticks, and a wooden drumstick – goodness knows where that had come from.

I sat back on my heels, feeling overwhelmed. Didn't Annie ever throw anything away? I rummaged right to the back. There were several cardboard boxes here, plus a couple of small suitcases. I pulled them out and opened them one by one. Piles of clothes met my eye. One box was full of old jumpers and skirts. Another was crammed with little girl dresses. I didn't remember wearing any of them. I guess they must have been Shelby's or Lauren's. I was trying to be systematic, but once all the clothes were on the carpet, it was hard to keep track.

'Madison, sweetie?' Annie's voice quavered from the doorway.

I spun round. I'd been so caught up in my search for a diary I hadn't even heard her come in.

'What are you doing?' she said, looking round at all the clothes on the carpet, her voice breaking into a sob.

I stood up. 'I want to know everything,' I said. 'I want to know why you used a sperm donor. I want to know who he is. And I want to know why everyone else except me knew about him for seven years.' I folded my arms and glared at her.

A tear trickled down her cheek. Her hands were shaking as she twisted them over each other. How I hated that gesture of hers. Sometimes, though it felt horrible to admit it, I hated Annie herself. She was always so weak and miserable. For as long as I could remember, I'd felt it was my job to look after her. But why should I have to do that? It wasn't fair.

'Madison, I realise what you heard was a shock,' Annie said. 'But I've kept certain things from you to protect you. Because I didn't want you to be hurt . . .'

My guts tightened into an angry knot.

'I get you've been trying to protect me,' I said, clenching my fists. 'But you need to get this: I'm not a little girl anymore, and what I overheard was something important about my dad.

18

You owe me an explanation, because I don't understand and that's worse than anything.'

We stared at each other. Annie blinked rapidly. She wasn't going to tell me. I could see the resistance in her eyes. I clenched my fists, ready to storm out. Maybe I'd go back to Lauren. Try and get the truth from her. And then Annie wiped her hand across her face, brushing away her tears. She looked up at me, clear-eyed and with a smile of resignation.

'You're right, Madison,' she said with a sigh. 'It's time you and Lauren knew the truth about your birth father. Please come downstairs. Lauren's here too. I'll tell you both everything I know.'

4

Allan Faraday

I followed Annie downstairs, into the living room, where Lauren was perched on the edge of the couch. She looked up as I walked in, her face scrunched up with misery.

'Mo?' she said.

'It's fine,' I said, without meeting her gaze. It wasn't fine, of course. Lauren had failed to tell me what she knew about my dad *and* that she was pregnant. But I didn't want a big fight with her.

I sat down across the room and waited, as Annie produced a small wooden box from the depths of the large scroll-top desk that stood in the far corner. With trembling fingers, Annie unlocked the box and drew out a sheet of paper. She turned to me.

'Lauren already knows this part: your dad and I tried to have a baby for over a year. We had some tests, and found that we couldn't have children together. I was fine, but there were problems with . . . with your dad. We talked about it for a while, then decided we should use a sperm donor.'

'Did you do IVF?' I asked.

Annie nodded. 'The donor was anonymous. All we were officially told were the things we'd been able to choose – like him having dark hair and eyes, the same as your dad, and being six foot . . . so the same height . . . and that he was twenty years old.' She hesitated.

'But you found out more?' I said. I glanced over at Lauren. She was sitting forward, listening intently, her hands folded over her swollen belly.

Annie nodded slowly. 'Like I say, that's all we were officially told, but when I was in the clinic in Evanport, having the treatment, I got friendly with one of the nurses. I told her how anxious I was about genetic problems . . . you know, things being inherited like diseases and conditions . . .'

I frowned. 'Don't they check out the sperm before they give it to you?'

'For some things,' Annie said, 'but not everything. It would be too expensive.' She hesitated again. 'Anyway, this nurse happened to be sympathetic. She thought the clinic was skipping even the basic tests and trying to do things on the cheap. So . . . well, she didn't want to make a fuss. She was scared of losing her job. But she gave me some extra information about our donor. Not much, just a name and an address, but it was enough to make it possible for me to hire someone to investigate. I had to know everything would be all right.'

Well, that made sense. Annie was such a worrier – though I could hardly imagine her having the drive actually to organise an investigation.

'Did Dad – Sam – know what you were doing?' Lauren asked.

21

'No.' Annie sighed. 'Your father was struggling enough as it was with the idea he couldn't have his own children. It was different after you were born but, back then, he couldn't have handled knowing the other man's name, let alone any other details.'

'So . . . what did the investigator find out?' I held my breath.

Annie handed me the piece of paper from the wooden box. 'This is everything I know,' she said.

I looked at the sheet. It was a report, typed in three paragraphs, on a man named Allan Faraday. I read the lines, but I couldn't take in any of the information. This whole thing felt surreal. I mean, how was it possible that this stranger was my biological father? I tried to read the three paragraphs again. This time I picked up the crucial bits of data: at the time of Lauren's conception, Faraday was twenty, and a student at New York State University. He had grown up travelling around various capital cities in Europe thanks to his dad's banking job and suffered 'the normal childhood illnesses' the report said. He was basically fit, healthy and a keen basketball player. He only drank in moderation, didn't smoke, didn't take drugs and had achieved good grades in his most recent set of exams. The only negative given in the report was that he tended to spend extravagantly – hence his attempt to increase his income by donating sperm.

I skim-read the next paragraph which gave details of Faraday's wealthy parents – his dad was American but his mother was from Britain – and their medical history, then the next, with data on the two sets of grandparents. All four individuals were still alive in their eighties. No indications of cancer, heart problems, dementia or degenerative diseases. I looked up.

'This is our real dad?' I said. 'This . . . Allan Faraday?'

'*Sam* was our real dad,' Lauren said firmly. 'This man just provided a . . . a genetic base for us.'

I shook my head. It was all right for Lauren. She had known Sam when she was my age. Plus, she had her adoptive dad as well. But I had no-one. I didn't even properly remember Sam.

Annie wrung her hands. 'Lauren's right,' she said, her voice all trembly. 'Sam took care of you and loved you and played with you. You *know* that, Madison.'

'Earlier, you said something to Lauren about finding out more about the sperm donor's medical history . . .' I said. 'Does that mean you think we should get in touch with him?'

'No.' Annie's eyes widened. 'Definitely not. I was . . . I was just surprised about Lauren being pregnant. But she was right, if there had been something wrong with him, it would have shown up in you or her by now.'

'Anyway, I'm going to have the baby in a few weeks,' Lauren said. 'That's going to happen whatever, and afterwards we can do any tests we want.'

'Don't you want to find this man?' I persisted. 'I mean, he's your blood father.'

'No.' Lauren shook her head. 'He doesn't mean anything to me.'

'But . . .' I frowned. 'But you wanted to know about *us*. About your original family. Why not your birth dad?'

'That's completely different, Mo,' Lauren said. 'I was stolen away from Annie and Sam – from my original family. This man just donated a bit of himself. It's . . . it's meaning-less by comparison.'

I couldn't believe it. Of all the people in the world, Lauren was the one I'd have expected to understand. She'd grown up away from us because she'd been kidnapped as a toddler and later adopted by another family. She had gone in search of her birth parents, just like I wanted to. Yet here she was, not getting it at all.

'I want to know him,' I said, my anger rising. 'I want to know my birth dad, if I can.'

Annie was on her feet, tears welling in her eyes. 'No, Madison, that's a terrible idea.'

'Why?' I protested. 'I've got a right to know him.'

'Mo, listen.' Lauren's eyes pleaded with me. 'I understand you want to find out about your roots. But Sam *was there* from the beginning. He *wanted* you. This man – Allan Faraday – he doesn't even know we exist. Remember, the sperm donation was supposed to be anonymous. He . . . he might not want to know you. And I'd hate to see you hurt.'

'Oh, so would I, sweetie,' Annie added.

I couldn't be more hurt by him than I have been by you two and your lies.

I thought the words, but I didn't say them. Instead, I looked down at the living room carpet. A tuft of wool stuck up by the leg of the couch where Lauren was sitting. I chewed on my lip. OK, so Annie and Lauren didn't understand why I needed to find Allan Faraday. Well, I wouldn't bother to talk to them about it anymore. I held out the piece of paper to Lauren.

'D'you want to look at this?'

'No thanks,' she said.

I folded it up and put it in my pocket.

'Madison, please promise me you're not going to do anything stupid like . . . like try and find this man.' Annie sounded on the verge of tears.

I turned to her. 'Course not,' I lied. 'Like you say, what would be the point? He might not even want to know me.'

Lauren left soon after this and I went up to my room. I did a Google search on Allan Faraday straight away, but it didn't come up with anything. I'd worked out the man must now be forty-three but the rest of the information I had – all the medical stuff – wasn't really much help. I slept badly that night, my dreams filled with dark shapes that loomed out of the shadows, then disappeared again, leaving me awake and trembling.

I finally dropped into a deeper sleep at about 5 am. I woke from this with a start just after 10 am and began my search again. This time, instead of just inputting Allan Faraday's name, I trawled all the social networking sites I'd ever heard of as well as several that I hadn't.

I came across scores of Faradays, but none of them fitted in terms of colouring, age or nationality. And then, after an hour or so, I stumbled across an entry on a media networking site called Bizznet. From the picture beside his job description – media consultant – this Faraday looked about the right age and he definitely had dark hair and eyes. I quickly clicked through to his full profile. My heartbeat quickened as I read on.

Allan Faraday, media consultant and freelance journalist. Dual US/UK nationality. Graduate of New York State University.

After this top line entry, there followed a list of the clients Faraday had worked for – loads of famous brand names among them – and then, at the end, a short biog.

Faraday, 43, lists among his interests soccer, film and basketball. You can follow him on Twitter @faradayall

It had to be him. All the details fitted, right down to the unusual two 'l's in 'Allan'. My fingers were shaking as I logged onto Twitter and searched for his username. *There.* The most recent entry was for this morning. It said:

Leaving London tomorrow but looking forward to Brisbane Media drinks first. See ya there!

I gasped. He was in London. Right now. It was fate. I *had* to find him. All I needed to know was where this drinks party he referred to was being held. I flicked quickly through to the person he'd sent his tweet to, then opened their conversation to see if I could find out.

It took another few minutes but I soon had the info I needed. My biological father, Allan Faraday, was going to be at the Houses of Parliament tonight for a drinks reception starting at 7 pm.

And so was I.

5

A Hitch

Getting away from home and Annie was the easy bit, despite Annie's overprotective habit of demanding to know where I was going and who I'd be with. I told her I was meeting my friend Rosa from school. I'm not exactly popular at school – I'm too shy and too serious for most of the airheads in my class – but Rosa and I genuinely get on. She comes from a majorly dysfunctional family too, with no dad and three older brothers, one of whom is in constant trouble with the police. Anyway, Rosa was quite happy to cover for me that evening.

I took the tube to Westminster then followed the map on my phone to the building with the designated entrance for the Brisbane Media drinks reception. The Houses of Parliament are huge and sprawling and it took longer than I'd expected. I didn't reach the building I was looking for until almost 7.30 pm.

I'd taken a lot of trouble over how I looked. I normally wear jeans and jumpers or T-shirts and never any make-up, but today I put on a proper skirt and one of Annie's silk shirts tied over a vest top. I was even wearing mascara and lipstick. As I walked towards the iron gate at the side of the big brick building, I could feel a million butterflies zooming around inside my stomach.

What was I going to say to Allan Faraday? I could hardly just march up to him and announce that I was his long-lost daughter. For all I knew, he might not even remember donating sperm over twenty years ago. Lauren's warning rang in my ears:

He . . . he might not want to know you. And I'd hate to see you hurt.

She was right, of course. But I was prepared for rejection. The most important thing was that I met him . . . that I knew who he was . . . It was, surely, like a total sign that he should be in London the very day I went looking for him. And I knew from his tweets that he was leaving tomorrow. So this was my only chance to find him and introduce myself. I'd deal with whatever happened next, once it actually happened.

I was so caught up with all these thoughts that I didn't notice the security guards at the gate until I was just a few metres away. They were really dressed up – in uniforms with . . . jeez, were they *guns*?

I stopped in my tracks.

Why hadn't I thought that it might be tricky just to walk inside a drinks reception? Especially one in a high security area like Parliament. As I watched, two women approached the gate. They showed the guards pieces of card. Invitations.

What was I going to do now? Even if it had occurred to me earlier that I might need a formal invite, I'd have had no idea how to fake one. The two women laughed at something the

28

guards said, then went inside. I backed away, looking around for an alternative entry point. There was nothing obvious. I could see a few ground-floor windows, but they were all closed – and all within the guards' sightlines. There were no other doors.

I sauntered away, trying to look like I was casually strolling about. I rounded the corner. Now the guards could no longer see me. I spotted a fire door and rushed over. I pushed at it, hoping against hope that it wouldn't be locked, but it was.

Of course it was, this was the Houses of Parliament for goodness' sake. Feeling defeated, I turned away. *Was this it?* I felt suddenly swamped with desolation. I'd been so close to Allan Faraday and now I was as far away from meeting him as ever. I knew I could hang around outside, waiting for him to arrive, but it was nearly twenty to eight now. He was probably already at the drinks reception. And I had no idea how long that was likely to last.

Jeez, I was so useless. When Lauren had gone looking for her birth family, she'd faced far harder obstacles than I was up against, including crossing the Atlantic, boarding a flight to a place she'd never been and breaking into a building in the middle of the night.

Lauren had faced down every single challenge, while I couldn't even get into a simple drinks reception in my adopted hometown. So much for wanting to be a journalist. I wandered back towards the guards. What was I going to do? I could try talking my way in, but I really didn't feel confident enough for that.

And then I spotted another door, on the other side of the guards. It was some way beyond them, though still clearly visible from where they were standing. A man – young, maybe early twenties – was standing outside, smoking a cigarette. From his stained apron and white cap – plus the steam issuing from the door behind him – I was guessing he had just stepped out from inside a kitchen.

I took a circuitous route that led me towards him without walking directly past the guards. As I approached, he looked up and smiled.

'Hey, beautiful,' he said, his eyes twinkling. His accent was heavily eastern European. 'You want cigarette?'

I shook my head, tongue-tied. I was useless at talking to strangers, especially male ones. Boys quite often tried to chat me up but usually gave up in the face of my shyness. It didn't much matter whether I liked someone or not, I could just never think of anything to say. 'I . . . I don't smoke,' I stammered. What on earth was I doing? This guy wasn't going to let me in anymore than the guards were. Unless . . . 'I'm looking for a job,' I said.

The young man raised his eyebrows. 'You don't want work here,' he said in a loud whisper. 'Pay is terrible and boss is worse.'

'Just a bit of part-time work?' I glanced along the building. A large group was approaching the two guards. Neither of them were looking in my direction. I forced a smile onto my face. 'Please?'

The young man stubbed out his cigarette. He winked at me. 'You know with all security screenings is more trouble than worth for part-time work, but I will ask the boss if he hiring,' he said. 'You wait here, beautiful. I come back.'

'Sure.'

The young man disappeared inside. He let the door shut behind him, but I caught it before it closed completely and peered inside. The young man was whistling to himself as he strolled towards a set of swing doors. Steam swelled up above the doors and I could hear the sounds of pans clanking and people shouting.

I looked in the other direction. The corridor disappeared round a bend. Surely that had to lead to the rooms where the reception was being held? Either way, it was my best chance to get inside. As soon as the young man vanished behind the swing doors, I darted inside and tiptoed along the corridor. Round the bend, I reached a short flight of concrete stairs. Up these and through a door to another corridor – this one oak-panelled and lushly carpeted. As I crept along, voices drifted towards me from the doors on either side – a series of low, male mumbles. Where on earth was I? And how was I going to find the drinks reception and Allan Faraday?

I headed for the door at the end of this corridor. Hopefully this would lead me back down to the rooms where the reception was being held. I wiped my palms on my skirt as I sped along. Behind me a door smashed open against a wall.

'Hey! Stop!'

I spun round. *No.* One of the guards from outside was just a few metres away, running towards me.

'Stop!' he yelled again.

Panic rising, I turned and fled for the door ahead. I reached it in a few steps. Yanked at the handle.

It was locked. The guard behind me pounded up. His hand slammed against the door by my head. I turned to face him. He was panting and puce in the face. His hand slid down to his gun. I stared at it in horror.

'What the hell do you think you're doing?' he demanded.

6

A Meeting

My mouth opened and shut silently. I gulped. What could I say? I was sure that, if she were in my place, Lauren would have come up with some ultra-convincing reason for being there. But all I could think to say was the truth.

'I was looking for my father,' I stammered. 'Allan Faraday. He's at the Brisbane Media drinks reception.'

The guard took a step back and looked me up and down. Faces were peering out from the rooms on either side of the corridor. I kept my gaze on the guard. His expression was softening, as if he were registering how young I was – and how frightened. He took his hand away from his gun and reached inside his jacket pocket.

'The reception is next door,' he said, taking out a walkie-talkie radio.

'I know but . . .' Again I searched for a good reason for entering the building. Nothing came. '. . . But I didn't have an invite so I didn't think you'd let me in.'

'What's your name?'

I told him.

'Any ID?'

I took out my student card. The guard studied it for a

moment, then tilted his head to one side and gazed at me thoughtfully.

'You don't have the same surname as your dad,' he said.

'I know.' I could feel my face burning.

'So why is it so urgent you want to get hold of him?' he said. 'Couldn't you just ring him?'

'I . . . I don't have his number . . . I just know that he's here for one night in London and . . . and I wanted to see him . . .' The words came out in a big, blubbery sob. Tears pricked at my eyes. I sounded ridiculous and I *hated* that I'd just given away so much personal, private information.

The guard sighed. 'Look, love, you can't go crashing about like this. There are national security implications for a start. What did you say your dad's name was?'

'Allan Faraday, but . . .' I stopped, unwilling to explain that Faraday would have absolutely no idea who I was.

Ignoring my hesitation, the guard spoke into his radio.

'Bob?' he said into the mouthpiece. 'I found the girl who snuck in. She says she's a Madison Purditt and she's looking for her father. Can you check him on the guest list . . . it's an Allan Faraday.'

The radio crackled, then a voice on the other end spoke.

'Yup, he's here, Jerry.'

'Right.' Jerry looked at me thoughtfully. 'Would you ask him to step outside, please?'

No. My mouth dropped open in horror. Apart from the fact that Allan Faraday was hardly likely to come outside to meet a daughter he didn't even know existed, this was so *not* the

34

way I'd imagined introducing myself to him. I'd planned to find him and study him for a minute or two first. Then, when I was ready, I would move over gracefully and ask for a quiet word. I didn't know what I was going to say after that, but I'd imagined I'd be able to introduce myself gently and carefully.

Not like this.

'Come outside.' Jerry led me back along the corridor and down the steps.

Outside the air seemed colder than it had before. My heart was totally in my mouth. I tried to move away, but Jerry gripped my arm.

'Don't think about running, love,' he said. 'That would be really stupid.'

I gulped. Suppose Allan Faraday wouldn't come outside? I'd probably be arrested. Annie would go into total hysterics.

Jerry led me along to the entrance to the drinks reception. I kept my head bowed. The light was fading now, casting shadows across our path.

We reached the entrance and stopped. The other guard was checking someone's invite and didn't look round.

'Wait here with me,' Jerry said. Now he'd stopped running his face had returned to normal colour and I could see that he was probably about thirty, with soft creases around his eyes.

The seconds ticked by. I kept my gaze on the grey pavement at my feet. And then a man appeared in the doorway. I noticed his shoes first – shiny and pointy and black. Very smart. I looked up a little, taking in the sharp creases of his designer suit.

35

'What's this about?' the man said. He had a strange accent – somewhere between English and American. 'They said someone wanted me.'

Oh my goodness. It was *him*. I still couldn't look up, properly, into his face.

'Are you Allan Faraday, sir?' Jerry asked.

'Yes.' The man sounded suspicious. 'Why? Who's asking?'

Jerry cleared his throat. 'I've got this girl here – Madison Purditt. She was caught trying to get into the reception. Says she's your daughter?'

The question hung in the air. I wanted to evaporate where I stood. This was totally humiliating.

'My *daughter*?' Allan Faraday sounded as shocked as I'd have expected him to. 'I don't have a daughter.'

'Ah.' Jerry's voice was a mix of embarrassment, confusion and anger. I could tell he was looking at me, though my eyes were still fixed on Allan Faraday's shoes. 'Sorry to have disturbed you, sir.'

Say something, Madison.

Allan Faraday's shoes took a step back. He was going back into the drinks reception and I was going to be arrested and I hadn't even looked at his face.

Allan Faraday took another step away from me.

I forced myself to look up, into his eyes.

He was tall with high cheekbones. Much better looking than in his Bizznet photo, with dark hair slicked back off his face and a look of Lauren about his mouth. He stared back at me, his forehead creased with a frown.

36

'Why are you saying I'm your father?' he said. 'I've never seen you before.'

My mouth was dry and my legs were trembling and my heart was hammering against my ribs. My whole focus was on Allan Faraday. I stared at him, forgetting Jerry and the other guard standing beside us. The distant traffic noises and the cool night air faded to nothing. This was my one chance.

I had to get it right.

'Mr Faraday, you . . . you . . .' I lowered my voice; this was *beyond* embarrassing, '. . . you donated sperm that was used by a clinic in Evanport, Connecticut. It was my mother who used it and . . . and . . . *that's* how you are my father.'

7

The Invite

Faraday's mouth gaped and his eyes widened as he took in what I'd said. I was aware of Jerry, the guard, hovering nearby, watching us intently. I couldn't believe I'd just blurted out the facts like that. And what if I'd got something so personal all wrong? What if this wasn't the same Allan Faraday? What if he denied ever donating sperm? Except . . . I looked at his mouth again. His lips definitely curved in the same 'bow' shape as Lauren's.

Faraday stared at me. 'Sperm donation is anonymous,' he said slowly. 'At least it was back then, when I did it.'

My heart leaped. That meant he was admitting being involved, didn't it?

'How old are you, Madison?' he went on. 'Where are you from?'

'I'm fifteen,' I said. 'My family was originally from Evanport in, er, in the States, but we live here now. That is, me and my mum live here – we moved here after my . . . my dad – the man who brought me up – after he died.'

I glanced at Jerry, the guard, wishing he wasn't watching me. Faraday followed my gaze. He cleared his throat, then leaned over and whispered something in Jerry's ear.

'All right, then, Miss Purditt,' Jerry said. 'You can go. But next time be more careful.'

Faraday indicated the path leading back to the street. 'Come on, then,' he said. 'Let's get to the bottom of this.'

My chest tightened as he led me towards the pavement. Had he believed me? What was he thinking? What was he going to say? He strode on, away from the building. I had to walk fast to keep up with him. As we reached the main road, he glanced down at me and stopped.

'So,' he said. 'You're looking for your birth father?'

I nodded.

'Well, you've successfully got me out of what was admittedly a rather boring drinks reception, so go on, tell me why you think it's me,' Faraday said. There was a hint of impatience in his voice, but his eyes were warm, almost twinkling, as if he were more amused by the situation than anything.

I took the sperm donor report Annie had given me out of my pocket.

'Here,' I said. 'This is you, isn't it?'

Faraday stared at the report. He let out a low whistle, then looked up at me. His expression was guarded. I got the distinct impression he was weighing up the situation, trying to decide if he was being conned . . . if I was about to make demands on him . . .

'I don't want anything from you,' I said quickly. 'I just wanted to meet you.'

The suspicious look faded slightly from Faraday's eyes. He smiled at me and, again, I was reminded of Lauren.

39

'I bet none of this is how you imagined,' he said with a chuckle. He held out his hand. 'Shall we start again? I'm Allan.'

I shook his hand. 'Madison.'

'It must have taken a lot of guts to find me . . .' Allan pointed to a café just along the road. 'Would you like to get a coffee?'

I nodded. 'OK.' I still wasn't sure what he was going to do or say, but at least he seemed to believe that I'd genuinely been looking for him.

The café was virtually empty. Allan bought a double espresso for himself and a hot chocolate for me. We sat down in the corner and Allan placed his hands flat on the table in front of him.

'How on earth did you track me down from this old address?' he said, nodding towards the sperm donor report.

I explained how I'd searched his name on a range of social networking sites. 'It wasn't that hard in the end,' I said.

Allan nodded. 'To be honest with you, Madison, I always wondered if this – someone like you – might happen along one day. But if your mother wanted to know so much about me in the first place, why didn't she try and find me sooner?'

'Oh, my mum just wanted to make sure you were properly healthy,' I said. 'She got a nurse at the clinic to pass on your name and address. But that was all back then, years ago.'

'You mean your mother doesn't know you've come to meet me tonight?' Allan's eyebrows arched with surprise.

'No, she . . . actually, she doesn't want me to try and find you at all.' I looked down at my hot chocolate. The cream was dissolving into the brown. I suddenly felt miserable. This whole meeting was completely surreal. Worse, this man, Allan, was a stranger. I realised I'd been hoping that when I met him, there'd be some way in which we felt connected. But the truth was: he could have been anybody.

I looked up. Allan was sitting back in his chair, arms folded. 'You realise I could sue your mother *and* that nurse for revealing my identity?'

I gasped. That hadn't even occurred to me. 'But it was so long ago,' I stammered.

Allan shook his head. 'I'm forty-three,' he said. 'I did the whole sperm donation thing when I was a student to make some extra money. That's only twenty-three . . . twenty-four years ago. Not long at all, in legal terms.'

I looked down again. Jeez, what had I done? The last thing I wanted was to get anyone into trouble.

Allan chuckled again. 'Don't worry, Madison, I'm not going to sue anyone. To be honest with you, I'm more intrigued than anything. And impressed . . . you've gone to a lot of trouble to find me. You've made me wonder how many other little Allans there might be out there.'

'There's Lauren,' I blurted out. 'She's my older sister. They used you for her too.' I paused. 'I . . . you actually look a bit like her. I mean, she looks a bit like you.' I tailed off, feeling I'd said too much and exposed myself again.

Allan watched me for a minute and, when he spoke again, his voice was more gentle than before. 'What is it you're looking for here, Madison?' he said. 'Why did you want to find me?'

I looked up, into his intense eyes. There were lines on his forehead and grey hairs at his temple. Despite that look of Lauren's around the mouth, I couldn't see myself in his face at all. It was still so hard to believe I was related to this man. Impossible to imagine having any kind of relationship with him.

'I just wanted to meet you once, before you left London tonight and went home . . .' I said quietly. 'I just wanted to know who you were.'

Allan made a face. 'What makes you think I'm leaving London?'

I frowned. 'It was on your Twitter feed. You said: "leaving London tomorrow" or something?'

'Leaving for a few days, sure,' he said with a smile. 'I'm away on business until Friday, but I'm back home then.' He took a sip of coffee. 'London is my home now. I live in Fulham.'

'Oh.' I didn't know what to say. 'Are you married? Do you have . . . you know, your own kids?'

'No and no,' Allan said. 'Never met the right lady, I guess.' He made another face. 'Why don't you tell me a bit about yourself, Madison? Home. School. What you do in your free time.'

I swallowed. I hated talking about myself. Still, I'd wanted this . . . I couldn't exactly expect Allan to tell me about himself if I wasn't prepared to confide a few personal details as well.

'School's OK,' I said. 'I like English and History best . . . I don't like reading out loud or doing sums and stuff like that. And I *hate* swimming.'

I paused, my head filling with the memories of nearly drowning – once when I was six and trapped on a boat and, a second time, two years later, in a bay with the rising tide threatening to pull me under. Ever since those experiences, water had terrified me, especially the sea.

I shook myself and turned my attention back to Allan. 'Anyway, most of the girls in my class are total airheads, but Rosa's nice, she's like my best friend, and Rory looks out for me.'

'Rory?'

'He's Lauren's brother, the one she grew up with after she was adopted. She was stolen away from us, her original family, when she was little.'

Allan's eyes widened as I told him the whole story. He listened carefully, just asking a few questions as I went on. I found myself talking about things I never spoke of: the near drownings and how I'd watched as Cooper Trent set fire to the building where Lauren, Shelby and Jam were trapped inside.

'So Shelby died, like my dad.' I paused. I couldn't really remember Shelby any better than Dad, but most of the memories I did have featured her being mean to me. Lauren says she had a hard time growing up, but it's difficult to feel sympathetic seeing as how Shelby took out her 'hard time' on me. Still, I didn't want to say all of that to Allan.

I looked up to find him watching me intently. 'The truth is that Shelby and my dad dying makes me different from everyone and sometimes I think they look at me like I'm a total freak . . .' I stopped, realising I'd been talking for ages. I bit my lip, feeling exposed yet again. I hadn't intended to tell Allan so much. It was just that he'd listened so well.

'That's a lot to go through for a little girl,' he said. And there was real kindness in his voice.

I looked down. The cream had totally disappeared into my hot chocolate. I took a sip. It was cold.

Allan checked his watch. 'I have to get going,' he said. 'But . . . look, would you like to meet up again?'

'Yes, um . . .' I realised that I hadn't asked him anything about his own life. 'What is it you do, exactly?' I said.

'I'm – well, since recently, I'm a reporter. I work mostly for *The Examiner* though I do other freelance work too – all sorts of things . . .' Allan waved his hand as if to indicate a wide sweep of work activities.

'Wow.' I was seriously impressed. This, right here, this *was* a proper connection between us. It couldn't be coincidence that my genetic father did the very job I most aspired to myself. And on a really impressive newspaper.

Allan smiled. 'I wonder . . .' He paused. 'No, you wouldn't be interested.'

'Interested in what?' I said.

'Someone I know through work is having a birthday party on Hampstead Heath. It's this Saturday, in fact, a big celebration with a circus theme, like a festival almost. There'll be

44

loads of teens there too. I know he's got four kids . . . I'm not sure how old they are, but all definitely teenagers. You'd be welcome to come along with me, if you'd like.'

I blinked. Was he seriously asking me to a party? Old ingrained warnings from Annie about accepting invitations from strange men sprang into my head.

It's too risky.

Allan clearly saw the anxiety in my eyes.

'Perhaps I should speak to your mother first?' he suggested.

'No.' Definitely not. Annie would go into hysterics at the mere idea of me being in touch with Allan. No way would she agree to me seeing him again.

I took a deep breath. This was surely exactly what I'd wanted . . . a chance to get to know my birth father. And he *wasn't* a stranger. Plus, the party would be full of people and Annie didn't need to know about it and . . . I looked at Allan's slightly lined face again . . . the man had a kind smile. My instincts told me he had no desire to hurt me.

'That would be great,' I said. 'Thank you.'

8
Circus Party

The three days until Saturday passed slowly. I didn't want Annie and Lauren to know I'd met Allan Faraday in case they tried to stop me doing it again. Anyway, I was still cross with both of them for not telling me I had a sperm donor dad for so many years. Plus, I was worried Annie would start freaking out that Allan Faraday knew she'd had him checked out. I was sure Annie and the nurse had acted illegally – and that although Allan had said he wouldn't do so, suing them was definitely an option.

I told Rosa, of course. I knew she would keep the secret for me. Then I spent hours agonising over what to wear. Allan had said we were going to a party. But he hadn't said how formal it was going to be. In the end, I decided on my smartest jeans and my most glamorous T-shirt: silky-soft, pale blue cotton with a slash neck. I put on a bit of make-up, like I had for the drinks reception, then set off. I was using Rosa as cover again – Annie didn't suspect a thing. She'd tried to talk to me about the sperm donor dad revelation several times in the past few days, but I'd brushed her off saying I wasn't ready to talk about it yet. Lauren, who understands me so much better, just sent a text saying:

Come round whenever you want. We can talk. Or not. Love ya, kiddo. Lx

Allan met me, as he'd said he would, at Hampstead tube station. He was wearing a different suit this afternoon – darker, with a crisp white shirt underneath. His hair was slicked back off his face and he smelled of a fresh, light, lemony aftershave.

'You look nice,' he said, offering me his hand again.

We shook hands. It felt a bit weird, but I was glad he wasn't being too familiar. I wasn't ready to kiss him on the cheek like I guess you might a real dad.

'Please don't be angry with my mum,' I said, as we walked along the road. 'She was just worried about using a sperm donor and she didn't think the clinic did proper checks . . . My mum worries a lot.'

Allan shot me an amused look. 'I told you I wasn't serious about suing her,' he said. 'Truth is, there are other ways you could have tracked me down, though it might have taken longer. Anyway, I'm glad you've found me. I'm glad to have met you, Madison.'

I could feel my face flushing. And yet, in spite of my embarrassment, I was pleased Allan had said that. Not because it proved Lauren and Annie wrong, but because it meant maybe he wanted to get to know me.

'What kind of stories do you write as a journalist?' I asked. 'When I Googled you, it didn't come up with any newspaper articles.'

Allan shrugged. 'I write all sorts. Campaigning pieces

47

mostly . . . investigative stuff into businesses. I often work undercover – that's why you won't see a byline.'

'A what?'

'The bit that says who the story is written "by".'

I nodded, taking this in. Allan was *really* cool. I was itching to tell him about my own ambition to be a journalist – and how I won a London-wide competition for a short story I did a couple of years ago. But I didn't quite have the nerve.

After a couple more minutes, we turned onto a quiet road opposite Hampstead Heath. A large house was visible about fifty metres away, with a huge marquee in the foreground.

'That's where the party is,' Allan said. 'I parked here earlier to get a good space, before I came to meet you. Now, the host's name is Declan Baxter. I checked on his kids. There's a boy of eighteen, twins of thirteen and a girl in between, about your age. Her name is Esme.'

I gulped. It sounded like Allan was going to expect me to socialise. This Esme probably had a load of fancy clothes to match her fancy name – it was obvious from one look at the house and marquee up ahead that Declan Baxter was loaded. I'd met a few rich kids in the past few years. Some were nice. Some weren't. But they were all irritatingly confident . . . compared to me, anyway.

As we walked towards the house, Allan squeezed my shoulder. 'Don't worry, Madison, you'll be fine.'

I shrugged, embarrassed that he'd seen through my anxieties so easily. We reached the large driveway. There was a bouncer on the door who asked politely for our phones. Allan rolled his eyes but gave up his mobile without complaint. I handed mine over too.

'Baxter is *very* protective of his privacy,' Allan whispered darkly as we went into the house. The entrance hall was huge . . . and decorated with streamers and balloons like a carnival. It was full of smartly dressed adults, all drinking and chatting. A woman in a white Lycra bodysuit with clown-style face make-up appeared with a tray of glasses. Allan took an orange juice for each of us.

'Need to keep a clear head,' he said with a wink. 'Let's go through to the circus.'

The way was wreathed with bunches of balloons and the same brightly coloured decorations as the hall. As we turned down a short corridor, the smell of fried onions wafted towards us. Another face-painted girl in Lycra, this one also wearing a red and pink apron, was handing out hot dogs from a huge oval platter. She smiled at me, offering the platter, and the big red paint circles round her eyes crinkled.

'Er, no thanks,' I said.

'Me neither.' Allan patted his stomach. 'Watching my weight.'

Allan steered me through the crowd. More adults, all talking loudly and clinking glasses. I hadn't seen a single person under twenty so far.

'Ah, there's Hobbs,' he said. 'He works for Declan Baxter; he'll be able to tell me when the man himself is most likely to be free for a chat. Won't be a second, Madison.'

Before I could say anything, Allan was across the room and talking with a middle-aged man wearing a waistcoat and a yellow tie. Hobbs didn't look that pleased to see him, although his manner was so stiff and formal it was hard to tell. After about thirty seconds, he walked off. Allan hesitated a moment, then left the marquee through an exit marked *Toilets this way*. I waited, feeling self-conscious. After what felt like ages but was only really a couple of minutes, he was back. He was still smiling brightly, but there was a new look of disappointment behind his eyes. I hoped it wasn't because I was here, making it tricky for him to talk properly to people.

'Are you going to be able to talk to Mr Baxter?' I asked.

Allan sighed. 'Not if Hobbs has anything to do with it. He was no help.' He paused. 'By the way, the loos are just out there.' He pointed to the door he'd just come through. 'If you need to freshen up. Er, I'm going to circulate for a bit. See if I can get close to Baxter another way. I won't be long. Will you be OK on your own for a bit?'

'Sure.' In fact, I wanted to tell Allan not to leave me, but it would have sounded really lame.

I watched him fight his way through the thickest part of the crowd. I had no idea which man was Declan Baxter. Almost everybody here was taller than me and I soon lost sight of Allan in the crowd. I walked past a stilt-walker and a man on a unicycle to where a group of acrobats swung from a row of long white rope-ribbons. Two of them were juggling with five balls. I stared, entranced.

'Not much of a show, is it?' a woman walking past sneered.

'This is just for decoration,' the man beside her said. 'Declan's saving the big stuff for the show, later.' They moved on.

Wow. There was *more*? Declan Baxter must be even richer than I'd thought. There was still no sign of anyone remotely my age. And Allan hadn't reappeared. Grown-ups kept passing me and staring. I was feeling more and more uncomfortable. After another minute of wandering about, I headed for the door Allan had pointed out earlier. He was obviously still trying to talk to Declan Baxter and I didn't fancy hanging around inside the marquee any longer. A few minutes in the bathroom would kill some time.

I left the marquee and found myself outside the main house. A makeshift *Toilets* sign had been propped on a window ledge beside the second door down. I stopped before entering to finish my orange juice, then stood the glass on the ledge and headed inside. The building felt cool and quiet. I was standing in a wood-floored hallway, with corridors leading off on either side. There was no further sign but the bathroom surely had to be through the only door opposite. My feet echoed round the walls as I padded over. I could hear a girl's voice coming from inside.

'That's stupid.' She sounded younger than most of the guests I'd seen so far and very posh. '*You're* stupid.'

That *must* be the toilet.

I pushed the door open and walked into a big room that bent round in an L-shape. There were no windows, but the wall lights were bright and the room was bathed in a warm,

51

yellow glow. The shelves nearest to me were filled with books and games.

This didn't look anything like a bathroom.

'Hello?' It was the girl. 'Who's there?'

I had no choice but to show myself.

'Hi.' Cheeks burning, I walked into the main part of the room. I could hear the door I'd just walked through swinging shut but I paid it no attention. All my focus was on the area in front of me. It was huge and filled with old sofas and an array of floor cushions. A girl and a boy were sitting on the rug in the middle of the stone floor. The boy sprang to his feet – he was tall and slim, with thick fair hair that fell in a fringe almost as full as mine.

The girl stayed sitting, but raised her eyebrows. She was strikingly pretty, with slanting dark eyes and a tumble of blonde waves cascading down her back. One look at both of them revealed they were wearing hugely expensive designer clothes – the boy in a suit, the girl in a shimmering gold dress.

'What are you doing in here?' the girl demanded.

'I . . . I was looking for the restroom.' Damn, why did I always fall back into the American terms when I was nervous? I'd worked so hard to lose my accent in the past few years, it was totally annoying when words from the States crept back into my vocabulary. 'I mean the bathroom, the toilets.'

'There's no bathroom here,' the girl said with a haughty sniff. 'This part of the house is off limits to party guests. The toilet's a separate entrance next door.'

'Sorry,' I said.

52

'It's f . . . f . . . fine.' The boy smiled at me. 'I'm Wolf,' he said. 'This is my friend, Esme.'

'Esme . . . Baxter?' I exclaimed. 'Is this *your* party?'

Esme rolled her eyes. 'It's *Dad's* frickin' party. We're hiding out in the Den. The door to outside was supposed to be locked.'

'OK, sorry,' I said again. I couldn't work out what had happened. 'I must have read the sign wrong.' I headed back to the door. I grabbed the handle and tried to yank it open.

But it was stuck. I pulled again. The door wouldn't budge.

'Are you all right?' The boy, Wolf, appeared beside me.

'Can't open the door,' I said, my guts twisting into an embarrassed knot.

Wolf raised his eyebrows. 'Let's have a go . . .' He turned the handle himself, but the door still didn't open. He frowned. 'What the—?'

'What is it?' Now Esme was here too. She was barefoot but still nearly a head taller than me and model-style skinny. Jeez, were those *real diamonds* in her necklace?

Wolf turned to her. 'The door won't open,' he said.

'*WHAT?*' Esme tried the handle herself. No movement.

She turned to me accusingly. 'Well done!' she snapped. 'Whoever you are, you've managed to lock us in.'

9

Escape to Danger

'I didn't do anything,' I protested.

Esme paced dramatically across the room. Wolf tried the door again.

'It's frickin' jammed or something,' Esme snarled.

'OK.' Wolf stepped back, frowning. I followed his gaze around the room. There were no other visible exits. 'Then we're stuck.'

'Yeah, thanks to her.' Esme pointed at me. 'You must have done something to the door.'

'I didn't, I swear,' I said. 'There must be some other way out, isn't there?'

'No.' Esme shook out her long blonde hair. I had the sense that, despite her surface display of anxiety-fuelled rudeness, underneath she was enjoying all the drama.

I shrank against the wall, not enjoying it myself at all. For a start, Allan would surely have noticed I wasn't in the marquee anymore and what would he think? That I'd run away? Things wouldn't improve once I was found, either. I'd only just met Allan and he'd been so nice to me, bringing me to this party, and now the daughter of the host clearly thought it was *my* fault we were locked in this room together.

'I'm really sorry,' I said. 'If I did jam the door somehow, it was an accident.'

'It's not your f . . . f . . . fault,' Wolf said. 'And there's no need to be so melodramatic, Esme. This isn't the end of the world; we can just phone someone to let us out.'

'*I* can't phone anyone,' Esme said with a theatrical flourish. 'I left my mobile upstairs.'

Wolf turned to me, his eyebrows raised in question.

'I had to hand mine in at the door,' I said.

'Ah, so did I,' Wolf admitted.

Esme glared at him. 'But you're my *friend*, Wolf,' she said. 'You didn't have to do that. You wouldn't normally.'

Wolf shrugged. 'Dad m . . . made me – he said it was the polite thing to do seeing as all the other guests had to.' He paused. 'It's not such a big deal, Esme. Someone will notice when we don't show up later. Then they'll come looking for us.'

'That could take *hours*,' Esme whined. 'We'll miss the circus show Dad has organised.'

'You mean the acrobats and people in the marquee?' I said.

'That's nothing,' Esme said. 'Dad has a high-wire act lined up . . . there's even a tiger somewhere. I saw the trainer earlier.'

'A tiger?' I stared at her. 'In a private house? Isn't that illegal?'

Esme shrugged.

'Money buys you everything,' Wolf said drily. 'What's your name, anyway?'

'Madison,' I said.

'As in Madison Avenue?' Wolf said. 'You know, the street in New York with the ad agencies?'

'Er, yes.' I could feel myself blushing. Wolf was taller than me by a good few centimetres. He wasn't outstandingly handsome compared, say, to Rory's friend Marcus. His nose was slightly crooked and his lips a little thin. But there was real warmth in his grey-blue eyes.

We stared at each other for a moment. I had no idea what to say.

'Hey, guys.' Esme had wandered across the room and was standing facing one of the big couches. 'If you could tear yourselves away from the geography lesson, I think I've found a way out of here.'

'How?' Wolf asked.

Esme pulled the couch away from the wall, revealing a small door. 'It's locked,' she said, 'and I don't have the key, but if we could force it open, I know it leads to the cellars that run under the whole house.'

'I don't know, Ez,' Wolf said slowly. 'Your dad won't like us breaking a door down, and we won't r . . . r . . . really know which direction to head in once we're down there.'

'I'll know.' Esme put her hands on her slim hips. 'Man, Wolf is *such* a bad name for you. You should have been called Chip, for Chipmunk or something, not Wolf for . . . for Wolfhound.'

Wolfhound? Jeez, was that his real name?

Wolf's pale cheeks pinked. He rubbed his thick fringe off his forehead. 'Stop it, Ez.' He turned to me. 'W . . . what do you think, Madison?'

56

I glanced at the little door, thinking of Allan. He would definitely be wondering where I was by now. I looked up. Esme was watching me, hands still on her hips. The light from the lamps around her shimmered on the gold of her dress and lit up the white-blonde highlights in her hair. She looked haughty and beautiful and more than a little scary.

'It's Esme's house,' I said, hesitantly. 'If she thinks it's OK to break down the door, then that's what we should do.'

'Yes.' Esme grinned and offered me her hand to high-five.

I slapped it, grinning back. Esme might be a little bit full of herself, but there was something about her I liked.

'Fine.' Wolf threw his hands in the air. 'Bring it on.'

It took another ten minutes to lever the door open. In the end, Wolf broke the lock by inserting the aerial from an old-style radio between the door and the frame, then kicking at the lock.

'Yes!' Esme clapped her hands together. 'Thank goodness Mum never throws anything away.'

'Your mum's like that too?' I said.

Esme rolled her expressive eyes. 'She's the *worst*. A total hoarder.'

Wolf peered through the little door. 'I can see steps down. It's dark, though.'

'Not a problem.' Esme raced across the room and fetched a box from one of the shelves. She took out one of those fortune-telling Magic 8-balls that light up when you spin them. 'We can use this.' She gave the ball a shake as she crawled through the small door.

57

The outlook is good, said the ball.

'W . . . well, that's encouraging.' Wolf smiled. There was a gap between his front teeth. I wondered if that was what made him stammer.

'It's frickin' filthy in here.' Esme edged towards the steps.

I peered after her. It did look dusty. I glanced down at my best and most favourite top. I'm no princess about clothes, but I loved this particular T-shirt and hated the idea I might ruin it.

'Here, take my jacket.' Wolf started shrugging off his suit.

'No.' How embarrassing that he'd seen what I was thinking. 'I'll be fine.' I peered after Esme again. She was crouched low, by the top step.

'Come on, guys,' she said impatiently.

Wolf was still holding out his jacket. He was wearing a black top with a crew neck and short, close-fitting sleeves. His arms were as slim as the rest of him, but the muscles were well-defined. He might not be buff, but he looked strong.

'Esme's dress is much more expensive than my top,' I stammered.

'Yeah, but Esme doesn't value her dress,' Wolf said. 'And your top is . . . it's nice.'

'OK, thanks.' I was still hideously embarrassed but it was easier just to take the jacket than to argue anymore. As I slid it over my bare arms, I felt the fabric. Light wool with a silk lining. Jeez, Wolf's suit was probably as expensive as Esme's dress.

I crawled through the door, crept along the low-ceilinged passageway and followed Esme down the steps.

Halfway down, the Magic 8-ball's light went out and we were plunged into darkness. I froze.

Esme shook the ball again. *Cannot predict now*, it said, its dim light glowing again.

'N . . . not so encouraging,' Wolf said behind me.

At the bottom of the steps we found ourselves in a large room. The ceiling here was only just high enough for us to stand up. I reached my hands up to the rough plaster.

'This way.' Esme padded, barefoot, across the cold, dusty floor. She led us through two more doors into two more rooms. The first was cramped, filled with wooden crates, while the second was more spacious again, and lined with racks filled with wine bottles.

'Wow,' I said, looking round. 'There must be hundreds of bottles here.'

'Yeah, Daddy collects them,' Esme said dismissively. She strode off, shaking the Magic 8-ball again. *Ask again later,* it said.

'"Daddy" collects lots of things,' Wolf whispered in my ear. 'His favourite hobby is spending money.' He paused, lowering his voice further. 'Don't let Esme f . . . f . . . fool you. She might look tough, but she was sent off to boarding school when she was ten. She's had lots of money, but hardly any time with either of her parents.'

I glanced round at him as we followed Esme through the next door. What was Wolf's relationship with Esme, I wondered. He'd introduced her as his 'friend'. Was that, like, posh-kid speak for 'girlfriend'? They didn't act like they were going out together. In fact, Esme had been quite rude to him. Still, how would I know what was normal behaviour? The closest I'd ever got to having a boyfriend was a totally embarrassing date in year ten with Samuel Jones, a gorgeous boy from the year above me at school. He'd spent the whole time talking about a band he was into and how great they were live. When he finally stopped speaking, I couldn't think of a thing to say to him. As usual. After our date, Samuel had promised to call me, but he never did.

'Is your full name really Wolfhound?' I whispered as we crossed the next room. I had the strong sense we were walking uphill now and the air was definitely cooler than before. Hopefully we were near a way out.

'No,' Wolf sighed. 'But the truth isn't any better.'

'Go on.'

Wolf threw me a sideways glance, as if to check I wasn't making fun of him.

'I'm interested,' I said.

'OK, my full name is Wolfgang William Alexander Manville Yates.' Wolf paused. 'Go ahead and laugh, everyone else does.'

'Whoa,' I said. Up ahead Esme was struggling with the next door. 'That's a lot of name.'

'You're telling me,' Wolf muttered.

We caught up with Esme, just as she managed to open the door. We traipsed through, into another draughty, dusty room. This one was just as dark as the others – though with a higher ceiling – and filled with a strange smell, something sour and musty.

60

'Pooh.' Esme turned to face me. She wrinkled her nose. The 8-ball cast a spooky glow across her face. 'What the hell is that?'

'God knows,' Wolf said. 'Are we nearly out?'

'Sure,' Esme said. 'We've come right round the back of the house. We're near the big tent in the back garden.'

'But the tent . . . the marquee . . . that was out front,' I said.

'There are *two* tents.' Esme swept off across the room.

Wolf and I followed. A second later, the 8-ball light went out again. A soft padding sound echoed across the room behind us.

'What was that?' I hissed.

Esme shook the 8-ball. It lit and spoke: *My sources say no.*

I turned around, peering into the shadows behind us. I could make out empty floor and the door. Nothing else.

And then a low growl filled the room.

Esme grabbed my arm. 'Look.' She pointed the 8-ball light at the door we'd just walked through.

I gasped, unable to believe my eyes. An animal was watching us, its eyes yellow in the dim light, pacing past the door.

'Oh my God,' Wolf said hoarsely. 'It's the tiger for the circus show.'

10

Circus Show

A piercing scream filled the air, nearly bursting my eardrums. It was Esme. Wolf slapped his hand over her mouth.

'Ssshhhh,' I hissed.

Esme's scream ended as suddenly as it had begun. The tiger stopped padding. It was looking in our direction, its eyes like orange discs.

'Don't run,' Wolf whispered. 'Walk slowly away.'

Nodding, I started backing away. The tiger was still watching us.

'Nice kitty, good kitty.' The breathless whisper tumbled out of my mouth. My heart was pounding so hard I could barely hear myself speak.

I glanced over at the others. Wolf was holding Esme's hand now, tugging her backwards with him. Esme's eyes – huge and terrified – were fixed on the tiger. It hadn't moved.

Yet.

As we walked, I wondered how many seconds it would take the tiger to reach us. From the look of those sleek, muscular legs, not many. I looked around. In the dim glow of the Magic 8-ball light I could just make out an iron gate a couple of metres ahead. It was one of those concertina types that you

62

can pull across and push back and was fastened with padlocks to iron bars on the walls either side.

This metal gate stood between us and escape from the tiger.

'What's that doing there?' Esme whispered. She had followed my gaze and was staring, shocked, at the iron bars.

'I imagine it's keeping the tiger in,' I said softly.

'So how do we get past those padlocks?' Wolf whispered.

We looked up and down but there was no way through.

'It's wall to wall,' Wolf said. 'There's no gap.'

'Oh, frickin' hell,' Esme breathed. 'Frickin' frickin' hell.'

The tiger was still watching us. Totally motionless. Unbelievably sinister. It was preparing to leap. I could *feel* it. But how on earth could we get away? The metal gate was impassable, while the tiger stood between us and the door we'd come through earlier.

'We'll be fine.' Wolf sounded convinced, but I could see in his eyes that he was as terrified as I was.

I looked up at the gate. It went right to the ceiling. No, there was a small gap. Right at the top. It didn't leave enough space for a tiger – or a grown man – to crawl over, but there was surely enough for me, Wolf and Esme.

'Climb,' I ordered.

'What?' Esme breathed.

'She's right,' Wolf said. 'Hurry.' He put his foot in the latticed metal of the gate, about a metre off the ground, and hauled himself up.

I looked at the tiger. It was still watching us, standing without moving in front of the door we'd walked through. It felt like hours had passed since we'd seen it, but it was only a few seconds.

'Come on,' Wolf urged.

As he spoke, the tiger moved. It was padding towards us.

'AAAGH!' Esme screamed again. She dropped the 8-ball. It landed with a clunk on the stone ground.

The outlook is good.

The tiger roared. Sped up. Wolf, Esme and I turned and flung ourselves at the metal mesh. Clawing at the bars, I hauled myself up. Hand over hand. Foot over foot. Panting, I climbed. I didn't look down until my hands gripped the top of the gate. The metal bit into my palms. Now I looked down, just as the tiger reared up. Its paws swiped at the gate, just centimetres below my feet.

'Madison!' Wolf was right beside me, straddling the gate. He just fitted between the highest metal bar and the ceiling. 'Move!' He held out his hand.

I glanced down again. Again, the tiger swiped at my leg with his paw, missing me by centimetres. I scrambled higher. Beyond Wolf, Esme was almost over the gate. As I reached the top, there was a ripping sound. A strip of Esme's dress hung from the metal bars but Esme herself was over. Another rip as she dropped to the ground. Wolf was waiting for me. I balanced on one leg, shifting my weight and moving the other leg through the gap. I found a foothold on the other side.

'You OK?' Wolf asked.

'Sure.' My whole body was trembling as I climbed fully over the gate. I took a couple of steps down. The tiger was right on the other side of the bars. Its low, rumbling growl made the metal vibrate.

Wolf was climbing down beside me. His feet were perilously close to the tiger's raised paw.

'Jump away from the fence,' I gasped. 'Jump now!'

'Together,' Wolf said. 'One, two . . . three!'

We jumped. Landed on the hard ground with a jolt. I put out my hands to steady myself. Wolf grabbed my arm. And then Esme was there and the three of us were holding on to each other, hugging and laughing and crying all at once.

The tiger roared. We all jumped. But we were safe. And then we hugged and laughed and cried again.

The light from the 8-ball – still on the other side of the gate – went out and we were plunged into darkness.

Esme squealed. But there was no real terror in her scream now.

'We're nearly out,' she said. 'The next door leads to the side passage opposite the kitchen.'

She held my hand, Wolf on her other side. We felt our way to the wooden door. It was locked. Wolf battered it with his palms.

'Hey!' he yelled.

'All of us together,' Esme commanded. 'Go!'

The three of us hammered on the door, yelling at the tops of our voices. I don't know how long we did that for – I'd completely lost track of time since we'd got into the first cellar.

At last a voice sounded on the other side. 'Wait a minute. Wait, let me get the key.'

We stopped slamming our fists against the door and stood, waiting. A few moments later, a key fumbled in the lock. The door opened, revealing the bright light of the passage and Baxter's man, Hobbs, in his waistcoat and yellow tie.

'Esme?' he said. 'Wolf?' His eyes glanced over me. 'What . . .?'

We stepped into the light, as Esme explained what had happened to us. All three of us were filthy. Wolf's face was smeared with dust and his shirt was torn, while the bottom of Esme's beautiful gold dress was in tatters. I looked down at my own clothes. Wolf's jacket was covered in dirty smudges but my T-shirt underneath didn't seem to have a mark on it. In fact, my jeans weren't too bad, either – just a bit dusty. I wiped my face with my hands, wishing I had a mirror.

'Let me fetch Mr Baxter,' Hobbs said at last.

'No, Daddy will just get cross,' Esme said.

I suddenly remembered Allan – and the bizarre circum-stances under which I'd come here. 'I need to get back to the marquee,' I said.

'I'll show you the way,' Wolf said.

'I must insist on fetching Mr Baxter,' Hobbs repeated. 'Or taking you to him. He has to know what has just happened. Apart from anything else, I need his authorisation to go down to the basement and check on the animal.'

Esme hesitated. 'OK, then,' she said. 'We'll all go.'

She leaned down, grabbed the torn hem of her dress and ripped the jagged edge off. Her dress now skimmed her knees at the front, a little lower at the back. It still looked stunning.

66

'Wow,' I said, impressed.

Esme gave a shrug, then led the way through the house. We entered a large kitchen – three times the size of mine – with two sets of double sinks and the biggest refrigerator I'd ever seen.

As I followed Esme through a very formal dining room with a long central table, I wondered how Allan would react when he saw me. I shucked off Wolf's jacket and handed it back to him. Wolf slipped it on in silence. His lips were pressed together and his forehead creased in a frown, as if he were worried about something.

Esme led us along a corridor, past several closed doors and out into the garden through a side exit. The front garden marquee was straight ahead. As we headed towards it, I glanced along to the door with the toilet sign beside it.

The door was there, along with my empty glass on the window ledge where I'd left it, but there was no sign. I peered again. Definitely no toilet sign. Had I imagined it?

'After you,' Wolf said. He was standing back, waiting for me to go inside the marquee.

I followed Esme inside. She was already drawing horrified gasps and astonished looks from the adults she passed. They were all still standing around with drinks, chatting loudly, just as they had been when I'd left. I could only have actually been gone about twenty minutes, but it felt like weeks had passed.

Esme headed for the thickest part of the crowd. People parted as she approached. I followed in her wake, with Wolf and Hobbs behind us. The party chatter stopped, as Esme walked up to a man in an expensively cut suit in the centre of a group. He was tall with thick grey hair and piercing eyes. This must be Declan Baxter, the party's host.

'Esme?' he said. He didn't smile.

'Daddy, we got trapped with the tiger,' Esme said, making her voice small and babyish.

Her father curled his lip. For a second he looked embarrassed, then concern filled his face.

'Darling, how awful,' he said, reaching forward to pat her shoulder. 'How on earth did it happen?'

'We were in the Den,' Esme went on, her lips trembling slightly, 'and then the door stuck after *she* came in.' She pointed at me.

Everyone turned to look at me. My face felt like it was on fire. I looked down.

'We went down to the cellars to try and find another way out,' Esme said. She was still making her voice all little-girly. 'We came through loads of doors and the tiger was behind one of them.'

'Goodness,' said one of the women standing in the crowd. A gasp ran round the others. There were loads of people watching us now.

'As luck had it, Mr Baxter, I heard them,' Hobbs said. 'They were hammering on the door of the shed that was built where the stable used to be.'

Declan Baxter nodded thoughtfully. The man beside him – shorter, with a mean look in his eye – shook his head.

I looked around. There was no sign of Allan.

'Go and check the door to the Den, Hobbs,' Baxter ordered.

His gaze flickered from his daughter to Wolf, then his eyes rested on me.

'And you are?' he demanded.

I gulped. Mr Baxter exuded an aura of absolute power. I could totally see where Esme got her scary manner from.

'This is M . . . Madison, sir,' Wolf butted in. 'She was great, actually, really h . . . helped when we were t . . . trapped.'

'Yes, she practically saved my life,' Esme said. 'Unlike Wolf . . .' she smiled, her voice returning to normal. 'Wolf screamed like a girl.'

What? I stared at her, shocked to my core. Wolf had been fantastic earlier. If anything, Esme was the one who had screamed. Esme was still smiling, as if the whole thing were a joke.

'There's a surprise,' the mean-eyed man standing next to Baxter said sarcastically. 'My son, rescued by a girl . . . two girls . . .' He glared at Wolf. 'What do you have to say to that? Is it true?'

Wolf went bright red. 'N . . . n . . . no, sir . . .' he stammered. 'W . . . w . . . we all h . . . h . . . helped.'

I felt myself blushing in sympathy. Wolf's stammer was ten times worse around his father. No wonder he'd looked worried about coming in here earlier.

His dad sneered. He had the same high cheekbones as Wolf, but his mean eyes and hard, cold demeanour were a million miles from Wolf's friendly manner. Wolf looked down at the floor.

This was *so* unfair. It was hard to speak up with so many people watching, but I couldn't let Wolf go undefended.

'Wolf *didn't* scream,' I insisted. 'He was very brave.'

'Really?' His father sniffed contemptuously, like he didn't believe a word.

'I checked the Den door,' Hobbs said, reappearing silently at Declan Baxter's elbow. 'It's working perfectly. Not locked at all.'

That was odd.

'The kids must have panicked,' Wolf's father said with another sneer.

'Madison?' I turned around. Allan was standing behind me, his mouth open in shock. 'What on earth . . .?'

I scuttled towards him, forgetting the others in my desire to explain what had happened. Allan's eyes widened as I told him about the door to the Den mysteriously jamming, then grew more horrified as I explained how we'd come across the tiger.

'Oh my God,' he said. He pulled me into a hug. 'Are you OK?'

'I'm fine.'

Allan glanced over at Declan Baxter. He was surrounded by people.

'Do you still need to speak to Mr Baxter?' I asked.

Allan shook his head. 'He's already ignored me twice,' he said with a rueful smile. 'Anyway, that's not important right now. What matters is that you're safe. Come on, you're white as a sheet, let's get you out of here. I've got my car, I'll run you home.'

70

He took my arm, ready to steer me away. I just had time to register how sweet he was being – especially compared to Esme and Wolf's fathers – when Esme herself appeared beside me.

'You're not running off, are you?' she said. 'Stay and watch the circus show. I'm going to get changed, but I won't be a minute.'

I bit my lip. Part of me was tempted to stay, but now that the euphoria of escaping the tiger had faded, I actually felt pretty shaky. What I wanted more than anything was my own home and a hot bath.

'Maybe another time?' Allan said. I smiled at him gratefully.

'Sure. Where d'you live? What's your number?' Esme produced a phone and we swapped details.

It wasn't until Allan and I had left the marquee that I realised I hadn't seen Wolf to say goodbye. I looked over my shoulder as we headed through to the main house, but there was no sign of him.

'What was Esme Baxter like?' Allan asked.

'Nice,' I said, then remembered the rather cruel way she'd humiliated Wolf in front of his father. I was sure she hadn't meant to be unkind, but it was certainly insensitive. 'Complicated, though.'

Allan nodded. 'Like father, like daughter.' He paused. 'It's great you might meet up again . . . seeing as you obviously hit it off.'

We passed a clown with a tray of drinks. Allan took a glass of water and offered it to me. I drank thirstily. I had the strong sense there was something Allan wanted to say. 'What is it?' I asked.

'Nothing.' Allan led me outside and we crossed the crunchy gravel drive.

'So how come Mr Baxter invited you to his party if he didn't want to speak to you?' I asked as we turned onto the pavement.

Allan grimaced. 'Oh, I'm way too far down the food chain for Baxter to take any notice of me. Still, I found something out . . . something that Baxter's done.'

I stared at him, deeply curious. '*What?*' I asked.

Allan lowered his voice. 'This is highly confidential, Madison. You *have* to keep it a secret, OK?'

'Sure,' I said as we walked along. Excitement thrilled through me. 'What has Mr Baxter done?'

'Nothing I can prove yet,' Allan said. 'But . . . look, when I said I knew him through work . . . well, it's true, but what I *really* meant was that I was investigating him . . . I didn't say before because I didn't want to put you in an awkward position at the party . . .'

My throat tightened. 'Investigating him for what?' I said.

Allan stopped beside a black car, parked on the side of the road. 'Get in,' he said. 'I'll tell you while I drive you home.'

11

Teatime Tension

I hesitated. Allan's car was large and shiny. I had no idea what make it was, but it looked as stylish as his suits, with its sleek wooden dashboard and elegantly curved bonnet. I stood on the pavement, Annie's endless warnings about getting into cars with strangers threading through my head, but Allan had already proved himself a decent and caring person. Hadn't he? Everything he'd said and done so far suggested he was simply interested in getting to know me a little.

'I can call you a taxi if you'd rather, Madison,' he said.

I took a deep breath. 'It's fine, thanks.' I got into the passenger seat as Allan pulled onto the road. As we drove off, a few spots of rain spattered the windscreen. I peered out of the window, surprised. I'd been so preoccupied I hadn't even noticed how much the sky had clouded over. It was still early evening – not yet 7.30 pm.

'Declan Baxter is a phenomenally successful business-man,' Allan said, his eyes on the road. 'But rumours about his criminal activities have been circulating for years.'

'Have the police looked into him?' I said.

Allan shrugged. 'I think there've been a couple of small-scale investigations, but nothing has ever come of them. I don't know whether that's because there was a cover-up or whether the police found no evidence of wrongdoing.'

I thought of Esme. This was her father we were talking about.

'Maybe he's innocent?' I suggested.

Allan gave a snort. 'Somehow I doubt that,' he said. 'There's no smoke without fire.'

'So . . . so what exactly are you investigating about him?' I asked.

Allan hesitated.

'I won't tell anyone,' I said. I wanted to explain how much I wanted to be an investigative journalist myself, but I still felt too shy. Allan was *so* cool. How could I tell him I aspired to the same job that he obviously did so well?

'OK.' Allan nodded. 'I know I can trust you . . . I'm trying to find out about some missing girls . . . that is, rumours of girls coming into the country and disappearing without a trace.'

'That's . . . isn't that called trafficking?' I said, trying to sound knowledgeable. Allan was actually sharing proper, grown-up information. Unlike Annie, who treated me like a child, he was talking to me as if I were an equal.

'There's no suggestion that the girls are being used illegally – no hint of prostitution or slave labour . . .' Allan went on. 'Just a bunch of rumours that Baxter pays them to enter the country . . . then "disappears" them.'

'Whoa.' I shivered. 'What was the new information you got today?'

74

'A name and a number,' Allan said. 'Miriam 21.'

'What d'you think it means?'

'No idea, I'm afraid.' Allan sighed. 'Maybe it's the name and age of the latest girl.'

We drove on for a while in silence. I checked my face for dirty smudges in the mirror above the passenger seat, and wiped away a couple of grubby smears. We were getting close to my house, when Allan cleared his throat.

'So, do you think you'll meet up with Baxter's daughter, Esme, again?'

'I guess.' I thought about it. Esme had acted a bit spoilt, for sure, and she'd definitely taken her teasing of Wolf too far in front of his dad, but she'd also been funny and interesting. Of course Esme herself wasn't the whole story. If I were honest, I wanted to see Wolf again too – he intrigued me as much as Esme – and the only way I could do that was through her.

'What about me?' Allan said. 'Now we've met and you've had a chance to hang out for a bit, would you like to get together again?' He paused. 'I don't want to do anything that will make you feel uncomfortable. I realise at this stage that I can't be any kind of conventional father to you, but . . .' He tailed off.

'Yes,' I said with a smile. It struck me that a lot of men would have behaved just like Lauren and Annie had predicted – running a mile in the face of a child they had never actively wanted – and that I was really lucky that Allan seemed genuinely to want to get to know me.

'Great.' Allan smiled back. 'I'll give you a ring, then.'

A few minutes later, he dropped me at the end of my road. As I walked in the front door, Annie was flapping about in the hallway.

'There you are, Madison,' she said, her face filling with relief. 'I was going to have to leave you a message. Did you have a nice time with Rosa?'

It took me a second to remember my cover story, so much had happened since I set off earlier this afternoon. Thank goodness Wolf had lent me his jacket. Without it, my top would have got dirty and then Annie would have been full of questions about what I'd been doing.

'Great, thanks,' I said. 'What was the message about?'

'Oh.' Annie's hand fluttered to her chest. 'Just that Lydia called with a last-minute invite for us to go for supper. I was supposed to be there fifteen minutes ago. I didn't think you'd be back in time, but now you are, you can come too.'

'Right.' I could tell from the slightly fake-smiley way Annie was speaking that she had some hidden agenda.

'Lydia will be so pleased that you can come,' Annie went on. 'Lauren's going to be there too.'

So that was it. I'd refused to talk to Annie about having a sperm donor father, so now she was hoping that I'd speak to Lauren about it.

'I need to take a shower first, though,' I said, hoping I could get out of the visit. Honestly, it was so typical of Annie to try and force the issue like this. Thinking it through, I was certain Lauren wasn't behind our meeting – she was letting things be . . . letting me come to her when I was ready . . . Why couldn't Annie do that too?

'Please, Madison.' Annie wrung her hands together, her voice suddenly all wobbly. 'It'll only be a couple of hours and Lydia will think it rude if—'

'Fine,' I said, my irritation rising. Why couldn't Annie ever say what she properly meant? 'But I still don't want to talk about *anything.*'

I stomped off to my room and splashed some water on my face. Considering our climb over the iron gate, my jeans didn't look too bad. I decided not to bother to change them. I'd have a bath when I got back.

Annie and I walked to Lauren's mum's house in silence. Annie tried to get me talking about the weather of all things. Again, it was so obviously a fake topic that I felt really resentful. Rory opened the door to us. He was in the living room with a bunch of his friends, including the gorgeous Marcus, who gave me such a sexy smile as I passed the door that I nearly fainted.

Lydia and Lauren were in the kitchen. Lauren's skin had that same peachy glow as before and her belly seemed even bigger than it had earlier in the week. She struggled to her feet as we came in and Annie immediately started fussing, saying she thought Lauren looked pale and tired.

'D'you think perhaps you're doing too much, Lauren sweetie?' she went on anxiously.

What was she talking about? As far as I could see, Lauren looked healthier than I'd ever seen her.

'I'm fine,' Lauren said with a hint of irritation in her voice. 'I'm going swimming every morning and—'

'Are you sure that's not too much?' Annie said.

Lauren's voice rose: 'Well, according to Chelsey Barton's pregnancy book, swimming is the best exercise you can do if—'

'Why don't I take you upstairs, Annie?' Lydia said quickly. 'I've just bought a new dress I wanted to show you.'

I met Lauren's eyes. We both knew Lydia was trying to get Annie out of the way.

'You girls stay here,' Lydia went on. 'This one's for middle-aged ladies only.' She left the room, Annie trailing in her wake.

Lauren sat down heavily at the kitchen table again and rolled her eyes.

'What is Annie like?' she said with a sigh.

'Tell me about it,' I said. 'I have to live with her.'

Lauren grimaced. She fingered the jewelled, vintage cross around her neck. 'You know she's been on the phone to me every day since I last saw you, worrying that you're not coping with this sperm donor stuff and begging me to try talking to you.'

I looked away.

'I've told her you're too sensible to go chasing some ridiculous dream, but she won't listen. She thinks you're going to try tracking down the donor dad . . .'

'*Our* donor dad,' I said, turning back to her.

Lauren threw me a sharp look. 'He won't want to know

78

you,' she said. Her blue eyes bored into me. She took her hand away from the cross around her neck and pressed it flat on the table for emphasis. 'If he'd wanted to know you, he wouldn't have been an *anonymous* donor, would he?'

What was Lauren saying? That I wasn't worth knowing? Well, she was wrong. Totally wrong. Allan *did* want to know me. Anger spiralled up inside me. How dare Lauren assume she knew what someone in Allan's position would think or feel or say or do? How dare she think she knew better than me about what *I* should do?

'Don't look at me like that, Mo,' Lauren said fiercely. 'I'm only looking out for you.'

'I can take care of myself.' I marched to the door, feeling really furious now. 'Tell Lydia I'm sorry about dinner and tell Annie I've gone home.'

'Wait—'

But I didn't stop to listen. Tears pricked at my eyes as I headed back to the front door and let myself out. I didn't know why I was so upset, just that everything with Lauren seemed to be changing now. It was partly the baby and partly her refusal to understand how I felt about Allan . . . it really hurt.

I switched off my phone, got home and had the long soak in the bath I'd been looking forward to. Annie arrived back about an hour later. Again, she was all concerned and wanting to talk, and again, I walked away, shutting myself up in my room and watching movies into the small hours.

I slept late the next day, Sunday, and it wasn't until I'd been awake for half an hour or so that I remembered my phone was still switched off. I turned it on, to find messages from Rosa and Esme. Rosa's was an invite to go shopping the next day. Esme's said:

Come over Thurs? No tigers! Ex

I texted 'yes' to both. Even if my family were really annoying, at least I had friends.

12

Undercover Mission

I enjoyed shopping with Rosa. She was full of questions about my meeting with Allan and wide-eyed with horror when I told her about escaping the tiger. I half thought of asking Esme if I could bring Rosa along to meet her, but it seemed a bit presumptuous. Anyway, I wasn't sure if they'd get on. From the short time I'd spent with her, it was already clear Esme wasn't everyone's cup of tea.

Allan rang me just before lunchtime the next day. He said he was about to fly to France on business, but that he'd be back in *The Examiner* offices on Friday morning.

'I'm in an all-day meeting with the editorial team,' he said. 'The desk editor is Matthew Flint.' He paused expectantly, as if I should know who this was.

'Wow,' I said, hoping this was the right response.

'Matthew's young but he's *really* building a reputation,' Allan said proudly.

'Actually, I've always wanted to be that kind of proper journalist.' I hadn't meant to tell him right then, but I couldn't stop myself. As the words gushed out of me, I blushed. What was Allan going to think of me now?

'That's fantastic,' Allan said. 'I'm thrilled you're interested.

Perhaps . . . when I'm back . . . we can talk about that . . . about the best way to get started?'

'Oh, yes, thank you.'

How cool was that? Allan was being really encouraging, like he thought it was perfectly realistic for me to want to be a serious journalist. Annie was so negative about everything . . . always seeing the potential problems in any course of action. It was wonderful to have someone listening to my hopes and dreams and sounding so enthusiastic.

I told Allan that I was going over to see Esme on Thursday.

'At her house?' he asked.

'Yes.'

'Great,' he said. 'That's . . .' He paused. 'That's great.'

I was sure there was something else he wanted to say. My mind ran over the possible options. Was he worried about me going alone to a house where a suspected criminal lived? Or was he hoping I'd have a chance to speak to Baxter himself?

'Mr Baxter will be at work, won't he?' I said.

'I would think so.' Allan hesitated again.

'Yes.' I frowned, still trying to work out what was on his mind. And then I thought I saw . . . I'd be in a brilliant position to try and find out more about the stuff on Baxter that Allan was investigating. If I could discover something useful, Allan would be really pleased *and* I'd show him I was serious about becoming a journalist.

'D'you want me to ask Esme if she knows anything . . . say, about Miriam 21?'

'No,' Allan said quickly. 'No, I'm sure she won't know and if she happened to mention you'd said something, it might put you in danger with Baxter himself.'

'OK, well, shall I just keep my ears open? See if anyone mentions it?'

'Only if you're comfortable doing that,' Allan said. 'I don't want you putting yourself at risk.'

Time passed slowly until Thursday afternoon. I arrived at Esme's house five minutes early so hung around outside for a bit. The marquee was gone from the front garden, and the house itself looked even bigger than before. It really was a mansion. Three floors high, plus the hidden warren of basement cellars, and at least six rooms across, with wings extending away, towards the back garden, on either side.

Esme let me in. She was wearing black leggings and a fitted orange top. I glanced at my own jeans and black T-shirt. Esme's clothes were just as casual as mine but, on her, everything looked amazing. That top was definitely designer, anyway. Esme flicked back her long blonde hair and grabbed my arm as she led me up two flights of stairs. She chattered non-stop.

'It's awesome that you've come round. I get so bored in the holidays. Bertie, that's my older brother, he's such a freak and the twins are a total nightmare. They're all out right now. Do you have brothers and sisters?'

I started explaining about Lauren – I wasn't quite ready to talk about Shelby – but I'd only said a few words before Esme was onto another topic.

'Wolf's coming over too. He kept bugging me about calling you.' Her eyes twinkled with mischief. 'I was starting to think maybe I should be jealous . . .'

'Oh, er . . .' I stammered, feeling embarrassed. 'Is he your boyfriend, then?'

Esme stopped and blinked at me. 'No, not exactly.' She lowered her voice to a conspiratorial whisper. 'I mean, I think he'd *like* to take things further but to be honest . . . well, don't get me wrong, Wolf's great, but we've known each other *forever.* I don't really think of him like that.'

I nodded, hoping my cheeks weren't as visibly flushed as they felt. It was kind of a relief to know I wasn't barging in on some boyfriend/girlfriend thing, but the news that Wolf might be into Esme made me feel strangely empty. I glanced over at her. Esme was wearing glittery eye make-up that would have looked ridiculous on me, but that on her looked sophisticated. The word 'sparkling' could have been invented for her.

Of course Wolf was going to be into her. What boy wouldn't be?

Esme turned off the stairs onto the second-floor landing. 'My room's along here,' she said, pointing to the corridor on our right. As we walked along, she explained what lay behind each of the doors we were passing. 'Spare room. Never used. Spare bathroom, if you need it.' She waved her hand to the left.

'What about back there?' I pointed to the other side of the landing and the corridor that lay beyond.

Esme made a face. 'Daddy's office is down there. We're not even allowed along the corridor in case we mess anything up.'

'Really?' My heartbeat quickened. Baxter's private office was surely the most likely place for him to keep data on his dodgy business dealings.

'Yeah.' Esme rolled her eyes. 'Daddy's a total control freak.'

We walked on. 'I'm in here.' Esme opened a door into the biggest, most elegant teenage bedroom I'd ever seen. Forget posters on the wall, Esme had *signed, framed* photographs of every major music or film star I'd ever heard of – and plenty I hadn't.

'Jeez,' I said, looking around. A lot of the pictures were old, of people in thirties and forties style poses. The effect was incredibly glamorous. All the photo frames were black and the walls behind were cream with a black lace effect at the top and bottom. There was a black lace cover on the huge double bed and a large walk-in closet at the far end of the room, past two red velvet sofas. 'Wow!'

Esme giggled. 'It's just a bedroom.'

Her phone rang. She muttered into it for a moment, then came off the mobile with a sigh.

'Mum's nagging me about sorting out some school stuff I left in the car. I told her you were here but she's insisting I go down and deal with it. I'll only be a few minutes. Eight or ten max. Why don't you wait here?'

'No problem.' I wasn't sure I could face Esme's mum yet. If she was anything like her husband or her daughter, I imagined she'd be pretty scary.

85

I stood at the door and watched Esme walk away. As she disappeared down the stairs, I glanced across the landing towards the corridor opposite, where Esme had said her dad's office was located.

Allan would give his right arm to be here now, with such an opportunity to investigate. I could just see him, creeping over to the office and looking for information on Miriam 21.

And then it struck me. Why shouldn't *I* go looking? Mr Baxter wasn't here. Esme wasn't going to be back for at least another five minutes. I could certainly have a quick peek . . . My heart pounded. It was reckless to even consider doing such a thing. But I wasn't really risking anything. If Esme came back and couldn't find me, I'd just pretend I went wandering about and had got lost. A thrill of excitement throbbed through me. Why shouldn't I investigate?

It was what a proper journalist would do. And it would be helpful to Allan. He'd be really impressed if I came back with information about Miriam 21.

Yes. That thought settled it. I took a deep breath and set off.

13

Miriam 21

Seconds later, I had crossed the landing. No sounds rose up from the stairs or along from the corridor. The whole house still felt deserted though it was so large that a party could probably have been going on in a different wing and I wouldn't have heard it. I scuttled along the forbidden corridor. The first door opened onto a bathroom – the mirror image of the one I'd just passed on the other side of the landing.

The second door led into an office: Baxter's private study. I took in the two long desks and array of computers at a glance. The room was almost entirely paper-free. A bookcase containing several rows of leather-bound hardbacks stood against one wall but there were no filing cabinets . . . no notes or pads . . . no diaries. If it wasn't for the three computers and ornamental pen set at the end of the desk, you wouldn't even know this *was* an office.

I raced across the room and tapped on the first computer's keyboard. The machine fired – to a screen requesting a password. It was the same with the other two computers. I sighed. What had I expected? That an eminent businessman would leave his work content unprotected?

I tugged at the shallow drawer that ran under the first desk. Empty, apart from a couple of Post-it notepads and two biros. It was the same with the second desk. I looked back at the computers and a strong sense of defeat swamped me. When Lauren had been investigating her birth family, she had broken into offices and found clues to her past . . . names and addresses and all sorts of useful data. I couldn't even get beyond the first hurdle of a password. I was certainly kidding myself if I thought I stood a chance as a proper journalist.

I wandered over to the bookcase again. A photograph of Baxter and a lady I assumed was Esme's mum stood on one shelf. Below was a row of other snapshots. One in particular stood out. It looked like a family shot, mum and dad plus four children: a blond boy with a sulky expression, two small kids in matching overalls and a little girl who was unmistakably Esme. She had positioned herself in the middle of the photo, her arms spread wide and a huge, beaming smile on her face. Her hair was shorter than now, but even blonder. She made the other people in the picture look somehow washed out.

I reached out to take a closer look at the photo and accidentally knocked the one next to it onto the ground. I crouched down to pick it up. Honestly, what was I doing? I really needed to get out of here and make my way back to Esme's room before she returned.

As my fingers curled around the picture I'd knocked onto the floor, the bottom row of books on the bookcase caught my eye. The leather label on one of the books was peeling. Surely real leather wouldn't come off like that? I touched the book.

The whole label came away in my hands, revealing a plastic frame behind. I gasped. The whole book was a fake. Just a fancy-looking cover. I scanned the entire bottom row. They were *all* fakes . . . false fronts of books in front of hollow plastic frames.

Why would anyone bother to stack a shelf with pretend books? I pulled at the plastic frame I'd first revealed. I was expecting it to be wedged in, but it came away easily in my hand. Gently I moved the book-fronted frame next to it. And the next. A small wooden tray was hidden behind the frames. Six memory sticks sat on the tray. I scooped them up and brought them into the light. My heart beat against my throat. Why was Baxter hiding stuff here?

Each stick was marked in highlighter pen with the letter 'M' and a number. I scanned them quickly: M15, M4, M16, M19, M8 . . . M21.

Was this *Miriam 21*?

I placed the other sticks back in the wooden tray and shoved the plastic frames and their false fronts into position. I replaced the leather label from the first frame and propped the family photo back on its shelf. Then I looked down at the memory stick in my hand.

A cold chill snaked down my spine. Should I try opening it on one of these computers?

'Madison?' The voice from the doorway made me jump.

I looked up, my fist closing over the memory stick. Wolf was standing, gazing at me with a frown on his face.

'What are you doing in here?'

'I . . . er . . . I got lost.' Jeez, the excuse I'd imagined using earlier sounded ridiculous now it was actually coming out of my mouth. I could feel my cheeks burning.

'Oh.' Wolf was still frowning. 'Esme's room is down there.' He pointed along the corridor. 'I just saw her downstairs. She was having a row with her mum but she said I should come up and keep you company.'

'Right. Great.' I was still holding the memory stick tightly in my hand. Should I leave it on the desk? Drop it on the floor? No. Even if Wolf didn't see, when Mr Baxter next came in here, he'd know someone had been snooping around. Anyway, I needed to look at what was on the stick.

Wolf led the way back to Esme's bedroom. I tucked the memory stick into my jeans pocket. How on earth was I going to examine its contents?

Wolf glanced round at me. 'How're you doing, Madison?'

'Great,' I lied. 'How about you?'

'Great,' Wolf echoed. He was dressed in skinny jeans and a longer-sleeved version of the black top he'd had on at the party. Like Esme, his clothes seemed effortlessly put together – almost as if he'd been styled.

As we reached Esme's bedroom, Wolf ran his hand through his thick fair hair. He seemed suddenly awkward and embarrassed.

'Er, thanks f . . . for sticking up for me with my dad the other day.' His face turned crimson.

I shrugged. 'Well, you saved us,' I said, my mind flashing back to the tiger. 'If you hadn't said to walk slowly, I'd have run and the tiger would have chased us and caught us before we'd got to the gate.'

'My dad hates me anyway,' Wolf said quietly.

I stared at him. Surely hate was too strong a word. Then I remembered how I sometimes felt about Annie. 'Why d'you think that?' I asked.

Wolf made a face. 'You've heard my name: Wolfgang William blah . . . blah . . . blah . . . I was called after Mozart and Shakespeare among others and . . . well, that's a lot to live up to. I guess my dad thinks I'm a f . . . failure.'

The atmosphere in the room tensed. I had no idea what to say to that. Luckily, Esme chose that moment to bounce in.

'Oh my *God*, my mother is *such* a nightmare. She kept me down there for *hours*. I'm so sorry, Madison. Hey, Wolf, shall we go to the music room? We could carry on with "Fever Light". What d'you think, Madison?'

I stared at her. 'What's "Fever Light"?' I asked.

'A song Wolf wrote. He's laid the backing track. I'm doing vocals.'

'Wow.' I looked at Wolf. He was still looking a bit awkward, but I was pretty sure it was because he was embarrassed about his dad. He had no idea I'd been snooping about in Mr Baxter's office. My hand drifted to my pocket. I could feel the memory stick pressing against my jeans. I *had* to find some way of looking at it, then returning it to its hiding place behind those fake books. Hopefully the music room Esme was referring to wasn't too far away and I'd be able to slip out while she and Wolf were busy and make my way back here.

91

Esme grabbed a laptop from behind one of the velvet red sofas. 'Come on,' she urged. 'I've written some new lyrics – they're on this.'

'I don't know about changing the lyrics,' Wolf said with a frown.

He followed Esme to the door. I hesitated. Maybe I could hang back and creep over to the office right now.

No chance.

'Come *on*, Madison,' Esme ordered.

I had no choice but to follow them both downstairs.

The music room was about as far away from Esme's bedroom as it could have been – on the ground floor and right round the other side of the house. I stood in the doorway, amazed at what I was looking at. Two rooms, one connected to the other by a soundproofed door, lay in front of me. The first contained a mixing deck and a computer. Through a large window, I could see the second was full of instruments: three guitars and a bass, plus a drum kit and two microphones.

'This is a proper recording studio,' I said.

Esme shrugged. 'One of Daddy's hobbies,' she said.

Wolf met my eyes. He raised his eyebrows as if to acknowledge my surprise.

'Cool, isn't it?' he said.

I nodded. Esme opened her laptop and fiddled with the keys for a moment.

'It's just an extra two lines,' she said in that little-girly, wheedling tone she'd used with her father at the party.

Wolf bent over her shoulder and read the words on the screen. 'F . . . fine,' he said. 'If you insist.'

'Yayy!' Esme raced into the room with the instruments and positioned herself in front of one of the microphones.

Wolf sat down at the mixing deck. 'Are you OK with all this, Madison?' he said. 'It's just when Esme gets an idea in her head . . .'

'It's fine.' I glanced at Esme's laptop which she'd left on one of the stools by the deck. Maybe I could use it to take a look at the memory stick before I returned it. 'D'you think it would be OK if I borrowed Esme's laptop for a minute?'

I held my breath.

'I'm sure Esme won't mind,' Wolf said. He picked up a pair of headphones and started talking to Esme in the other room.

I dragged a stool to the back of the room, took the laptop and opened it up.

Wolf and Esme were busy talking. Neither of them were looking at me. Palms sweating, I pulled the 'M21' memory stick out of my pocket and slid it into the USB port.

As I'd suspected, a folder marked *Miriam 21* appeared on the screen. So this *was* the clue Allan had been following. I opened it up. It contained just one file.

The Miriam Project: Miriam 21
Natalia K. 19. 5ft 4in to: Flat 4, 30 Burnside Road, NW3. Due July 26.

Fear rose inside me. Was Natalia one of the missing girls Allan had talked about? She was obviously being sent to this Burnside Road address on July 26? *Wait*, today was the 27th. Did that mean this Natalia K was already there? How long would she be held? NW3 was Hampstead, the same area as Baxter's house, so the address must be nearby. I looked up. Wolf was still chatting with Esme. I felt sick with sudden fear. Should I call the police? No, that was crazy. I had no basis, other than Allan's suspicions, for thinking that the details on this memory stick were anything other than entirely harmless. I should just call Allan. Tell him what I'd found out. But first I *had* to put the memory stick back. I slid it out of the laptop and into my pocket, then I shut the laptop and put it back on the stool.

Wolf glanced round. 'We're ready. Esme's about to sing. The track's laid underneath.'

Esme's voice filled the room. Pure and sweet, it suited the soulful acoustic accompaniment though Esme had a habit of drawling the lyrics so I couldn't actually make out any of the words she was singing.

After a minute or so, she stopped. 'What d'you think?' she asked.

Wolf turned to me. 'Madison?'

'It sounds amazing,' I said truthfully. My hand felt for my pocket, where the memory stick nestled next to my mobile.

'Thanks.' Wolf blushed slightly. Esme grinned.

'D'you want a go, singing?' she asked.

'Me? No way.' I shook my head, desperate to think of some excuse for getting back to Esme's bedroom. 'Er, I think I left something upstairs. I'm just going to go back for it.'

'OK.' Esme wasn't listening properly. She'd picked up the bass and was picking out a line of notes.

Wolf stared at me. 'What did you leave upstairs?' he said, slowly.

'Er, my phone.' I tried to keep my gaze on him steady.

'OK,' he said. 'Can you remember the way?'

'Sure,' I said.

I slipped out of the room and hurried away. In spite of what I'd said, I got hopelessly lost. It was ten minutes before I found the right staircase and made my way to Mr Baxter's office. I replaced the memory stick then headed back to the music room.

As I walked, I tried Allan's number, but my call went straight to voicemail. I didn't want to leave a message about something so confidential. Anyway, there was nothing Allan could do from where he was in France.

I Google Mapped the Burnside Road address. As I'd thought, it was just around the corner. If Natalia K *was* there, she might be moved on at any moment. I really wanted to speak to her. I mean, if she was connected with the *Miriam Project,* she would surely know all about it – *and* about the missing girls.

Maybe I should check out the address myself?

No, it was crazy to think about getting involved. I kept walking and, a few minutes later, I reached the music room, where Esme was singing again.

I stopped, spellbound for a second by the haunting melody. Wolf was still hunched over the mixing deck. He smiled as I walked in. 'Find it?' he said.

'Er, yes.' Jeez, I'd almost forgotten about my supposed missing phone. I held it up. 'Here.'

I spent the next hour letting Wolf show me how the sound system he was operating worked, while Esme sang a couple more songs. Then the three of us went to the kitchen, where Esme ferreted about in a cupboard and produced some delicious chocolate cake.

At about 6 pm, Wolf said he had to get home for a family dinner.

'OK,' Esme said with a yawn.

'I should go too,' I said. I had the impression Esme was ready for us both to leave. Anyway, I was still feeling guilty about snooping in her dad's office.

Wolf and I said goodbye on the corner of Esme's road. I headed towards the High Street and the underground station. I knew from the map I'd looked at online that Burnside Road was on my way. I could easily stop off and take a peek at number 30.

No, that was stupid. Dangerous. I should just wait until I could get hold of Allan, let him decide what to do. Except . . . Allan wouldn't be back in the country until tomorrow and, for all I knew, Natalia K might be moved to a new address by then. Plus, I was literally seconds away from Burnside Road. I kept walking. The turning I needed to take for the High Street was here, on my left. The turning for Burnside Road was on my right. I stood at the crossroads, hesitating.

Was Natalia K there? Was she a missing person? Was she in danger?

I didn't know the answer to any of those questions. I glanced along Burnside Road. It was tree-lined, full of smart, attractive houses. Two women were talking in posh, clipped accents on the corner. The sun was still shining. It was a quiet, warm summer's evening. Impossible to imagine anything bad happening. I would take a quick look . . . just so I could report back to Allan . . . I wouldn't go inside.

There would be no danger.

I took the right turn and headed along Burnside Road.

14

Natalia

I walked along the pavement, looking at the houses. They were set closely together and all built over three floors. Very smart and elegant. I peered through the windows as I passed. An elderly lady was busy vacuuming on the ground floor of number 22. A few doors down, two young men were talking animatedly in a first-floor room. The house next door to them seemed empty. No, a girl was sitting at the window on the second floor. She was peering out, gazing up and down the street.

With a jolt, I realised she was inside number 30, the very house I was looking for. I drew closer. This house was just as designer-looking as the others, with frosted glass at the windows and gleaming white paint on the woodwork. There were four bells beside the door, corresponding to four flats. I looked up. Presumably flat four was at the top. I squinted up to the second-floor windows. The girl was still peering down from the top window on the right. She turned her head slightly. She saw me. Her mouth opened slightly. Even from down here on the pavement I could see her face was drawn and her eyes were wide with fear. Was that Natalia? Was *I* scaring her? Or was she afraid because she was trapped inside the flat? I glanced around. The road was deserted. I looked up again, but the girl had vanished behind the curtain.

I turned away. Whoever she was, the girl up in flat four definitely didn't look happy. I took a couple of steps, then stopped. Part of me wanted to run away, but part of me felt bad not to at least check out the situation. I mean, maybe I'd got the whole thing wrong. Maybe the girl in the flat wasn't even Natalia.

I looked back. The girl was peering through the window again. This time she didn't duck away behind the curtain. Instead, she smiled. A timid, trembly kind of smile. It felt like an invitation. Without thinking about it any further, I walked to the front door and rang the bell for number four. There was a long pause, then a voice sounded over the intercom.

'Hello?' The voice was hesitant, with a light European accent.

'Hi,' I said. 'Are . . . are you Natalia?'

I could hear the sharp intake of breath on the other end of the line. 'Who are you?'

'I'm Madison,' I said. 'I just came from Mr Baxter's house, I—'

The intercom buzzed, drowning me out, and the front door jerked off its lock. I pushed at it with my fingers and it opened into a smart communal hallway. There were two doors: one on either side of the hall. They were marked '1' and '2'. The entrance to '4' was obviously upstairs – and the girl inside was clearly inviting me in.

I gulped. Should I go? Again, I thought of Lauren and how brave she had been all those years ago, travelling around the east coast of America and risking danger to find out about her past. I shook myself. If Lauren could cope with life-threatening adventures in icy woods and run-down neighbourhoods, then I could certainly speak to a girl in a flat in the heart of sophisticated, wealthy north London.

I ventured up the stairs, past flat three on the first floor and on, up another flight, to flat four. The wooden staircase gleamed with fresh paint and there were elegant prints on the walls. Everything smelled faintly of floor cleaner. Despite all these reassuring signs, my hand was clammy on the banisters as I reached the second floor. I faced the door to flat four. It swung open and the girl with the drawn face peered out. She looked about nineteen or twenty, only a few years older than me.

'Are you alone?' she whispered.

I nodded. 'Natalia?'

'Yes.' She stepped into the doorway and my mouth fell open with shock.

This girl was pregnant. Heavily so – she looked twice as big as Lauren had the other day. And there was absolutely no glow about her at all. Her face was really pale and there were dark shadows under her anxious eyes.

'Come in,' Natalia said.

She turned away from the door and I followed her inside feeling completely confused. She led me along a narrow passage which opened out into a huge, square living area. It was full of designer furniture – two leather sofas, a big plasma TV on the wall, lamps with triangular-shaped shades, a striped rug on the wooden floor.

Natalia sat on one of the sofas. She looked up at me anxiously.

'You said you came from Mr Baxter's house?' she said.

I nodded, feeling even more bewildered. Allan had said girls were disappearing . . . which kind of implied being kidnapped or made to suffer in some way. But Natalia was clearly living in a luxurious flat. And, OK, so she was pregnant, which I hadn't suspected, and she definitely looked tired, but she had just let me in, and could obviously let herself out of the building – so no way was she a prisoner.

'What does Mr Baxter want?' Natalia asked.

I frowned, then I realised that she'd misunderstood me.

'He didn't *send* me here,' I said quickly. 'I . . . that is, someone told me you might be here, so . . . well, I happened to see the address and I thought . . .' I hesitated. It sounded ridiculous to say I was investigating on behalf of a freelance journalist, even if he was my father. 'I . . . I just came to see if you were all right,' I finished lamely.

'Oh.' Now Natalia was frowning. 'So . . . how . . . what's your connection with Mr Baxter?'

Now what did I say? I took a deep breath. 'The truth is, someone told me that a number of girls had gone missing and . . . and I got it into my head you were one of them. But you're obviously not a prisoner here so . . .' I tailed off again.

101

Natalia bit her lip. She rested her hands on her swollen belly and stared at me. I got the strong impression she was trying to decide whether or not to tell me something. What was it? She was dressed in leggings and a lilac top that draped artfully over her bump. Apart from the fact that she wore no make-up, she looked as expensively dressed as Esme. Certainly no kind of victim.

Allan had clearly got the whole thing wrong. I still didn't understand what the name 'Miriam' meant, or why I'd seen other memory sticks with different 'M' numbers on them, but, as I stared at Natalia, I suddenly thought I saw the connection between her and Baxter. Something that made sense of everything.

'Oh.' My hand flew to my mouth. 'Oh, it's *his* baby, Mr Baxter's.' My face burned as I thought through the ramifications of this. Mr Baxter was having a baby with a girl half his age, barely older than me – or Esme. It was revolting. I stood up, wishing I hadn't come in. Now I had a great big secret to keep from my new friend.

'Mr Baxter is *not* the father.' Natalia's face expressed genuine shock.

To my horror, her eyes filled with tears. She looked down at the floor and her voice wobbled as she spoke.

'OK,' I said. 'I'm sorry.'

I gulped. I *was* sorry for upsetting her, but I didn't believe Baxter wasn't the dad. I mean, what other explanation for her living in this nice flat so close to his house could there be? Still, it was none of my business. I took a step towards the door.

'Please don't go,' Natalia said shakily. 'I haven't talked to anyone for months . . . not properly . . . *please*.' She looked up. The pain in her dark brown eyes was so intense I could barely meet her gaze.

Now I felt confused again. Maybe she *was* telling the truth.

'Does Mr Baxter own this flat?' I said. 'Does *he* know you're here?'

'Yes.'

'But he isn't the father?'

'No,' Natalia said with a sigh. 'But he wants my baby.'

'Sorry . . . I don't understand,' I said.

Natalia hesitated. I got the strong sense that she was fighting with herself again. That she knew talking to a total stranger was a terrible risk, but that she was so desperate she couldn't help herself.

'If I tell you,' she said softly, 'will you promise to help me?'

'Yes,' I said. 'But what do you need help with?' I looked around the sophisticated living room. 'You don't exactly look like you're being badly treated.'

'I'm not,' she said. 'Mr Baxter provides food and clothes and a doctor comes every day to check I'm OK. But it's time . . . it was time yesterday . . . for the baby to come. That's why they moved me here.' She held my gaze, and the horror in her eyes was totally genuine. 'And when the baby is born, Mr Baxter is going to take him away. Forever.'

15

Getting Out

'Slow down,' I said. 'Are you saying Mr Baxter is looking after you until your baby's born – then he's going to *take* him?'

Natalia nodded. 'I saw it happen before, with other girls. Mr Baxter calls it the Miriam Project after some woman in the Bible. He takes the babies as soon as they're born to give to childless couples. I'm the twenty-first girl.'

Miriam 21. I stared at her, bewildered. *This* was the explanation behind Allan's suspicions – a surrogacy business.

'Baxter pays a doctor to check on us and there are several nurses who stay with us in shifts,' Natalia went on. 'I'm waiting for the next nurse now. She'll be here soon. You see, my baby was due yesterday, so he'll . . . it won't be long until he's born now.'

I gasped, remembering the 'due' date on the memory stick file. I thought of the other sticks with their 'M' numbers.

'You're saying Mr Baxter has done this with twenty other girls?' I asked.

'Yes.' Natalia clasped her hands together. 'He picks on girls away from home, who don't have jobs or money . . . girls with no family. He offered me ten thousand pounds to do IVF for him . . . to get pregnant.'

'So you agreed to give up your baby,' I said. 'You actually agreed to do it?'

'Yes, because I was desperate. I was all alone and it was awful, so I said yes, because back then the baby was just an idea. But now I can feel him moving inside me. I . . . I can't bear the thought he'll be taken away from me.'

'Where will Baxter take him?'

Natalia sniffed. 'If it's the same as the others, he'll take the baby as soon as he's born. He'll have a couple all lined up, ready to pay. My friend Lana told me how it works: the couple get a baby just a few hours old without having to travel abroad or do mountains of paperwork. There're official-looking documents that say it's all legal, but it's not . . .'

I couldn't believe it. I'd stumbled across the whole story that Allan had been investigating. For a second I imagined how pleased he was going to be when I told him what I'd found out. That editor he was working for at *The Examiner* – Matthew Flint – would surely be impressed too. Maybe my efforts would even help me get some kind of work placement there. No. I shook myself. It was selfish of me to focus on what I could get out of Natalia's suffering. My main priority should be to help her.

'So you agreed to carry a baby before you were pregnant, but now you'd give up all the money if you could keep your baby?'

'Yes.' Natalia looked around her. 'I know this place is all designer and everything, but I've been forced to live in flats like this since I was four months pregnant,' she went on. 'There was another girl with me for a while, Lana, but they took her

105

away and she promised she would call me, but I haven't heard a thing. I don't know what's happened to her.'

A shiver snaked down my back. 'Why don't you just walk out?' I said.

Natalia rolled up her leggings to reveal a thick black ankle bracelet on her left leg. 'Baxter put a tracker on me. If I leave the house, he'll know. He'll find me. Then he'll take the baby anyway. Maybe . . . maybe worse.'

'Worse?'

'At first he said if I ran away or talked to anyone, I'd lose the baby and all my money, but now that I can't get hold of Lana, I . . . I . . . think maybe he killed her for trying to escape.' Natalia leaned forward, her head in her hands. Tears leaked out from between her fingers. 'I'm so scared. Whichever way I look, I'm *so* scared.'

I looked at her. My heart was beating fast. 'Come on.' I held out my hand. 'I know someone who can help you.'

'Who?' Natalia peered up at me from between her fingers.

'His name's Allan Faraday. He's . . . well, he's actually my dad . . .' The words sounded strange as I spoke them. 'He's the one who suspected Baxter was doing something illegal.'

Natalia gulped. She suddenly seemed much younger than before. I felt older . . . responsible . . .

'But . . . but . . . the tracker . . . Mr Baxter will know where I am.'

'Allan will know what to do about that.' As I spoke, I remembered Allan was out of the country until tomorrow. I hesitated.

106

'I can't,' Natalia said. 'I can't leave here if he can trace me. Lana tried to do that. She didn't get as far as the end of the road.'

'OK.' I thought fast. 'I'll call the police.' *Yes.* I should have thought of that in the first place. If Baxter was conning girls into giving up their babies, he was clearly acting against the law. The police would rescue Natalia and arrest him.

But Natalia shook her head. 'If Mr Baxter knows I've gone to the police, then he'll come after me, take my baby *and* kill me.'

'But the police will arrest him before he can do any of that,' I insisted.

'No.' Natalia's eyes welled with tears again. 'Don't you see, he's kept himself out of anything illegal. Lana told me before she ran off. There's no money in his name. It's all done through different accounts. It'd be years before the lawyers sorted it all out and in the mean time he'd be free to take revenge on me for talking to the police.'

'But we'll explain what really happened,' I insisted.

'Don't you see? Baxter has covered his tracks too well for that. There's no proof. Everyone will think I'm just trying to put the blame on him, but the money *I* took will be easy to find,' Natalia sobbed. 'Didn't you hear what I said before? There's nothing illegal about surrogacy except accepting lots of money to do it. And I've already taken thousands of pounds. *I'll* be sent to jail before Mr Baxter even goes to trial. And then I'll *never* see my baby.' She dissolved into tears again.

I stared at her, feeling helpless.

Natalia wiped her eyes. Her fingers trembled as they brushed over her cheek. I suddenly saw how completely and utterly terrified she was.

She looked up at me with a wan smile. 'You should go,' she said. 'The nurse will be here soon.'

'Right.' I tried to pull my thoughts together. 'So . . . so if I could find some way of getting the tracker off you here, so Baxter won't know you've left, that's the only chance of you getting away from him. No police. No lawyers. Just escape.'

'Yes, but you'd need proper equipment to do it, and . . . and there's nothing in the whole flat I can use.' Her voice cracked. 'It's hopeless. There's no scissors, no sharp knives – not that they'd be strong enough – this plastic is tough.' She paused, clearly trying to calm herself. 'Anyway, even if I could buy some time by getting rid of the tracker, I'd need more money than I can get my hands on to get out of the country.'

'OK,' I said. I thought it through. Surely Allan would help me, if I could just get hold of him. 'What if I could bring tools to get the tracker off *and* some money? What if I came back tomorrow with all that?'

Natalia stared uncertainly at me. 'Would you really go that far to help me? I don't understand. Why would you do all that? You don't know me.'

I shrugged, feeling awkward. To be honest, I didn't really know the answer to that question. All I knew was that Natalia needed help and that Allan and I appeared to be the only ones who could help her.

'What time will your nurse leave in the morning?' I asked.

'Ten am,' Natalia said. 'There's an hour's gap between shifts at the moment. It used to be longer, but now the baby's due . . .' She looked at me hopefully, her tears glistening on her cheeks. 'Will you really come back? Will you really help get me out?'

'Yes.' I took a deep breath. 'Yes, I promise.'

'Thank you.' Natalia gripped my hand and squeezed it tight. 'Thank you.'

I said goodbye and stumbled down the steps of the apartment building and out onto the pavement. The sun was still shining, low in the sky. I looked up and down the street. No sign of Natalia's nurse. There was only one other person on the road – a shapeless figure with a cap pulled low over his face, half hidden by a tree further along the street. He looked kind of out of place – suspicious even – but I wasn't worried. He was staring in the opposite direction and didn't seem to have noticed me.

I walked along the street, my stomach churning with anxiety.

Why had I gone inside? What had I been thinking? And what on earth had I done, promising to help like that? Part of me just wanted to run away and pretend I'd never heard of Miriam 21 or found that memory stick or visited Natalia. But how could I? The poor girl was trapped and terrified.

I *had* to get hold of Allan. He would surely know what to do. I dug my hand into my pocket, took out my phone and called him. He still wasn't answering and I didn't want to leave a message about something so important, so I rang off without speaking. I was nearly at the end of Burnside Road – just a couple of minutes from the tube station.

Suppose I couldn't get hold of Allan before tomorrow morning? What would I do? Somehow I still had to help Natalia. I thought of Lauren – less pregnant, but just as attached to her baby – and how meanly I'd reacted when she made her announcement. Maybe helping Natalia was a way of making up for being selfish with Lauren.

I turned the corner and headed for the High Street. Money didn't have to be a problem. Annie kept some emergency cash in a jar in the kitchen – only a hundred pounds or so, but it would at least help Natalia get out of London. But how could I get rid of that tracker? That was the priority. Yes. Unless I could find some way of removing it, Natalia would be as trapped as ever.

A shiver ran down my spine. I had the sudden sense I was being watched. I glanced over my shoulder. The guy in the cap was walking a few metres behind me. Was he following me? I shook myself. Surely I was just being paranoid.

I turned onto the next road. I was close to the High Street now. I looked around. Jeez, he was still there.

I sped up. Glanced backwards again. The man was speeding up too, his face hidden under his cap. Panic swirled inside me. I broke into a run. Faster. I was almost at the High Street. Footsteps pounded behind me. He was following. Chasing me.

And then I felt his hand on my shoulder. I opened my mouth to scream as he spun me round.

We were face to face.

'What the hell are you doing here?' he said.

16

Tracker

It was Wolf.

The scream died in my throat as I gazed into his eyes. He looked totally bewildered, his forehead creased with a frown.

'What are you doing here?' he repeated, taking off his cap.

'Nothing,' I stammered. 'I'm not doing anything.'

Wolf shook his head. 'You were snooping about in Mr Baxter's office for a start, then you acted all weird afterwards. And then you said you were going straight to the tube, but you came here instead.' His eyes bored into me.

'You think I was acting weird?' I said, desperately trying to think up a cover for my actions.

'I was watching you,' Wolf said. His eyes softened as he spoke next and his voice lost its accusatory tone. 'Actually, I couldn't stop watching you.'

My heart thudded.

Wolf sighed. 'You have absolutely no idea how beautiful you are, do you?' he said.

What? I stared at him. Today had already been surreal enough without Wolf making bizarre comments like that out of nowhere.

'I don't understand,' I stammered.

Wolf looked away. All the force he'd spoken with before seemed to evaporate . . . all the confidence. He stared down at the pavement.

'I know you're out of my league,' he mumbled. 'Look, let's forget it. Just tell me what you were doing in Mr Baxter's office. You stole something, didn't you? Was it money?'

'No.' I stared at him, my head whirling with confusion and outrage. I couldn't make sense of anything he was saying. In the same breath he was accusing me of being a thief and virtually telling me he had a massive crush on me. Except that last thing *had* to be a joke. Wolf might not be obviously good-looking with his thick fringe and his skinny arms, but he was rich and stylish and he hung out with *Esme* for goodness' sake. She was way more beautiful than me. I decided to ignore this part of what he'd said.

'I didn't steal anything.' I blushed, thinking of the M21 memory stick. Still, I'd only borrowed that to read. I'd put it back afterwards. I turned on my heel and set off for the tube station, hoping Wolf would go away, but he followed me.

'So what were you doing?' he persisted.

'It wasn't anything.' I kept walking, not looking at him. 'I was just checking something out. My . . . my dad's a journalist and he'd heard a rumour. Well, more than a rumour really . . . to do with Mr Baxter . . . I was just looking into it for him.' I stopped. Jeez, I was probably making my situation here far worse by admitting to spying, yet only hinting that Baxter had done anything wrong.

113

I expected Wolf to demand more information – or to accuse me of using him and Esme – but, to my surprise, he just made a face. 'Baxter is into some really dodgy stuff, isn't he?'

'Yes.' I didn't know what else to say. My head spun. Why couldn't I ever think quickly, like Lauren always did?

Wolf glanced over his shoulder, back towards Burnside Road and the flat where I'd found Natalia.

'Is he doing something illegal in that flat you just left?'

I bit my lip. 'I'm not sure how illegal it is, but I know it's wrong.'

We reached the High Street. The tube station was just a few metres away now. Wolf stopped and turned me to face him. He tilted his head a little to one side. 'Wrong?' he said. 'How?'

God, he was persistent. And I didn't have any clever explanations or excuses up my sleeve. In fact, I had nothing . . . no idea what to say now . . . no idea what to do to help Natalia . . . and – with Allan still not answering his phone – no-one to turn to . . .

I looked away, along the High Street. Traffic was whooshing up and down the road, shoppers and commuters bustling along the pavement.

'You can trust me, Madison,' Wolf said, his voice suddenly much gentler. 'I'm sorry if I sounded rude before, it's just I really thought you might have stolen something from Esme's house.'

'OK.' I took a deep breath and turned back to face him. There was genuine kindness in his eyes. 'It's about some girls

114

who've gone missing. Mr Baxter is keeping the latest one in that flat. He's paying her to have a baby, but she's changed her mind and now she—'

'What? Slow down.' Wolf's eyes widened with horror.

'Listen,' I said. I explained everything. I told Wolf all about the *Miriam Project* and how Natalia was Miriam 21. I even told him how I'd tracked Allan down and how he had brought me to Baxter's party.

Wolf stood completely still, listening while I spoke. After I finished, he let out a long, slow breath. 'Whoa, this is serious,' he said.

'I know,' I said miserably. 'I'm kind of in over my head here. I can't get hold of Allan, but I've promised to help Natalia. But Natalia says she can't get away or go to the police because of the tracker . . . that Baxter will trace her. She thinks he'll punish her if she goes against him *and* he'll take her baby away.'

'So we need to get rid of the tracker around her ankle?' Wolf asked.

'Yes, but . . .' I hesitated. 'Are you saying you'll help?'

'Of course.' Wolf took my arm and started leading me towards the tube. 'I don't think it should be too difficult to get rid of this tracker thing. We just need the right tools. My dad has got loads at home. I can go and get something now. Shall I meet you back here in thirty minutes?'

My heartbeat quickened. 'No, wait,' I said. 'Natalia said her nurse was coming over. She's probably arrived by now.

115

Natalia said she'll be there until tomorrow morning at ten. We'll have to come back then.'

'OK, well, describe the tracker so I know what I need to bring.'

I told him exactly what the plastic bracelet around Natalia's ankle had looked like. 'It'll need a saw or something,' I suggested. 'And Natalia will also need lots of money. I'm sure Allan will help her, but he's not back in the country until tomorrow so . . .'

'No problem,' Wolf said. 'I've got plenty of money. Let's swap numbers. I'll call you later to arrange a time to meet.'

Feeling stunned, I handed over my number. This was all happening so fast. Could I really trust Wolf? Still, what option did I have? I had no access to any tools myself – and wouldn't know how to use them if I did. Anyway, tomorrow Allan would be here. Surely if Wolf and I could take Natalia to him he would know what to do from there?

Wolf walked me down to the tube station. 'I'll call you in a few hours, Madison,' he said.

'Thanks, er . . .' I hesitated. 'Er, why are you helping like this?' I asked. 'I mean, you don't know this girl, Natalia . . .'

'No.' Wolf smiled. 'But I know you.' He turned and walked away.

I went into the tube station, more confused than ever. Was he saying he was helping in order to be with me? A thrill wriggled through me at the thought. I pushed it away. I couldn't be sure Wolf really meant what he said. Anyway, he was the least of my worries. I was more concerned that my getting

116

involved hadn't got Natalia into any greater danger than she was already facing.

It was all down to tomorrow.

I was back in Hampstead, as arranged, at 9.30 the next morning. I'd made yet another excuse to Annie to spend time away from home. I didn't like lying to her about where I was going, but it was really her own fault. If she didn't push me so much about everything, I wouldn't be forced into concealing the truth from her. At least – thanks to Wolf's generosity – I hadn't had to take the emergency money from the kitchen jar.

Wolf was waiting for me outside the tube station. He had a small canvas bag in his hand.

'What's in that?' I asked.

'A Stanley knife and a hacksaw.' He grinned. 'If the first doesn't work, we'll get the tracker off with the second.'

'Right.' Now we were here, I could feel my anxieties building inside me. Natalia might have given birth during the night and no longer be in the flat. Even if she were still there, our plan might not work. What if we couldn't get the tracker off after all? What if we couldn't get Natalia safely to Allan? I'd called and left a message for him saying I needed to speak to him urgently, but he still hadn't called back. At least I knew he'd be back in England today. He'd told me before he left that his plan was to go straight from the airport to *The Examiner* offices in west London. I was planning to take Natalia to him there.

We walked round to Burnside Road. Natalia had said the

117

nurse who stayed overnight would leave at ten, giving us an hour before the next nurse arrived.

We stood at the end of the road and waited. At 10 am precisely, a woman in a dark coat left number 30. Wolf squeezed my arm.

'Is that her?' he said.

'I think so.' We crept closer to the house. I looked up. Natalia was peering out of the window. When she saw me, her eyes lit up.

Seconds later, we were inside the flat.

'This is Wolf,' I said as Wolf shyly followed me inside. 'He's got the stuff we need to get your tracker off.'

Natalia trembled as she thanked us. Her eyes looked red and sore from crying.

'Don't thank me yet,' Wolf said sheepishly. 'Let's see if this works first.'

Natalia sat down and hitched up her leggings again. She peered anxiously down, over her bump.

Wolf crouched beside her ankle. He took his Stanley knife in one hand and Natalia's leg in the other.

'OK, now keep very, very still.' Wolf shot me a nervous glance. I nodded back encouragingly.

Wolf placed the knife over the tracker. Natalia flinched.

'Hold still,' Wolf warned.

Natalia screwed up her face, closing her eyes tight shut. Wolf applied the knife to the plastic. He made a stroke. Then another. He looked up. 'The knife isn't sharp enough,' he said. 'I'm going to have to use the saw.'

118

Natalia's face paled as he took the hacksaw out of his bag. Its serrated edge glinted in the sunlight shining in through the window.

'Oh, God,' she said shakily, shrinking away.

'Don't look,' I said, taking her hand. 'As soon as this is done, we're going straight to find Allan. He's the journalist who put me onto Baxter in the first place.'

'He's a *journalist*?' Natalia's face creased with a new anxiety. 'Won't he want me to tell him about what Baxter has done? Won't he want quotes and my name and—?'

'I'm sure he can keep everything anonymous,' I said, hoping this was true. 'And once we've got the tracker off you, Baxter won't have any idea where you are.'

I looked down. Wolf's forehead beaded with sweat as he positioned the saw over the tracker.

'Keep t . . . totally still,' he ordered again. 'I don't want to cut your leg.'

Natalia whimpered.

I gulped. 'Have you thought about names for the baby?' I said, trying to distract Natalia.

Natalia kept her frightened gaze fixed on my face as Wolf sawed at the plastic tracker band. She ran through the various names she'd been considering, but I wasn't listening properly. My mind had wandered to Lauren and *her* pregnancy. Why hadn't I thought to ask her and Jam about names? Jeez, I really had been so selfish before.

'Done.' Wolf held up the two pieces of the tracker.

'Let's go,' I said.

Natalia got up. She grabbed a small backpack from the floor and led the way downstairs. I followed, feeling numb. This whole business was totally surreal. I caught Wolf's eye as we walked out of the house.

'How long d'you think we've got before anyone notices she's gone?' he said quietly.

'The nurse isn't due for forty minutes or so. The tube's only round the corner.'

We hurried along the pavement. Reached the end of the road. Natalia was panting for breath even though we were only walking briskly.

'You OK?' Wolf asked.

'The station's not far,' I said.

'I know,' Natalia moaned. 'But it's hard to go fast when I'm so big.'

As she spoke, the sound of tyres screeching to a halt filled the air. I glanced over my shoulder. A thickset guy in a leather jacket was bounding out of a silver Mercedes, heading for Natalia's flat.

'Oh my God,' she gasped.

'That's one of Baxter's staff,' Wolf said. 'I recognise him from the house.'

'Nooo,' Natalia wailed.

'Come on.' I grabbed her wrist. 'Run!'

17

Handing Over

Wolf took Natalia's other arm. Between us we half dragged, half carried her along the pavement. Natalia was sobbing, clutching at her belly and gasping for breath. I looked over my shoulder as we turned onto the High Street. Baxter's leather-jacketed henchman was looking up and down the road. As I watched, he caught sight of us and broke into a run.

'Hurry!' I yelled.

Wolf sped up, taking more of Natalia's weight.

'I *can't*,' she cried. 'The baby.'

'I know but we have to,' I panted, running hard to keep up with Wolf.

'Oh my God,' Natalia wailed.

We reached the tube station. I glanced over my shoulder again. Leather Jacket was just metres away, fighting through a crowd of tourists.

'My pocket ... travelcards ...' Wolf panted, holding Natalia as she wept.

I reached into his pocket and drew out two travelcards, one for him and one for Natalia. I fumbled for my own. Seconds later, we were through the barrier and standing by the lift. I kept my eyes on the entrance. Leather Jacket would be here any second.

'It's on its way.' Wolf's eyes were fixed on the arrow above the lift. It was signalling an elevator was rising from the bowels of the station.

'Come on, come on,' I muttered.

Leather Jacket appeared at the station entrance. I froze.

The lift was arriving. People gathering around, ready for the doors to open. I kept my eyes on Leather Jacket. He spotted us. His eyes widened, his lips curling into a snarl. As the lift doors opened, Leather Jacket rushed for the ticket barrier.

'Get inside,' Wolf ordered. 'Pregnant lady! Make way!'

I pushed my way in after him. Leather Jacket leaped over the barrier.

'Oy!' called the ticket inspector. 'Stop there!'

Leather Jacket ignored him. He was running over. The doors were closing. Our eyes met as his fists lunged forward. He couldn't hold back the doors. They shut.

We were safe.

Except . . . 'He'll take the stairs,' I said, remembering the emergency spiral staircase.

'Maybe the ticket officers will stop him,' Wolf suggested.

'Maybe.' We looked at each other. I could tell Wolf wasn't convinced.

'Get ready to run again, as soon as the doors open,' I said.

Natalia nodded. Seconds passed unbearably slowly. If Leather Jacket was coming down the platform via the stairs, how far had he got? The lift landed. With a beep, the doors opened. Wolf and I raced out, holding Natalia between us.

'Here, she shouldn't be rushing like that—' said a woman from inside the lift.

Ignoring her, we hurried on.

'Get on the first train,' I gasped.

We reached the platform. A train was due in one minute. We headed for the far end, past a group of Italian schoolkids, all talking at the tops of their voices.

I kept my eyes peeled, scanning the platform as the train roared in. The tube doors opened. Still no sign of Leather Jacket. We got on board. Wolf ushered Natalia to a seat. I kept watch, my heart thudding against my ribs.

Close the doors. Close the doors, I muttered under my breath.

Leather Jacket darted onto the platform. He looked up and down. He hadn't seen us. Couldn't be sure we were on the train. As he hesitated, the doors shut, leaving him outside.

I sank into the seat opposite Wolf, my whole body shaking.

'Jeez, that was close,' I said.

'How did they know so fast?' Natalia said, her hands trembling as she laid them on her belly.

Wolf leaned forward. 'Cutting the tracker off must have activated an alarm. I thought it might, but I was hoping we'd have more time before they realised.'

I bit my lip. It hadn't even occurred to me that it would be a problem. Thank goodness Wolf was here. I'd never have got Natalia away from the flat without him. It was the same at the station. If Wolf hadn't thought of buying her a travelcard in advance, we'd never have got her through the barrier in time. My skin erupted in goosebumps as I thought how easily Leather Jacket could have caught us. I turned to Wolf, eager to thank him, but, before I could find the words, Natalia spoke.

'So where are we going, Madison?' she said, her forehead creased with an anxious frown. 'I mean, are you sure your . . . Allan . . . will help me?'

'Absolutely,' I said. 'He said before he left that he'd be going straight to his newspaper office from the airport this morning so I'm sure he'll be in when we get there.'

'OK,' Natalia said. She stroked her bump.

'Thank goodness for that.' Wolf sat back, looking relieved.

I felt relief too. It was good to know we'd soon be able to hand Natalia over to Allan. He'd know how to help her without necessarily involving the police.

We had to travel right across central London to get to Kensington, where Allan's paper was based. We kept a careful watch as we switched trains, but there was no sign of either Leather Jacket or Baxter himself.

'How could there be?' Wolf reasoned. 'They don't know which stop we're planning to get off at, or how long we were going to stay on the tube. We've lost them for now.'

For now.

The words stuck in my head. With all Baxter's money, I knew he still had the resources to track down Natalia if she went anywhere too public, like a hospital. We just had to hope she didn't give birth until we'd got her to Allan.

We got off the train at High Street, Kensington and walked up the road and round the corner to Allan's newspaper offices. As we got nearer, Natalia grew very pale.

'I feel sick,' she said, reaching for my hand.

I exchanged an anxious glance with Wolf. 'Should we call an ambulance?'

'No.' Natalia squeezed my hand. 'It's just all the stress. Maybe a glass of water . . .'

I glanced at the café across the road. 'Why don't you take Natalia in there while I find Allan?' I said to Wolf.

'Sure.' He helped Natalia along the street.

I headed into the newspaper offices. Reception was behind a huge pair of sliding glass doors. Security guards stood posted in front of two escalators, also behind glass doors, which led up to the first floor. I gulped; it was all really intimidating.

The guards let me through to reception. A stylishly dressed woman with pointy-edged glasses peered down her long nose at me.

'Yes?' she said rather snootily.

'I'm Madison Purditt. I'd like to see Allan Faraday, please,' I stammered. Damn, I could feel my cheeks reddening.

The snooty receptionist checked her computer.

'So sorry but he's not registered,' she said, in a tone that implied she wasn't really sorry at all.

'Not registered?'

'As an employee.' The woman cocked her head to one side. 'Does he work here or not?'

125

'Er, no, not exactly,' I said. 'I mean he's freelance, not an employee. He said he'd be here today, though. He works with . . . for . . . one of the editors . . . er, I think the name is Matthew Flint.'

The receptionist checked her screen again. 'Mr Flint is in; would you like me to tell him you're here?'

'Er, yes.' I gulped. 'But he won't know who I am . . . you'll have to say I've got some information for Allan Faraday.'

'Information?'

'Like . . . like a story . . . for the paper . . .' I said.

The receptionist tapped her nails on the counter as she put in the call. She turned away as she spoke . . . talking quietly so I couldn't hear what she said.

I looked through the glass windows and across the road to where Wolf and Natalia were sitting by the window of the café. Natalia was sipping at a glass of water, her head propped in her hand. Wolf was watching me. He raised his hand in a wave. I waved back. Then Natalia said something and Wolf looked away.

'Mr Flint says you should take the escalator. He'll meet you at the top.' The snooty receptionist handed me a visitor pass. I clipped it to my T-shirt.

The security guard smiled as he let me pass through the glass doors and onto the escalator. My hands felt clammy on the handrail as I travelled to the top. A huge atrium opened above me with a high glass roof. Wow. The building went up for several more levels.

I got off the escalator and wandered over to the sofas opposite. I waited a couple of minutes, trying to work out how I was going to begin explaining everything to Allan. Hopefully Matthew Flint would bring Allan with him when he came out to meet me.

'Madison?' I turned round.

A short, slight man with a high forehead and glasses was smiling at me. He looked a bit older than Jam and Lauren, but not much.

'Hi, I'm Matthew Flint,' he said, looking at me with a sceptical expression. 'I understand you've got a story from Allan Faraday?'

'No, er, not exactly,' I said, anxiety clutching at my guts. Wasn't Allan here? 'It's a story *for* Allan. Actually, it's much, much more than that.'

Matthew Flint narrowed his eyes. I got the strong impression he was sizing me up. 'How do you know Allan?'

'He's . . .' I hesitated. It was all very well telling people who didn't know him about Allan being my dad, but maybe it wasn't fair for me to explain our relationship to someone he worked for. 'Allan's a family friend,' I said at last.

'And you're an aspiring journalist?' Matthew Flint raised his eyebrows. He looked even more sceptical than before. 'So what's this story you want to give Allan, then? I hope it's a better lead than the last load of nonsense he tried to sell me.'

I bit my lip. 'Couldn't I speak to Allan directly?' I said.

Matthew Flint frowned. 'He's not here.'

What? 'But . . . he sent me a text saying he was working here today.'

127

'Working here today?' Matthew Flint chuckled. 'Allan's not working here. I'd be surprised to find out that he's ever worked anywhere.'

'What do you mean?' I thought of Natalia waiting outside in the café. A chill ran down my spine. Allan had *definitely* said he would be here.

'I mean that Allan Faraday isn't here today and won't be here tomorrow.' Matthew Flint drew himself up. 'In fact,' he said, 'Allan Faraday has *never* worked here.'

18

A Matter of Trust

'Allan Faraday has never worked here?' My voice sounded faint to my ears as I echoed Matthew Flint's words.

'That's right.' Mr Flint nodded. 'He's tried to sell me a few ideas over the past couple of years, but . . . to be honest . . . he's a bit of an idiot.' He frowned at the look of shock that was clearly all over my face. Allan was being called an *idiot*. How was that possible?

'But he . . . he said he was an investigative reporter . . .'

Matthew sighed. 'He *plays* at being one. He's written a few things I suppose, though they were mostly write-ups of social events. He comes from a wealthy family – his parents left him a huge income which he spends on going to the latest parties and buying the latest gadgets.'

I thought of Allan's designer suits and easy, charming manner. 'So he is a writer at least?' I said.

'Sort of. Like I say there's the occasional article, then he networks, he blogs, he does some PR . . . He's tried to get me interested in some stories in the past – leads he's picked up from his wealthy friends – but he never follows anything through.'

I couldn't believe what I was hearing.

'I'm sorry,' Mr Flint went on, 'but I only came down here because reception said you looked very young and very scared, so I thought you genuinely might have something to tell me, but if you don't, then . . .' He shrugged.

'Wait, no, I *do* have something.' My mind was in freefall. I didn't want to put Natalia in any more danger than she already was, but if Allan had lied to me, then he wasn't going to be of any help anyway.

Should I tell Mr Flint what I knew? I couldn't decide.

'Madison?' Mr Flint sounded impatient. 'What is it?'

My eyes filled with tears. I hated myself for being so weak, but I couldn't help it. After so long without a father, I'd finally found Allan, and since I met him my life had changed in these huge ways I could never have foreseen. I'd thought he was so cool. I'd tried so hard to impress him. Everything I'd done, since hearing about Miriam 21, had been aimed at being the kind of investigative journalist I thought Allan was . . . making him see that I could be that sort of person too. In a world where Annie was scared for me to take a single step on my own, I'd wanted my birth father to believe in me. And he had. At least I thought he had.

But I'd been wrong. And now I didn't know what to do.

I turned to Mr Flint. This was simply too big a decision to take by myself. I needed to speak to Wolf and Natalia first.

'There are other people involved,' I said. 'I need to talk to them. They're just over the road.'

Mr Flint rolled his eyes. 'Get them here now.' He checked his watch. 'You've got five minutes.'

I gulped. Wolf answered his phone straight away.

'You have to come over here,' I whispered. 'I don't know what to do.'

'OK,' Wolf said. 'Don't say any more, we'll be right there.'

I paced up and down at the top of the escalator. Less than a minute later Wolf appeared. He was alone. Mr Flint had called down to reception to let him through and was now on another call on his mobile. I only had a few more minutes to work out what to tell him.

Wolf raced up the escalator.

'Where's Natalia?' I said.

'She was still feeling really faint, so I told her to wait and have a cup of tea while I came over and found out what was going on.' Wolf frowned. 'Where's your . . . where's Allan?'

Tears bubbled up in my eyes again as I explained how Allan didn't work here after all. 'The features editor – Matthew Flint – said Allan gave him a few ideas for stories, but nothing that worked out.'

'Oh, man.' Wolf's eyes widened. 'This is bad.'

'I can't believe Allan lied to me,' I went on. 'Why would he do that?'

Wolf's cheeks reddened slightly. 'I don't know. Maybe he was trying to impress you, you know, make out he's something more than an expensive suit or something . . .' He frowned. 'That doesn't matter right now. What on earth are we going to do with Natalia?'

'I don't know,' I said. Anxiety clawed at my chest.

Mr Flint appeared by my side. 'Time's up,' he said. 'Either

131

you tell me what this lead of yours is, or you have to leave now.'

I gulped. I still had no idea what to do.

'Tell him about Baxter's surrogacy operation,' Wolf said. He put his hand on my shoulder. 'There isn't another option.'

He was right. I didn't want to betray Natalia's trust or put her in danger, but there was no way Wolf and I could handle this by ourselves. I turned to Mr Flint. 'You know the businessman Declan Baxter?'

Mr Flint nodded. 'Of course.'

'Well, we've found out he's involved in illegal surrogacy arrangements between wealthy clients who want babies and poor girls coming from abroad mostly who are prepared to give up their babies for money.'

Mr Flint's eyes rounded. 'Seriously?' he said. 'Do you have proof?'

'Yes, there's a girl—' Wolf started.

I laid my hand on his arm to stop him revealing Natalia's name. 'One of the girls Baxter has been using is in the café opposite. She'll talk to you, but I think you'll have to keep her name out of it. She's scared Baxter will come after her if he thinks she's gone behind his back.'

Mr Flint frowned. 'Sounds like she should be going to the police.'

'That's what I think too,' Wolf said.

'She's too scared to do that,' I insisted.

There was a pause.

'She's in the café opposite?' Mr Flint said.

'Waiting for us,' I said with a nod.

'Come on, then,' he said. 'Let's go and speak to her.'

We headed downstairs. As we crossed the road opposite the café, Wolf and Mr Flint strode on ahead. I hung back, worrying what Natalia would think. I'd promised her Allan with his offers of help and money. And now I was bringing her Mr Flint who clearly was more interested in Natalia's story than her actual situation.

I followed the others into the café. It wasn't big – a scattering of tables on either side of a small glass counter selling cakes and sandwiches and coffee.

There was no sign of Natalia.

Wolf looked around. 'She's gone,' he said.

I rushed over to the man behind the counter.

'Where's the girl who was here?' I asked.

'What girl?' the man said. He narrowed his eyes.

Beside me, Mr Flint shuffled impatiently.

What was going on?

'The girl I was here with just a few minutes ago,' Wolf said, his voice rising as he spoke. 'She was pregnant.'

'I don't know what you're talking about,' the man said.

He turned away. I met Wolf's eyes. He looked as terrified and confused as I felt. What was happening? Why was this man lying to us?

And where was Natalia?

19

Allan's Secret

The café fell silent. Mr Flint frowned.

'OK,' he said slowly. 'So your entire story is based on a far-fetched claim about a successful businessman . . . and you have absolutely nothing to back it up with whatsoever?'

I looked down at the tiled floor of the café. The customers at the nearest table and all the waiting staff were staring at us.

Mr Flint sighed. 'I'll admit there are a lot of rumours about Declan Baxter, but nothing has ever been proved. And I've never heard he's involved in trafficking girls . . . or baby farms or whatever.'

I blushed, unable to meet his gaze. He was basically saying I was lying – or exaggerating. It didn't really matter. He didn't believe me.

Wolf reached for my hand. I let him squeeze my fingers, but the gesture made me feel no better. I'd done everything wrong . . . taken off the tracker so Baxter knew straight away Natalia had gone . . . left her with Wolf instead of bringing her into the newspaper office. And now, if Baxter's men had kidnapped her, anything might happen to her. And *I* was the one who'd persuaded her to run away in the first place. It was my fault.

'Someone's bribing that guy to lie to us,' Wolf insisted, pointing to the man behind the counter.

'Right,' Mr Flint said sarcastically. 'So tell me, Madison, how do you even know Declan Baxter?'

'I don't,' I stammered. 'But I know his daughter. I've been to his house . . . that's where I found out about Natalia . . . about Miriam 21.'

'Oh for goodness' sake.' Mr Flint took out his wallet and removed a business card. He shoved it into my hand. It contained his name, mobile and email details. 'Call me if you have a real lead, OK?' he said. 'And tell Allan Faraday not to send a kid next time. In fact, tell Allan Faraday to stay the hell away from me.'

He marched out of the café. Wolf gave a low growl.

'That wasn't fair,' he said. 'He should have believed you.'

'Why?' I said, my emotions whirling inside my head. 'I kept telling him things that turned out not to be true. Or at least looked like they weren't true.'

Wolf strode over to the man who was still lurking behind the food counter. 'You lied just now,' he said angrily. 'I *was* here with a girl before, a pregnant girl.'

The man shook his head, but he didn't meet Wolf's eyes. 'Get out!' he muttered.

'Come on.' I took Wolf's hand to lead him out of the café. A large van zoomed past as we stood on the pavement. I suddenly felt self-conscious we were holding hands and let Wolf's fingers slide away from my grasp.

'D'you think Baxter's men got to Natalia?' I asked.

'I guess so,' Wolf said.

We walked towards the main road. The traffic was heavy and shoppers crowded the pavement. I felt terrible. Anything could be happening to Natalia. And I had no idea where to go for help.

'Should we call the police now?' Wolf asked uncertainly.

'I don't know,' I said.

As we reached the corner, footsteps sounded behind us. A girl with straggly hair tied back in an elastic band rushed up. 'I'm from the café,' she panted.

I stared at her. I hadn't noticed her before.

'I remember you.' Wolf raised his eyebrows. 'What—?'

'He was lying to you. The girl you were with, she gave my boss money to say she'd never been there.'

'Money?' I said. 'Natalia didn't have any money.'

The girl shrugged. 'She had a leather wallet. She gave him fifty quid out of it.'

Wolf gasped. He reached inside his pocket.

'My wallet,' he said. 'It's gone.'

'Natalia stole it?' I said, disbelieving.

'I gotta get back.' The straggly-haired girl flew away along the pavement.

Wolf shook his head. 'She wasn't taken. She left of her own free will and she took my wallet.'

'*Why?*' I said. 'I don't get this. Why would she run off? What did she say when you left the café?'

'Nothing, but she looked kind of agitated,' Wolf said. 'I just thought she was anxious about keeping the baby safe from Baxter . . .'

'She must have decided talking to a journalist was too risky,' I said. 'She mentioned not wanting to give her real name before. Maybe she thought she'd be forced to reveal who she was . . . that if her name appeared, Baxter would know she'd grassed on him and take revenge . . .'

'You mean she didn't trust us,' Wolf said, heavily.

I nodded. Once again, I felt a total failure.

My phone rang. *Allan calling.*

I hesitated. Wolf peered over my shoulder.

'Talk to him,' he said. 'He owes you some answers.'

I wasn't sure. I mean, of course Wolf was right, but I didn't know if I could face Allan right now.

'Go on,' Wolf urged.

I took a deep breath. 'Allan?' I said into the mobile.

'Madison, I'm sorry I didn't get back to you earlier.' Allan's voice was smooth and gentle. It sounded fake. Why hadn't I heard that phoney note before? He was a con man. And I was really stupid to have trusted him. Anger filled me.

'You said you were a proper journalist,' I snapped. 'You said you worked at that newspaper, but they told me you just do a bit of blogging and PR stuff – that you've never actually worked there in your life.'

Allan sucked in his breath. 'You *went* there?'

'Yes,' I said. 'I went to find you. We had Natalia . . . the girl from the *Miriam Project*. Miriam 21. She's pregnant. Baxter was keeping her locked up so he could take her baby.'

'What?' Allan said. 'Say that again.'

'Why should I tell you anything?' I said. A sob rose in my throat as anger gave way to misery. Allan had lied to me.

'Listen, Madison.' Allan's voice was low and intense. 'I exaggerated my job because you turned up wanting me to be something special and I didn't want to let you down.'

'You're saying lying to me was *my* fault?'

'No, of course not. I'm saying that I wasn't trying to trick you. The truth is that . . . that I wasn't getting anywhere with Matthew or *any* of the other editors and—'

'And you used me.' My mind was in overdrive now, piecing it all together. No wonder Allan had been so warm and friendly. 'You didn't want to get to know me at all. You only invited me to that party at Baxter's house so that I'd meet Esme . . . as a way of getting back into the house later as her friend.'

'That's not true,' Allan insisted. 'I was invited to the party because of my PR work. Baxter has no idea I'm investigating him. As I'm sure Matthew Flint has told you, I haven't really broken through as a reporter so Baxter doesn't know me and I was in the perfect position to get close to him without him suspecting anything.' He paused, a note of shame creeping into his voice. 'I admit I *hoped* you might make friends with one of his children, but everything else that happened was spur of the moment . . .'

Everything else? What did he mean? In an instant I remembered how I'd watched Allan speaking quietly to Baxter's man, Hobbs, in the waistcoat and yellow tie. It was straight after then that Allan had gone to the loo, then come back and more or less suggested I used the toilets myself. I gasped.

'You got Hobbs to tell you where Esme was, then moved the toilets sign from outside the actual bathroom to outside Esme's Den. You meant me to go in there and, when I did, you locked me and the others inside.'

'When I found out where Esme was – well, it was too great an opportunity to miss,' Allan said quickly. 'Honestly, I only meant to leave you in there for fifteen mintues or so. Just enough time to start making friends. I unlocked the door again before you came back.'

I froze, the High Street and Wolf's anxious face a blur. Allan was admitting it. He had moved the sign and locked me in. That explained why Esme had said the bathroom was next door and how, later, the sign had vanished and the door to the Den had been found unlocked.

'We were trapped with that tiger,' I said. 'We nearly *died.*'

'I didn't know about the tiger,' Allan persisted. 'And I *do* want to get to know you, Madison. None of that was a lie.'

My breath was coming in big rushes. I could barely take this in. Wolf tugged at my arm.

'Madison, listen,' Allan said, his voice urgent. 'We can still make this work. From what you said it sounds as if Baxter is up to his eyes in something illegal. Pregnant girls, selling babies . . . and if you've got one of the girls he's using, you've got proof about—'

'Natalia's gone,' I interrupted. 'She ran off while I was talking to Matthew Flint. We don't know where she is.'

'OK,' Allan persisted. 'We just need to find her . . . she can't have got far. Then we can take her to Matthew Flint and explain everything.'

Wolf tugged at my arm again.

'I think Natalia ran away because she was scared her name would come out if her story got into the press,' I said. 'She's terrified Baxter will find her and take revenge. But you don't care what happens to her, do you?'

'Of course I do,' Allan persisted. 'I want to help Natalia. Going to the press *will* help her. She'll get money for her story *and* they'll make sure she talks to the right people at the police. *Straight* to the right people, so Baxter has no time to get to her.'

'Even if we find her, she won't want to talk to the police.' I took a deep breath. 'And you know what, Allan? I don't want to talk to *you*.' I switched off the call – and my phone.

I stared down at the pavement. It swam in front of my eyes. I felt all churned up. Natalia had run away and Allan had lied and nothing was working out like I'd thought it would.

Wolf pulled on my arm for a third time. 'Madison?' He sounded hoarse.

'What?' I blinked away my tears and focused on him at last.

His face was drawn and pale. 'Look,' he said.

I followed his pointing finger to the end of the road. A figure on a stretcher was being loaded into an ambulance. Despite being several hundred metres away and covered with a blanket, the huge pregnant bump that rose up from the stretcher gave her away.

140

'Oh my God,' I breathed. 'It's Natalia.'

'Come on.' Wolf grabbed my hand and, together, we ran towards the ambulance.

20

The Chase

Wolf clutched my hand. We ran so hard that I practically flew along the pavement. We still weren't fast enough, reaching the end of the road just as the ambulance containing Natalia drove away.

'Damn,' Wolf panted.

We stopped running. I bent over, gasping for breath. Wolf turned to an elderly lady watching the ambulance *nee-naw-ing* away along the street.

'What happened?'

'A young girl . . . pregnant . . . she was unconscious, poor thing.' The lady offered up a sympathetic sigh.

Wolf and I exchanged a look. Had Baxter's men somehow found Natalia and knocked her out? No, there was no way they could have caught up with her so fast. Even if they had, surely they would have bundled her quietly into a car – not organised an ambulance.

'Did you see her collapse?' I asked. 'Did something happen to her?'

The old woman shrugged. 'I don't know, love.'

I looked around. The crowd which had gathered was fading away. There were no indications that any kind of struggle had taken place, but it was impossible to be certain what had really gone on.

'D'you think Baxter got to her?' I suggested. 'Maybe he or one of his men ran her down in their car.'

'How could they have known where she was?' Wolf said. 'We took off her tracker. Anyway, why would they risk being seen attacking her in such a public place?'

'I don't know,' I said.

The elderly woman was wandering off along the pavement. I chased after her.

'Do you know which hospital they took her to?' I asked.

'Probably Kensington General,' she said. 'It's quite close. Is she a friend of yours?'

But I was already running back to Wolf.

'Let's try Kensington General,' I said.

'OK, but I don't have any money anymore, so we can't take a taxi,' Wolf said.

'Then we'll walk. It can't be that far.'

It took thirty minutes and several anxious checks of the GPS on Wolf's phone to get us to the hospital. Along the way my imagination had been working overtime, wondering if Natalia was OK.

'The more I think about it, the more Baxter trying to hurt Natalia doesn't make sense.' Wolf paced along beside me, frowning with concentration as he worked it through. 'Even if he knew where she was and came after her, what Baxter wants most is her baby. He certainly wouldn't want to risk a public showdown with people crowding round – and where Natalia might end up being taken to a hospital and telling the doctors all about his illegal surrogacy business.'

'She wouldn't tell. She'd be too scared.' I thought of Natalia's terrified face earlier and, again, felt a stab of guilt. I'd encouraged her to escape – and now she was unconscious and in as much danger as ever.

'Maybe she wouldn't say anything,' Wolf mused. 'But Baxter can't know that for sure.'

We hurried on. I turned my phone back on. It rang almost immediately. Annie. I let her go to voicemail, then listened to the message. It was classic Annie – all breathless and nervy – asking in an irritatingly timid *I don't want to upset you* voice when I would be home. 'I'm just so worried about you, sweetie, we've hardly talked for days and you were gone when I woke up. Please give me a call . . .' and so on. I sent a text – *am fine, see you 18r Mx* – then switched my phone off again.

Ten minutes later, Wolf and I arrived at Kensington General Hospital. It was massive – completely bewildering – but at least the Accident & Emergency department was clearly marked. We followed the large red sign into the building and found ourselves in a huge waiting area. It was crowded, though plenty of seats were still available. There was no sign of Natalia on the chairs. My heart thumped.

'What now?' I said. 'If she was brought in unconscious, she wouldn't have been able to give her name. How are we going to find her?'

144

'She'd give a false name, anyway,' Wolf said. 'She won't want Baxter to trace her.'

'Or us,' I added.

For a moment I wondered if we were being stupid trying to track down Natalia. After all, if she didn't want our help, why were we persisting in offering it? But in my heart I was certain she'd only run away from us because she was scared that she couldn't trust the newspaper to conceal her name. And she'd probably been right. All that mattered now was trying to help her get away from Baxter.

Wolf pointed to the swing doors that led to the treatment area of the A&E ward. A male nurse in a smart blue uniform emerged. He looked around the waiting room and called a name.

'Natalia could be through there, in one of the cubicles,' Wolf said. 'The doctors might be examining her.'

I nodded, watching as an elderly man, stooping over his cane, shuffled towards the male nurse. They vanished through the swing doors. I followed them and peered over the doors into the treatment area. Two rows of cubicles, divided from each other by long blue curtains, stretched away from me. The male nurse was helping the old man into one of the cubicles. I gulped. Time to start putting on an act. When I was younger – around the time I met Lauren – I thought it would be cool to be an actor, to spend the day pretending to be other people, getting right inside their heads. Of course, as I got older, I realised that performing meant having people look at you, which I hated.

However, right now, I needed to do some acting. 'Wait here,' I hissed at Wolf. Then I waved through the swing doors as if to the old man. 'We're coming, Granddad,' I cooed and, without looking round to see if anyone in the waiting area was watching me, I headed through to the cubicles.

Once past the doors, I tried to look like I belonged. Most of the curtains around the beds were at least partially open. I passed two, three, four cubicles on both sides of the aisle. No sign of Natalia. I reached the end of the row. The nurses' station was up ahead, just around the corner. The nurse on duty was frowning, talking in a low voice to a man in a sharp suit with his back to me.

'I'm afraid you'll have to ask at reception,' she said icily. 'That's *outside*, in the waiting area.'

The man raised his hands in protest. I caught sight of his profile. My breath caught in my throat.

It was Baxter.

I stared, frozen to the spot.

'She's my PA and she's heavily pregnant,' Baxter was saying, his voice rising with indignation. 'I've been ringing around the hospitals and this is the only place that's admitted an unidentified pregnant girl of her age in the past hour. Admin sent me down here, so . . .'

I backed away, round the corner, then turned and fled through the swing doors, back into the waiting room.

'He's in there,' I said, grabbing Wolf's arm and pulling him out into the hospital lobby. 'Baxter. He's traced Natalia already.'

146

'Oh, man.' Wolf's eyes widened. 'Was *she* there?'

'I don't know.' I felt numb with fear. Baxter was so close.

'Maybe they sent her up to the maternity ward already,' Wolf said thoughtfully.

'But if she came in unconscious, she'd still be in A&E.'

'Maybe she *was* conscious. Maybe she just refused to give her name.' Wolf drew me over to the board that explained which department was in which wing and on which level. It was bewildering.

'Everything's colour-coded,' I said.

'How does anyone find their way anywhere?' Wolf said.

I pointed to the sign for the maternity ward – RED wing, level 3. 'I have no idea how to get there,' I said.

'Come on.' Wolf pointed to the red marker tape on the floor.

We followed it along the corridor and up two flights of stairs. Several long minutes later, we found ourselves outside the maternity ward. The doors were locked, with a keypad to the side. I looked through the glass panel of the door to the nurses' station along the corridor ahead. I was hoping to catch the eye of the nurse standing there, but she didn't see me. A moment later, a harassed-looking man, clutching a bunch of flowers in one hand and a little girl in the other, appeared. He pressed the button under the keypad.

'Martin Rivers to see Angie Rivers,' he said.

I tugged at Wolf's arm. 'I'm going in. Keep watch out here,' I hissed.

Wolf nodded, as the nurse at the station buzzed the man and the little girl through. I took a deep breath and followed them.

147

My heart was racing, but neither the man nor his daughter noticed me. The nurse didn't even look up from her station. I ducked behind the first cubicle curtain I came to. Two hospital trolleys were stacked inside, but otherwise it was empty. I tried to focus on what I was going to do.

Walk along the ward like you belong. If anyone stops you, say you're looking for your sister.

I emerged from behind the curtain and walked along the corridor. I held my head up high as I reached the nurses' station, but the woman on duty was busy on the phone and barely glanced in my direction. As soon as I was past her, I came to a room with several beds, all occupied. I looked quickly around. No sign of Natalia.

I moved on, to the next room. *There*, in the end bed by the window: Natalia was sitting up, hugging her knees. Her eyes widened as I rushed over.

'Oh, Madison,' Natalia gasped. 'You found me.'

'Yes – and so did Baxter,' I said. 'He's downstairs now.'

Natalia clutched my hand.

'Come on,' I said, grabbing her coat off the chair by the bed. 'We have to get out of here.'

Holding Natalia's arm, I scurried across the ward.

'Why did you run away?' I hissed.

'I'm sorry.' Natalia's voice filled with tears. 'I felt so ill and I was scared of speaking to the journalist . . .'

So I'd been right.

Gritting my teeth, I steered Natalia out onto the corridor. The nurses' station was a few metres to our left. This time the

148

woman on duty looked up. She saw me with Natalia's coat and frowned.

'Just getting some air,' I said, forcing a smile.

I turned away and led Natalia in the other direction. There was a fire door at the far end of the corridor. We headed towards it.

'Are you OK now?' I said as we walked.

'Yes,' Natalia said. 'I felt really weird in the café. I think it was the running that made me ill. I'm better now.'

I looked at her. She didn't look so sick as before – her cheeks were pink and her skin clear. I was reminded of Lauren and how glowing and healthy she'd seemed with her belly all big and taut.

'I fainted as I was walking down the street to the underground,' Natalia went on. 'Just for a moment, but someone passing by called an ambulance. I didn't have a choice. I *had* to come here.'

Right. Well, that explained everything, though it was still scary that Baxter had managed to trace her so fast.

We reached the fire door. I pushed it open and led Natalia onto the fire escape. The sun was shining brightly, glinting off the iron steps that led down two flights to the concrete car park below.

'Are you sure you're well enough to leave the hospital?' I said.

Natalia turned to me, her eyes intense. 'I'm not letting Baxter take my baby. I was thinking about it: there is someone in Scotland . . . an old friend of my mum's. I could go there now. Baxter won't find me – he won't have her name.'

149

'OK,' I said. 'So you need to get a train?'

Natalia nodded. 'I'm really sorry I took your friend's wallet, but I was panicking and—'

'Don't worry about it,' I said. 'I think Wolf will understand.'

As I spoke, I realised I was sure that he would . . . that Wolf had already been incredibly understanding and helpful . . . and my heart gave a funny little skip. I shut the fire door and switched on my phone to call him. There were missed calls and texts from Annie and Allan and Lauren and Rosa and Esme, but I ignored them all. I was scrolling to Wolf's number when he rang me himself.

'Wolf?' I said.

'Baxter has just gone into the maternity ward. He didn't see me and he's on his own, but you need to leave.'

My guts twisted into a knot. I had to get Natalia away from the hospital. Now.

'On our way. See you on the street.' I started hurrying down the iron fire escape, beckoning to Natalia to follow me. Down and down we scrambled. As we reached the parking lot below, I could hear the fire door above us scraping open. That *had* to be Baxter. I didn't look up.

'Hurry!' I hissed.

We sped up. Natalia was walking very fast, letting me take some of her weight. As we raced along, she squeezed my arm. 'Thank you so much for helping me, Madison.'

'Wait 'til you're on the train before thanking me,' I muttered.

We reached the street. I glanced up and down. Wolf was there, just outside the main hospital entrance, frantically flagging down a black cab. I hurried Natalia towards him. As she followed Wolf into the taxi, I looked back, over my shoulder.

Baxter ran onto the street.

Our eyes met. His mouth fell open as he saw me. Even from twenty metres away, I could see the fury on his face. He started running towards me. I jumped into the cab and slammed the door shut.

'Go!' I shouted. As we roared off, Baxter pounded along the pavement after us. He stopped running, but as I looked out the back of the cab, he was still watching us drive away.

Watching me.

21

Running Away

By the time we arrived at Euston Station Natalia had returned Wolf's wallet and apologised for stealing it – and I had apologised to her over Allan. I still felt embarrasssed when I thought about how he'd tricked me.

Wolf kept very quiet during the journey. He insisted we stopped the cab to allow him to take five hundred pounds out of a cashpoint machine to give to Natalia. I couldn't work out whether it was more astonishing that Wolf had access to so much money or that he was prepared to give it to a complete stranger who had robbed him just hours before.

'I'll pay you back,' Natalia said with a sigh. 'I promise.'

'It doesn't matter,' Wolf said gruffly. 'It's just money.'

I stared at him. Only people who have a lot of money ever think that it's not important. I'd seen from his clothes that Wolf was well off but, because he wasn't as flashy with it as Esme, I hadn't appreciated just how rich his family must be.

'Will you contact the police when you get to Scotland?' I asked Natalia.

She shook her head. 'I want to put everything that's happened with Baxter behind me. If I don't make trouble, perhaps he will leave me alone.'

I bit my lip. Not only was that risky, but it didn't seem quite right to me, either. Baxter should surely be punished for manipulating Natalia – and his baby farm racket should be exposed too.

'I have to think about him.' Natalia put her hand protectively on her belly. 'Having a baby is a huge responsibility. Nothing else matters more.'

My mind shot to Lauren and her pregnancy. Her baby would be due soon. That was a big responsibility for her and Jam and, so far, I hadn't exactly been very understanding.

The cab pulled up at Euston Station and Wolf and I helped Natalia to buy her ticket and find a seat on her train.

There was no sign of Baxter and yet I felt uneasy. He hadn't seen Wolf's face, but he'd seen mine. Had he recognised me from the few seconds we'd spent in each other's company at the party?

I could only hope he hadn't.

I switched my phone back on as we left the station. More missed calls, texts and messages from Annie, Allan – and Esme. Until this minute, I hadn't considered how what I'd learned about Baxter might affect my newfound friendship.

I glanced at Wolf. 'Guess I won't be going back to Esme's any time soon,' I said.

Wolf offered me a sympathetic smile. It struck me that, for him, the dilemma was far worse. He had been friends with Esme for ages and, by telling him what I knew about Baxter, I'd put him in a horrible situation. Not just with her, but also with his own father who was one of Baxter's friends.

'Will you tell . . . anyone what we found out about Mr Baxter?' I asked.

'I don't think so,' Wolf said slowly. 'I mean, what would be the point? Esme would only get upset, that's if she even believed me. Dad would say I've got no proof . . . plus, he'd find some way to turn it all round to make me look stupid.'

He sounded bitter. I thought back to the way his dad had humiliated him at the party.

'Will your dad mind that you took all that money?' I asked.

'Yes.' Wolf looked away, across the street.

I didn't know what to say. As we stood on the pavement, the Euston Road traffic roaring past, my phone rang. It was Allan.

'Hello,' I said warily. Allan was really the last person I wanted to talk to.

'Did you find that girl, Natalia?' he asked breathlessly. 'It's just I've been on to Matthew Flint at the paper. I'm sure I can get him to hear her story. I'll come with you to the police too, if—'

'She's gone,' I interrupted. 'Natalia's left. She didn't . . . doesn't want to talk to anyone.'

'Oh.' Allan fell silent.

Anger rose inside me. All he had cared about was getting the story on Baxter. He'd totally used me to find out information.

'Madison, listen,' he said.

'I told you already I don't want to talk to you,' I said.

'OK, OK, but just be careful. All right?' Allan's voice was low and intense. 'Baxter has a reputation – all rumours, of

154

course – but . . . look, just be careful. If he has any idea you've gone against him, he might try and take revenge.'

'Right,' I said curtly. 'Thanks.'

I rang off, feeling suddenly depressed.

'Are you OK?' Wolf asked.

'I'm fine,' I said.

There was a pause.

'What would you like to do now?' Wolf said.

I sighed. I should really call Annie back – she'd left so many messages – but I couldn't face talking to her, or going home and seeing her face to face. In fact, right now, I didn't want to speak to or see anyone.

'I don't want to go home,' I said.

Wolf smiled. 'Me neither, but I kind of have to. My parents are giving a dinner party and I'm expected to be there for the pre-dinner drinks. It's . . . it's like . . . well, I have to be there . . .'

'Oh, OK.' For some reason, the thought of having to leave Wolf now made me feel more depressed than ever. 'OK, well, I'll see you.'

'You could come back with me.' Wolf spoke so fast the words almost ran into each other. 'To my house, I mean. For the drinks thing. We could hang out after.'

'Oh.' I flushed.

'No, don't worry.' Wolf was blushing too. 'That was a stupid idea, it'll be so boring for you and—'

'Actually,' I said, 'I'd like to come.'

'Great.' Wolf beamed at me.

We walked along the road. I'd assumed we were heading towards the tube station, but a moment later, Wolf stuck out his arm to hail a passing black cab.

'Another taxi?' I said, 'Can you afford it?'

Wolf was still smiling. 'I'm in so much trouble already, a few quid more won't make any difference.'

The cab pulled over and we got in. Wolf chatted away, more animated than I'd seen him before. He asked me what music I liked and told me about a new band he'd seen the week before. I noticed he didn't stammer once. In fact, now I thought about it, he'd stopped stammering at some point earlier today. I relaxed as we chatted. After all the turmoil of the past twenty-four hours, it was nice to talk about normal stuff.

However, as we pulled up outside his house in St John's Wood, Wolf grew quieter again. It was a big house and our footsteps sounded loud as we crunched across the drive.

I was kind of hoping we could slip inside without Wolf's mum or dad noticing. The thought of this pre-dinner drinks session suddenly seemed really intimidating and I was hoping that, if they didn't know I was there, I'd be able to make some excuse and stay out of the whole thing.

No such luck. Wolf's dad was in the hall as we walked in. His eyebrows nearly shot up to his hairline as he saw me.

'Who's this?' he barked.

'My f . . . f . . . friend, M . . . Madison,' Wolf said, not looking directly at his father.

I stood stock-still, feeling awkward.

156

'Right.' Wolf's dad peered down his nose at me. 'Well, she can't come to drinks dressed like that. See if your sister can lend her anything.' And he stalked away.

My mouth fell open. I looked down at my jeans and T-shirt.

'You look *great*,' Wolf said. He sounded furious. 'I'm so sorry. My dad is unbelievably rude.'

'That's OK,' I said uncertainly. 'I wasn't sure about the drinks thing anyway.'

Wolf hesitated. I couldn't work out what he was thinking. Did he want me to leave? Or was he wondering if he could persuade me into his sister's clothes?

Embarrassment filled me – and irritation. I didn't want to go to his dad's stupid drinks party anyway – and I certainly wasn't borrowing someone's clothes.

'I'd better go,' I said.

'Wait.' Wolf opened a door to what looked like some kind of library. I'd never seen so many books in one family home before. He beckoned me inside and closed the door.

'Madison?' He hesitated again.

'What?'

'Do you have a boyfriend?'

'What?' I stared at him, confused. 'No, why?'

Wolf just looked at me. Was that sweat on his forehead? My heart raced with anxiety. I liked Wolf, but right now I felt really uncomfortable. 'What about Esme?' I said, quickly. 'You hang out with her a lot. I thought you liked her . . .'

'No,' Wolf said. His eyes were still fixed on me – dark and intense. 'I mean, of course I like Esme. We've known each

other forever. But everything about her is just so . . . so . . .
big.'

'What?' I didn't understand. 'She's really slim. I don't—'

'Not her body,' Wolf interrupted. 'I mean her hair . . . her
laugh . . . her personality. It's all so "out there", filling up
space . . . but you're different.' He paused, still fixing me with
his gaze. 'I've never met anyone like you. You . . . you almost
disappear into yourself.' He moved closer. I froze. 'As soon
as I met you, I wanted to know where you went . . . to follow
you . . . God, I'm not making any sense. But I don't stammer
when I'm talking to you. And . . . and I think you're so beautiful. Ten times more beautiful than Esme. You're the most
beautiful person I've ever met.'

He stopped talking, his face really near mine now. He was
flushed, holding his breath.

A million emotions swirled in my head. I couldn't take in
what he was saying . . . what he meant . . . but it was over-
whelming. Scary. I felt sick.

'No.' I backed away, fumbling behind me for the door. 'No.
Sorry. No.'

I turned and fled out of the room, across the hall and away
from the house. I didn't stop running until I'd put two streets
between me and Wolf's mansion. Then I took out my phone
and spent a moment working out where I was. Just a couple
of minutes from the nearest station. I ran straight there and got
on a train. I was home in less than an hour. Annie was fluttering by the door when I walked in.

'Oh, sweetie, I'm *so* glad to see you. Are you all right?'

158

'Hi.' I forced a smile onto my face and headed for the stairs. 'I'm good, thanks, but I have loads of homework.'

Annie frowned. 'But it's the summer holidays,' she said plaintively. 'I thought we might go to see a movie this evening?'

I gripped the stair rail. The usual annoyance was welling up inside me. The last thing I wanted was to go anywhere with Annie fussing over me. I had a sudden flashback to Wolf's dad's sneering face as he'd looked at my jeans and T-shirt, then Wolf's intense eyes when he'd looked at me and said I was beautiful. A shiver slithered down my spine. I needed time *alone*. Time to go over everything he'd said . . . to make sense of it.

'It's *coursework* I have to do,' I said, trying to sound as patient as I could. 'Art coursework. There's masses of it.'

Annie nodded. 'OK, of course,' she said. 'I'll bring you up a drink in a moment.'

I resisted the impulse to snap that I didn't want a drink. She was only trying to be nice and the calmer I kept her, the sooner she'd get off my back.

'Thanks.' I went up to my bedroom and flung myself on the bed. Thoughts crowded my head. Natalia would still be on her train to Scotland. I hoped she was OK. I could see from my phone that Esme had sent me a couple of texts demanding that we should meet. Wolf hadn't called or messaged . . . Well, of course he hadn't. I'd more or less run out on him.

My phone beeped and I snatched it up. Maybe that was him texting now.

159

I looked at the message:

I saw you, Madison. This isn't over.

My heart thudded. The sender's name and number had been withheld. But I was sure who it was. Declan Baxter. He was not only rich, powerful and a criminal.

He was threatening me.

22

Falling Out

I closed the message and sat, trembling, on the edge of my bed. How had Declan Baxter got my number? Presumably he'd taken it from Esme's phone, quite possibly without her knowing. It didn't matter. What mattered was what I did now.

But how on earth did I work out what that should be? I thought about it for a moment. There was only ever one person I turned to when stuff got seriously hardcore: Lauren.

It wasn't important that things had been a bit strained between us the last time we met. I mean, I was still upset that she hadn't told me she was pregnant or explained the truth about our birth father, but I knew Lauren hadn't intended to hurt me. The bond between us was surely strong enough to survive a couple of well-meant deceptions.

I picked up my phone and called her.

'Hey, Mo.' Lauren's voice on the other end of the line was immediately reassuring. For some reason I wanted to burst into tears on the spot. I tried to pull myself together.

'Is it a good time?' I asked. 'Are you still at work?'

'Naah, I got home about half an hour ago. In fact, I just started my maternity leave. It's ace. I'm gonna be able to sleep in and swim every day.' I could hear the grin in Lauren's voice. It was like there'd never been any distance between us.

A tear of relief trickled down my cheek. I could feel my whole body sinking lower on the bed, my shoulders relaxing. I hadn't realised how tense I'd been.

'So . . . so can I come round?' I said.

'Absolutely, Mo.' Lauren's voice softened a little. 'It'll be lovely to see you.'

Feeling calmer and more cheerful, I grabbed my bag and headed for the door. Annie heard me on the stairs and materialised from the kitchen.

'Where are you going?' she asked. 'What about all your coursework?'

Jeez, I'd completely forgotten my earlier excuse to keep her at arm's length.

'There's stuff for my art that I need at Lauren's,' I said. It was only a partial lie after all – and a well-meaning one. I didn't want Annie to feel hurt because I was confiding in Lauren rather than her.

To my relief, Annie visibly relaxed. 'You're going to see your sister?' Her eyes filled with tears. 'Oh, sweetie, that's wonderful.'

Irritation swelled inside me again. Why did she have to make such a big deal out of everything? I wanted to snap that it was perfectly normal for sisters to visit each other, but I held myself back. Long years of dealing with Annie's feelings meant I knew she'd get into a total state if I got cross – and I didn't want to have to handle her in floods of tears right now.

162

As I hurried to Lauren and Jam's flat, I read the threatening text message again.

What did 'this isn't over' mean? If I didn't go to the police – and there was no point doing that without any proof about Natalia and the *Miriam Project* – then why would Baxter bother with me anymore?

This isn't over.

I wanted to believe it was an empty threat. But inside I was scared. At least I was nearly with Lauren. She would listen. She would be sympathetic. She would know what to do.

However, when I arrived, I found Lauren's flat busier than I expected. Jam wasn't there – he was still at work – but Lauren's adoptive mum, Lydia, and brother, Rory, were both in the kitchen.

Lauren made a face as I walked in. 'They just turned up,' she whispered. 'I don't think they'll stay long.'

'It's fine,' I said. My stomach was still tied in knots, but I was going to be able to speak to Lauren soon . . . everything would be OK.

We sat in the kitchen and drank tea. Lauren and Lydia were chatting about the latest news on the baby and all the stuff that Lauren had bought: baby clothes and changing mats and a pram. They were both really excited and clearly expected me to be excited too. I did my best but the truth was that Baxter's threatening text was preying on my mind. I kept glancing at Rory. He was sitting in the corner, looking bored. It wasn't fair; nobody expected him to go all gooey over a pair of yellow booties.

'That's lovely . . .' I said for about the fifth time. Lauren seemed like a different person, all wrapped up in baby stuff as she was. She was wearing the blue tunic she'd had on when she'd announced she was pregnant. I'd never seen her look so happy or be so relaxed and chatty with her mum before. While Lauren showed Lydia how her new pram folded up, Rory beckoned me over.

'What are you doing here?' I said.

'Mum made me go shopping with her,' he moaned. 'We ended up just around the corner from here so of course we *had* to pop in.' He rolled his eyes. 'At least I'm meeting Marcus later . . . d'you want to come?'

I stared at him. Was he serious? A few weeks ago I'd have given my right arm to be included in a night out with Marcus. I thought back to that wink he'd thrown in my direction the other day and how it had made me blush with embarrassment. Then I thought of Wolf's intense gaze and the way his voice and his words had made me shiver earlier. That wasn't about being embarrassed, at least only partly. So why had I shivered?

You like him.

The realisation hit me like a slap in the face. *Oh my goodness.*

'Madison?' Rory was frowning. 'So, d'you want to come out with us or not?'

'Er, no. Thanks, but no.' I knew I was blushing and turned away, worried that Rory would be able to see what I was thinking. I didn't understand. Wolf wasn't the best looking boy I'd ever met and I hadn't spent much time with him, either. I hadn't even thought I fancied him. And yet . . .

'Bye, Madison.'

I jumped. Lauren's adoptive mum was standing over me, all ready to kiss me on the cheek. I hadn't even noticed her walk across the room.

'Er, bye,' I said, feeling completely covered in confusion.

I sat down at the kitchen table as Lauren showed Lydia and Rory out. I suddenly remembered why I'd come here. As I looked at the threatening text message again, I pushed Wolf firmly out of my head. It didn't matter if he liked me or if I liked him back. I'd run away from him, which would have put him right off me and was probably a good thing under the circumstances. Now I had to focus on what I should do about Declan Baxter.

'Sorry about that, Mo.' Lauren came back into the kitchen. 'D'you want some more tea?'

'No thanks.' I took a deep breath. I didn't want to waste any more time. 'Lauren, I did it . . . I tracked down my birth dad. I met him—'

'You did *what*?' Lauren looked so shocked that I stopped talking. 'What were you thinking, Mo?' she went on, her eyes wide and anxious. 'How did you find him so fast? God, are you sure it was really *him*? Don't you know how dangerous it is to go off and meet strange men you don't know? He could have been *anybody*.'

My mouth fell open. 'Of course it was *him*. I got his name from Annie. Allan Faraday. You saw the report she had. It

165

was easy to find him – he even *looks* like you. He admitted it straight away too. You know, he didn't have to show any interest in me at all, but he *did*.' I stopped, feeling my emotions whirling up again. It wasn't just the memory of how Allan had used me. I was also upset by Lauren's attitude. How could she have so little faith in my ability to look after myself?

'It was still really dangerous to go off on your own without telling me,' Lauren snapped.

'Well, you don't tell me everything – you didn't tell me about being pregnant.'

'That's different. I already explained . . . I didn't want you to have to carry such a big secret around . . . Anyway, that's irrelevant. I just need you to see what a big risk you took going to see a strange man without any back-up.'

'Stop calling him a "strange man",' I said. 'He's our birth father. *Yours* as well as mine. Jeez, Lauren, you travelled halfway across the world to find Annie and Sam when you were my age.'

'Don't exaggerate.' Lauren glared at me. 'It wasn't halfway round the world.'

I stared back, feeling mutinous. Lauren wasn't giving me a chance to explain *anything*. She was all angry and overprotective. And I'd had enough of people worrying about me to last a lifetime already.

'You're behaving just like Annie.' The words shot out of me.

Hurt radiated from Lauren's eyes. 'That's not fair, I just care about you.'

We sat in silence for a moment. I felt bad. I knew I'd been

166

mean saying that. And yet something held me back from apologising. I'd been so sure that Lauren would listen to me and she wasn't hearing me properly at all.

'So what was he like, this Allan Faraday?' Lauren asked.

'I told you, he was nice.' I hesitated, not wanting to explain how Allan had tricked me into coming to Baxter's party so that I'd meet and befriend Esme. 'He exaggerated his job a bit . . . but I think that was just because he was trying to impress me.'

'So he's a bit of a loser, then?' Lauren said.

I looked away. Why was she being so nasty?

'Did you tell him about me?' she asked.

'A little,' I said.

'Did you tell him I was having a baby?'

'Er, no . . .' I admitted. I thought about Baxter's threatening text message again and how desperate I'd been just a few minutes ago to tell Lauren all about it. This conversation was *so* not going as I planned.

'Do you care, Mo?' Lauren asked.

I looked up at her. 'What d'you mean?' I said. 'Care about what?'

'Do you care about me being pregnant?' Lauren's lips set in a thin, unhappy line. 'It's just I noticed you haven't mentioned it. Not once since you found out.'

I looked down at the kitchen table. A stain from a coffee mug stood out, dark against the wood. I traced my finger round the stain's outline.

'I told you I'm pleased you're having a baby,' I said quietly.

'Right.' Lauren sat back in her chair. She clearly didn't

167

believe me. 'So are you going to see Allan Faraday again?' A note of sarcasm crept into her voice as she said his name.

No, I thought. *Because he used me and got me into a really dangerous situation that I don't know how to get out of. But I'm not telling you that. Not now.*

'I don't know,' I said.

We sat in silence for a few more minutes. I didn't know how to fill in the huge hole that had opened up between us. After another few minutes, Lauren started saying how she was thinking about taking a bath soon so I took the hint and left. As I walked back to the tube station, I was too depressed even to cry. There had never been a distance between me and Lauren before.

And, after everything else that had happened, I had never felt so alone in my life.

Several days passed. I spoke to no-one. Well, I had a quick chat with Rosa before she went on holiday, giving her the briefest outline of what I'd been up to (though playing down the danger I'd been in) and, obviously, Annie was always starting conversations with me – but I didn't speak to Lauren again and Wolf didn't attempt to get in touch, either. Esme sent me a couple more texts, but when I didn't reply, she stopped. Allan also tried to call me. He left several messages in fact, but I deleted them all without even listening to them. Why should I make any effort with him? I'd wanted to make him like me, and he'd just let me down.

People always let you down. Allan had. Lauren had. I was sure Wolf would, if I gave him half a chance.

Better not to care about anyone in the first place.

At least then I wouldn't get hurt.

I got another threatening text a few days after the first.

This still isn't over. Say nothing to anyone.

I ignored that too. To be honest, the second text bothered me a lot less than the first had done. After all, nothing had happened to me yet even though Declan Baxter clearly knew who I was and could easily find out from the telephone directory where I lived.

I spent my time thinking about Wolf. He crept into my head in a really annoying way when I wasn't focused on anything else. I also threw my energies into the Art GCSE coursework I'd only pretended to be interested in before. At least Annie was pleased I was working hard.

It was the Thursday of the first week in August, just over a fortnight since I'd tracked down Allan Faraday. I'd been working hard on an essay on the influence of Christian values on art in the Victorian period. I was hungry and tired and came down to the kitchen to make a sandwich.

I wasn't expecting Annie to be there, but she was, chatting on the phone to someone.

'So she talked to Jam before she went?' she was saying.

My ears pricked up. It sounded like she was speaking about Lauren.

A minute later, Annie came off the phone. She walked towards me.

169

'That was Lydia,' she said. 'Apparently Lauren's taken herself off to a hotel in the country for a few days. She spoke to Jam and asked him to pass on the message.'

'Oh,' I said. I wasn't sure why Annie looked so worried. After all, Lauren tended to avoid talking to Annie for the same reasons I did. Annie knew that, even if she didn't like it much. 'So?'

'Well, it just seems a bit strange to me,' Annie mused. 'I mean, she's heavily pregnant and the hospital where she's having the baby is here and her family is here and—'

'Do Jam or Lydia think it's odd?' I asked.

Annie shook her head. 'Jam was adamant there was nothing wrong. Lauren just wanted a day or two by herself in the countryside. She's gone to a hotel just an hour and a half outside London. Jam's going to join her when he finishes work tomorrow night.'

'There you are, then,' I said. 'I'm sure Lauren's fine.'

'I suppose, I just don't like her being all alone.' Annie wandered away.

I headed to the fridge, intent on making my sandwich. As I opened the door, my phone rang.

Absent-mindedly I took the mobile out of my pocket – caller details withheld. Immediately on my guard, I put the phone to my ear.

'Madison?' The whisper was so low it was impossible to make out any accent or even whether the speaker was male or female.

'Yes?' I froze. Instinct told me the caller was Baxter.

'You were told to say nothing,' the menacing whisper went

170

on. 'Now I have your sister. Soon she will pay. An eye for an eye.'

The line went dead. I stood, stock-still, the phone still held against my ear . . . the fridge door still open in front of me.

An eye for an eye. That was from the Old Testament. I'd just been writing about it. It meant revenge. Baxter must think I'd talked to someone about Natalia and the *Miriam Project* – and he was taking the most terrible revenge possible.

An eye for an eye. I'd rescued Natalia – and now Baxter was going to hurt Lauren to pay me back.

23

The Clue

I raced out of the kitchen. I had no idea why Baxter thought I'd told anyone what he'd done to Natalia and the other girls – or how he even knew I had a sister. Esme might have mentioned it, of course, I distinctly remembered telling her about Lauren that day I went round to her house and there were loads of news stories on the internet about me and both my older sisters from years ago. I shivered. It didn't matter. Lauren was in some sort of danger and I had to help.

Annie was drifting about upstairs. I could hear her humming to herself as she wandered from the airing cupboard to her bedroom. For a moment all I wanted to do was to go up there and confess everything. However, long experience of my mother had taught me that turning to her for support gener-ally made whatever situation I was in worse. Annie's response to most problems was to panic. I needed to talk to someone who would believe me . . . who would stay calm . . . and who would know what to do.

Jam. As soon as I thought about calling him, I felt relieved. Jam would be as worried about Lauren as I was. Once I had explained everything, he would act . . . he would take responsibility.

I ran into the living room so Annie wouldn't overhear the call. With fumbling fingers, I found Jam's number on my mobile. He took a few rings to answer and when he spoke, his voice had that slightly self-conscious air that almost certainly meant he was at work.

'Jam, listen,' I said. 'I think something's happened to Lauren. There's a man called Declan Baxter. He knows I found out about an illegal operation he was running and he's taken her. He's planning on hurting her . . . doing something to her as revenge.'

There was a stunned silence on the other end of the line. Jam sucked in his breath. I could hear the murmur of voices in the background.

'What are you talking about, Mo?' His voice lowered. 'Lauren's fine. I talked to her less then half an hour ago.'

'Oh.' I remembered Annie telling me the same thing just a few minutes ago. 'Lauren must have been *made* to say she was OK. But I had a call. It's this man, Declan Baxter, I—'

'Listen to me, Mo,' Jam said gently. 'Lauren called me earlier and said she wanted to go away for a few days to Craven Manor. It's a spa hotel an hour or so outside London . . . got a big swimming pool apparently. I'm going to join her there tomorrow night.'

'No, it's a trick,' I persisted.

'Is this you talking, Mo?' Jam asked. 'Or is it your mother?'

I gasped. What was he saying? And then it struck me – Jam

173

was implying I was being overanxious and hysterical, like Annie.

'It's not like that, Jam.' Tears bubbled up behind my eyes. I desperately needed him to believe me. 'I was investigating this man and—'

'Who? Why would you do that? Is this something to do with your birth dad?' Jam sounded even more sceptical than before. 'Lauren told me you'd tracked him down.'

'Never mind Allan,' I said, feeling desperate. 'This is about someone else: Declan Baxter. I found out that Baxter has been paying pregnant girls to give up their babies so that other families can adopt them and—'

'You mean a surrogacy operation?' Jam interrupted.

'Yes, but—'

'Surrogacy isn't illegal, Mo,' Jam said. 'This Declan Baxter probably isn't doing anything wrong. D'you have proof of anything illegal?'

I hesitated. Natalia had made the same point: girls choosing to give up their babies wasn't against the law.

'Some of it *might* be legal,' I conceded, 'but if the girls change their minds and want to keep their babies, he won't let them go. Natalia said that when one of the pregnant girls tried to escape a few weeks ago, he caught her and Natalia never heard from her again . . .'

'So why hasn't this Natalia gone to the police now she's free?' Jam said.

'She . . . she was too scared . . . and also Baxter paid her a lot of money, so she's kind of part of the illegal side of it,'

I explained. Jeez, this was all coming out wrong. 'Look, the point is that I helped Natalia to escape and now Baxter's taken Lauren as revenge.'

'Are you sure, Mo?' Jam asked. 'Was this call you received even definitely from Baxter?'

'He didn't say it was him,' I admitted. Baxter hadn't identified himself on the phone. I hesitated. 'But he said "your sister will pay".'

'OK,' Jam said wearily. 'It sounds like a prank call, but if you're worried, I'll call Lauren again.'

'OK.' I rang off and waited.

Five minutes later, Jam called back. 'I just spoke to Lauren,' he said. 'She's fine . . . about to go swimming.'

I gulped. I was sure Lauren was being made to lie – probably to protect herself and us – but I couldn't see how I was going to convince Jam.

'Don't you think it's a bit odd, Lauren wanting to go to a hotel on her own?' I said.

'She's pregnant, Mo.' Jam sighed. 'Believe me, this is nowhere near the oddest thing she's done in the past few months. She's got a bunch of weird ideas from that Chelsey Barton pregnancy "bible" she's always quoting.' He paused. 'Now stop worrying and when we're back, I want you to come over. Lauren told me what happened the other day – it's crazy you two falling out.'

I agreed, my heart sinking, and we ended the call.

Now what did I do? Annie was still upstairs, humming to herself. I took my phone and dialled Lauren directly. The call went straight to voicemail. Still, if Jam was right, that wasn't surprising. According to him, Lauren had been about to go swimming. I left a message asking her to call me and redialled for Craven Manor. The receptionist confirmed that a Lauren Purditt had indeed checked in though she wasn't answering the phone in her room at this moment.

That proved nothing. *Anyone* could check in pretending to be Lauren. I paced across the living room. Clearly no-one was going to believe me without more evidence that she was actually missing. I stopped walking. If Lauren had been kidnapped, the chances were high that she had been abducted from her home. Annie and I had a set of spare keys. I should go there right now – see if I could find any signs of a struggle that might help prove Lauren had been taken against her will or any clues to where she might be now. I shouted up to Annie that I was popping out, grabbed the spare keys from their hook in our kitchen cupboard, then raced over to Lauren and Jam's flat.

I passed their car, parked outside, on my way in. That was strange, wasn't it? Surely Lauren would have driven herself to the hotel? As I let myself in, I couldn't help but remember the last time I'd been here and the argument we'd had. Suppose those words turned out to be the last we ever spoke to each other.

It was unthinkable. Unbearable.

I darted from room to room. Everything looked just as it normally did – clean and tidy. It was funny . . . Lauren was always moaning about how neat and uptight her adoptive

176

mum, Lydia, kept her house, but Lauren's own flat wasn't that different. A complete contrast to the way Annie lived, in perpetual chaos.

I whizzed from the kitchen to the bedroom to the living room. Nothing seemed in the slightest out of the ordinary. And then I saw the spilled drink – an upturned glass of orange juice on the low table in the living room, just by the sofa where Jam and Lauren sat to watch TV. The wood of the table was still damp and sticky and the juice had left a dark stain beside the bowl of dark green apples that stood there.

It was odd Lauren hadn't wiped the juice up.

Her pregnancy book – the Chelsey Barton 'bible' that Jam had mentioned – was on the sofa. I picked it up and fingered its worn pages.

It was, surely, also odd that Lauren had left this behind.

The hairs on the back of my neck prickled as I walked through the flat again. Nothing else seemed out of order. The only room I hadn't checked was the bathroom. It was clean and tidy, as usual. A picture of me with Lauren taken the year we met, when I was six and she was fourteen, hung on the wall by the door. I looked around. Everything was just as normal – from the blue and white striped towels hanging on the towel rail, to the red enamel mug at the sink containing Jam and Lauren's toothbrushes.

I glanced at the bath. Now that *was* weird. In the centre of the bath sat an apple with a large bite taken out of it and the vintage cross Lauren had been wearing the last time I'd seen her.

What on earth were they doing in the middle of the bath?

I picked up the cross. Jam had bought it for Lauren last Christmas – it was made of silver and studded with little coloured jewels. I remembered the three of us stifling giggles and trying not to catch each other's eyes as Carla had claimed she could sense its 'aura'. Why was it off its chain? And what was it doing in an empty bath alongside a half-eaten apple?

I took both items and carried them out to the hall. The apple clearly came from the bowl in the living room. Maybe Lauren had been eating it when she was kidnapped. And she could easily have been wearing the cross.

I gazed from the living room to the bathroom to the front door. Suppose Lauren had begged to be allowed to use the bathroom before she was taken away? She could have left the apple and the cross in the bath as some kind of sign.

Yes. I didn't understand what they meant, but I was certain these things were a clue.

24

The Trail

My heart was beating fast. I stared at the apple and the cross again.

What had Lauren been trying to say with them? Information about what had happened to her? I puzzled over it but got nowhere.

After a few minutes, I shoved the apple and the cross into my bag. If I was going to track Lauren down, I needed money, which meant going home and raiding Annie's emergency jar. I set off, hoping I'd be able to work out Lauren's clue on the way.

It only took twenty minutes to get home, and as I turned onto my road, I wasn't any closer to working out what Lauren had been trying to communicate. I rounded the corner. There, just ahead of me, standing outside my house, were Wolf and Esme. I stopped, a feeling of dread swamping me. What were they doing here?

Esme ran over as soon as she saw me. Wolf hung back.

'Why haven't you been in touch?' Esme pouted. She was wearing a silver jacket over a short black dress, black tights and pumps. She wouldn't have looked out of place at a cocktail party.

179

'I . . .' I stopped, wondering what on earth to say. I had so hoped Esme would just take my silence as a whopping hint that I was backing away from our embryonic friendship. I didn't want her to think I didn't like her – but it was equally impossible to tell her what I knew about her dad *or* to be friends with her without mentioning it. Now I was certain her father was intending to hurt Lauren, I felt even more awkward.

'I've been really busy,' I stammered.

'What?' Esme made a face. Her blonde hair was tied off her face in two long, thin plaits. They made her look younger than usual – despite the simple sophistication of her dress. 'Is it a boy?' she demanded. 'Come on, *tell* me. Don't be so frickin' mysterious. You know, that's what Wolf and I call you . . . Mysterious Madison . . .' She giggled.

I sighed. Esme had to be the most confident person in the world. Anyone else faced with a friend withdrawing contact would surely have wondered if they'd done something wrong. But Esme just assumed I'd been preoccupied with a boyfriend. I glanced ahead, where Wolf was leaning against the low wall of my front yard. He was looking in our direction and, though I couldn't properly make out the expression on his face from here, I could tell from the way he held himself that he was feeling awkward.

Was that because of the way we'd left things when we last spoke?

'How did you know where I lived?' I asked as Esme linked arms with me and led me towards Wolf and the house.

'You told me when you were leaving my dad's party the other day,' Esme said. 'At least you told me the area – and there aren't any other Purditts who live in N10.' She lowered her voice. 'I know I could have called, but I really wanted to see you in person.'

I nodded. The sun came out from behind a cloud as we reached Wolf. He glanced at me without properly meeting my eyes.

'Hey,' he said.

'Hey.' I swallowed. My palms felt all clammy just standing next to him. It felt like everything came into sharper focus when I looked at him . . . like I could see everything, from the expensive cut of his jeans to the yellow stitching in his top, to the natural golden-red highlights in his thick fair hair. Which was the last thing I needed. I *had* to get inside, get my money and work out Lauren's clue. Which meant I had to get rid of Esme and Wolf, not be distracted by them.

'Let's go inside,' Esme said brightly.

'Er . . .' I couldn't think of a way to say 'no' so . . . 'OK,' I agreed reluctantly.

We trooped indoors.

'I'm going to have a nose around,' Esme said with a grin. 'I love looking at other people's houses.'

Before I could say anything, she sped off, into the kitchen.

I exchanged a glance with Wolf. This time he met my gaze. He rolled his eyes.

181

'She's kind of an unstoppable force,' he said quietly.

I led him into the living room. We sat down, side by side on the couch. I was itching to get Lauren's clues out of my bag and see if they made more sense now.

'What's wrong, Madison?' Wolf asked.

I couldn't tell him. I didn't want to confide in him. And yet I didn't have anyone else to turn to . . .

'My sister's been kidnapped,' I whispered, hardly able to say the words. 'At least I think she has. Everybody else thinks she's fine, off on some spa weekend, but . . .'

Wolf's eyes were wide with shock. 'What? *Why?*'

I hesitated. I didn't want to tell Wolf the whole story, but maybe he could at least help me decipher Lauren's clue. I could hear Esme crossing the hall and tramping up the stairs as I took the apple and the cross out of my bag. I laid them on the couch, explaining I'd found them in Lauren's bathroom.

'I'm sure she left them there deliberately as a clue,' I said. 'But I have no idea what they mean.'

Wolf's face paled. 'Why would anyone want to kidnap your sister?'

I ignored his question. 'So do they mean anything to you?' I said. 'I've tried all the combinations of the words I can think of . . . but nothing makes sense: "Apple Cross", "Cross Apple", even "Bath Apple Cross". None of them mean anything.'

Wolf picked up the apple. 'Suppose the clue she was leaving wasn't "apple" but the *type* of apple this is?'

'OK, but . . .' I stared at the dark green fruit. 'What type is it?'

Wolf shrugged. 'I don't know,' he said. 'I've heard of Golden Delicious and Cox's Orange Pippins and Russets, but I don't think this is any of those.'

I shook my head. 'I don't think Lauren would know about types of apples.'

Wolf put down the apple. He fingered the cross. 'That doesn't have a brand name anyway.' He looked at me. 'Why don't we Google the words, see what comes up?'

I tapped 'apple' and 'cross' into my phone's search engine. The result flashed up instantly:

Appleton Cross.

I gasped, clicking through to the entry. 'It's a place – a tiny village based around an old monument on . . . on the outskirts of Linton in Cambridgeshire,' I said.

'A place?' Wolf sucked in his breath. 'Do you think it's a clue to where Lauren's been taken?'

'*Yes.*' I stared at him. That *had* to be it. Excitement thrilled through me.

Wolf smiled. A dimple I hadn't noticed before appeared in his cheek. My stomach did a backflip. 'Thank you so much, Wolf,' I said, feeling myself blushing again. I stared back at the information on my phone. Lauren's clue totally made sense now. I was certain that she *had* been taken to Appleton Cross by force, but I still had no proof. Which meant trying to find and rescue her was down to me.

183

'Er, Madison,' Wolf said. 'I've g . . . got something I have to tell you.'

I froze. Surely not another declaration of his feelings? Not now.

'It's n . . . nothing like that,' he said, clearly reading my expression. 'It's just that I kept quiet for ages about Natalia and how we rescued her. I never said anything to Esme, but in the end I told my dad. I was trying to help, to stop Baxter and—'

'*You?*' A cold weight settled in my guts. 'When did you tell your dad?'

'Last night,' Wolf went on. 'My dad was furious with me. He didn't believe any of it, said I was attention-seeking . . . spreading lies . . . it was horrible . . .'

I stopped listening. Baxter's threatening voice on the phone earlier filled my head: *'You were told to say nothing. Now . . . your sister will pay. An eye for an eye.'*

So *that's* why Lauren had been taken. Because Wolf had told his dad what we'd done to help Natalia, his dad had told Baxter and Baxter thought that meant I'd defied his order to keep quiet about his surrogacy operation.

I stood up. 'Get out,' I said, my hands trembling.

'What?' Wolf stared at me. 'Why?'

'It's *your* fault Lauren's been kidnapped,' I spat. 'Your dad obviously told Baxter what you said and— Get out of my house now.'

Wolf's mouth gaped open.

'You mean you think *Baxter* has taken your sister?' he said. 'To this Appleton Cross place?'

184

I looked away, furious with myself. I hadn't meant to reveal so much.

'Go away.'

'Madison, I'm so sorr—'

'I said leave it.' I tugged at his arm, half shoving him to the door. 'I don't want to talk about it anymore. I just want you to go.'

Wolf looked shell-shocked as I propelled him into the hall and out the front door. I'd almost forgotten about Esme. She appeared, trotting down the stairs, just as I was walking back across the hall. 'Nice house,' she said politely.

I gritted my teeth. 'Sorry, but I'm afraid I've just remembered I have to be somewhere, so you'll have to leave.'

'OK.' Esme looked around. 'Where's Wolf?'

I shrugged. 'He had to go too.'

Esme raised her eyebrows. 'Don't think I don't know something's going on between you two.' She gave me a hug. 'Well, *call* me, Madison. *Soon.*'

'Sure.' I drew back. I was still so angry with Wolf I could barely speak. But I didn't want to explain any of it to Esme. Except . . . 'Hey, Esme, your family doesn't have any holiday homes, does it?'

'Loads.' Esme waved her hand as if to indicate she had lost track of the many places involved. 'We have homes in the States and Tuscany and the south of France. There's a cabin in Sweden for skiing and—'

'What about England?' I asked.

'Sure, though most of those are investment properties. Daddy buys places in upcoming parts of the country hoping they'll go up in value or something.' She wrinkled her nose. 'There's too many to count.'

'OK, thanks.'

Esme gave me a curious look. 'Why are you asking?'

I shrugged. 'Just wondering.'

Esme grinned. 'Mysterious Madison, enigmatic as ever. Well, see you soon.' She swept out of the house.

I went into the living room and picked up my phone. Esme hadn't exactly confirmed my suspicions, but knowing Declan Baxter owned lots of properties certainly made me more determined than ever to find the best – and fastest – way to Appleton Cross.

Half an hour later, I had checked out all my options and was waiting for a train at Liverpool Street Station. I was going to have to change at Cambridge and find a bus or maybe a taxi to Appleton Cross. Once there, I would have to ask around to find out if any of the locals had heard of Declan Baxter. It seemed likely that he owned a property in the area and, if his Hampstead mansion was anything to go by, I was hoping it would be memorable in some way.

The train pulled slowly into the platform. There were quite a lot of people already waiting to board. A shiver prickled at my neck. I looked around, feeling spooked as the door in front of me opened. I waited for the arriving passengers to get off, then stepped inside. As I took my seat, I shivered again. This time I knew exactly what was spooking me.

Someone was following me. I could sense it.

25

The Hideaway

I looked around but no-one was watching me. The carriage was filling up – a group of students stood at one end, making a lot of noise, while the other passengers, mostly businessmen and women in suits, sat buried in their papers and laptops and iPads. An elderly couple took the seats opposite me. I stared at them suspiciously, but the old lady gave me such a soft, sweet smile in return that I blushed for my rudeness and tried to smile back. My mouth muscles felt stiff. In fact, my whole body was tensed. I peered up and down the carriage again. I still had the sense I was being followed. Jeez, maybe it was just my imagination playing tricks on me.

I sat back and took a few deep breaths. *Calm down.* The train started moving. I gazed around yet again. Everyone had taken their seats. No-one was looking at me. I took out my phone and did a proper search on Appleton Cross. The history of the place wasn't particularly striking, but I did find out that there was an Appleton Manor. That sounded just the sort of place Declan Baxter would buy. But then I read on and discovered that the manor had fallen into disrepair after the First World War and was now a ruin, owned by the council.

As I read, my phone rang. Another call from Allan. I

hesitated a second, then switched it off. I didn't want to talk to him. He had lied to me . . . tricked me . . . Anyway, what was the point? Allan didn't care about me. And he surely cared even less about Lauren. I stared out of the window, watching as east London's tower blocks gave way to red-brick houses, then open fields. Was she all right? My guts twisted every time I thought about her. Lauren was the bravest, most resourceful person I knew, but would she be able to cope – all alone and heavily pregnant? What was Baxter planning to do to her? I heard his menacing whisper in my ear again:

An eye for an eye.

I considered dialling 999 and demanding the police investigate. But they were no more likely to believe me than Jam: strategically placed pieces of jewellery and fruit didn't exactly amount to solid evidence.

The journey passed quickly. As I stepped onto the platform at Cambridge, I looked around again to check if anyone was following me. I saw no-one and sensed nothing . . . Maybe I had imagined it after all. I knew from my research that Appleton Cross was nine miles outside Cambridge. I had enough money to take a cab, but I didn't know if I'd need the cash later so I headed for the information desk to find out if there was a bus that would take me closer.

As I waited in line, the hair on the back of my neck stood on end. I had the same sensation as before – that someone was watching me. I turned around, scanning the concourse. He was standing just a few metres away, beside a coffee shop with chairs and tables set out in front.

Wolf.

Our eyes met and he started walking towards me. I watched him come closer, my legs suddenly shaking. Butterflies zoomed around my stomach.

Wolf reached me. He stood in front of me. His eyes were intense, his expression determined. 'Hi,' he said.

I stared at him, unable to speak.

'Please don't shut me out,' he said. 'I want to help.'

'You followed me?' I gasped at last. So that was why I'd had the spooked feeling earlier.

Wolf nodded. 'I'm really sorry that me talking to my dad has put your sister in danger, but I was only trying to do the right thing,' he said. 'And you can't do this alone. I'm coming with you. Like I said, I'd like to help.'

I hesitated. Part of me wanted to tell Wolf to get lost. And yet it was a relief to have someone else to help find Lauren . . . a relief to be with Wolf. Plus, as he'd said, he was only trying to do the right thing when he talked to his dad. If Annie wasn't so useless, I'd surely have talked to her too.

'What makes you think you can help?' I muttered.

'I've got plenty of money, for a start,' Wolf said.

I frowned. 'I thought your dad was mad at you for taking all that money for Natalia last week?'

'He was,' Wolf acknowledged. 'In fact, he cut off my allowance.' He took his wallet out of his pocket. 'I took this from home.'

'You *stole* it?'

'We should get a taxi to Appleton Cross,' Wolf went on.

'It's nine miles away – once we're there, we can try and find exactly where Baxter's taken Lauren.'

This was true, a taxi would be much quicker than the bus. I could feel my anger seeping away. Wolf was so sure of himself . . . so determined to help, and to make up for what he'd done in putting Lauren in danger.

'OK,' I said slowly. 'OK, let's go.'

Appleton Cross was exactly as described online – a tiny village with a central green containing a stone cross. Four roads led off from the green – two tarmacked thoroughfares and two rough country lanes.

We stood at the crossroads. There wasn't much to see: a few houses, a pub and two newsagents, one of which was also a grocery and a post office.

'Let's go in there and ask if they've heard of Baxter,' Wolf said.

'OK.' I followed him inside the little shop. It was crammed with produce, the shelves rising right up to the ceiling on all sides. A large, elderly woman with grey hair all bouffed up and swept off her face was bustling about behind the counter as we walked in. She smiled as she saw us.

'Hello there,' she said. 'How are you?'

I tried to smile back, but I was sure it looked forced. Jeez, I was used to London shops where people ignore each other. Wolf clearly felt more confident.

'Hello,' he said. 'We're fine, thanks.'

'Down for the day, is it?' the woman went on.

191

'That's right.' Wolf walked over to the counter. 'We were looking for a Mr Baxter. We think he might own a house around here.'

The woman smoothed her hair back. 'Ah, now, Mr Baxter's property is a little way down the lane to the left of the green.'

I gasped. So Baxter *did* have a house around here.

'It's not far, you can't miss it . . .' the woman continued, lowering her voice to a conspiratorial whisper. 'It's *very* modern.'

Wolf made a face. 'Too modern?' he asked.

I marvelled at his confidence. He was so comfortable talking to this woman. And, I realised, he hadn't stammered since I'd met him earlier.

'Too modern for my taste,' the woman went on. 'Anyway, like I say, you can't miss it.'

'Thank you very much.' I spoke at last. My heart was racing. We were on the right track, getting closer and closer to Baxter – and Lauren.

The woman beamed, then the smile faded from her face. 'Except . . .' She paused.

'What?' I said. 'What is it?'

'Now I'm thinking about it . . . that's not Mr Baxter's house after all.'

'What do you mean?' I asked.

I could feel Wolf move closer. We both stared at the woman.

'It *used* to be owned by Mr Baxter,' she said, folding her arms. 'They rented it out, but they sold it two months ago.'

'So who owns it now?' Wolf asked.

'No idea,' the woman said with a shrug.

26

House and Grounds

I stared at Wolf in horror. Had we got the whole situation wrong? If Baxter no longer owned a house at Appleton Cross, then how could Lauren be here?

I stumbled out of the shop in a daze. The sun was shining brightly. The day had really warmed up, but I was shivering. Wolf put his arm round my shoulder. I pulled away. I didn't want his sympathy. I was still certain Lauren was in terrible danger. But I appeared to be further away from helping to rescue her than ever.

'We must have got the clue wrong,' I said, tears pricking at my eyes.

'Just because Baxter sold the house doesn't mean he couldn't still use it,' Wolf said. 'He might be in league with whoever he sold it to. We don't know for sure, but—'

'We don't know *anything* for sure.' The words shot angrily out of me, all my frustrations and fears whirling up inside. I caught my breath. It wasn't fair to be cross with Wolf.

Wolf touched my arm. 'S'OK. Hey, as we've come all this way, why don't we check out the house anyway? The lady in the shop said where it was – it's only a minute or two up the road.'

'All right.' I turned to face him, feeling bad I'd just shouted. 'I'm sorry . . . I didn't mean to get angry. I'm just frightened for Lauren and . . . and I feel stupid that . . . *if* we've come all this way for nothing.'

Wolf took my hand and led me across the small village green and along the country lane that the shop lady had pointed out. His hand felt warm and strong. I wasn't used to holding hands with anyone, but walking along in the sunshine with Wolf, it felt like the most natural thing in the world.

We found the house easily. I hadn't been sure what the shop lady had meant when she'd said it was 'very modern', but after a couple of cottage-style properties with their sloping slate roofs and ivy-clad walls, Baxter's former house stood out in contrast. It was low and sprawling, with only part of the building raised up to a first floor, and made entirely of glass and wood. The whole effect was very pared-down and designer.

The house was sheltered from the road by a gate and a row of trees. We climbed the gate easily enough and walked round the house. Thanks to all the glass, it was possible to see inside almost the entire building. There was plenty of chic furniture and abstract art to look at, but no sign of life.

'It's all really tidy,' Wolf whispered.

I nodded. 'I don't think anyone's here,' I said.

Wolf pointed to the alarm box on the front wall. 'That'll make a lot of noise if we try and break in.'

'Break in?' I stared at him. 'Would you really go that far?'

Wolf shrugged. 'Your sister could be inside.'

I pursed my lips. It seemed unlikely. Surely Baxter wouldn't leave Lauren here without a guard – certainly not when the house was so easy to see into.

'Let's look around a bit more,' I said. The truth was I had almost entirely given up on finding Lauren here – but I wasn't ready to admit it. Not to Wolf and not to myself.

Keeping a careful lookout, we wandered through the grounds. The back of the house led into a patch of woodland. Sunlight filtered through the leaves, casting drifting shadows across the earth.

'D'you think this is part of the property?' I whispered, marvelling at the size of the place. How amazing to have a private wood on your doorstep.

'Yes,' Wolf said. He frowned, looking back at the house. 'You know, there's something that feels familiar about this place. I'm sure I've seen the house before.'

'Did you ever come here . . . with Esme, maybe?' I asked.

'No.' Wolf shook his head. 'Definitely not. It's not that . . . I don't know . . .'

We walked deeper into the trees. It was silent, just the swish of the breeze in the branches and the occasional traffic noise in the distance.

'It feels like we're miles from anywhere,' I said.

Wolf pointed at a small wooden hut that rose out of the ground to our right. Part hidden by bushes, it had been carefully designed to fit in with the natural land-scape around it. It was much older than the house nearby; the green paint on its wooden walls was blistered and peeling.

'What's that?' I said. 'Some sort of garden shed?'

'I guess.' Wolf walked closer and looked round one side of the hut. 'There aren't any windows,' he said.

I peered along the hut's other side. 'None here, either. That's odd, isn't it?'

Wolf shrugged. We walked over to the door. It was made of iron and brown with rust.

'Doesn't look like anyone uses it,' Wolf said thoughtfully.

A scrap of blue cloth was trapped between the door and the frame. I tugged it out, a sense of dread creeping down the back of my neck. Lauren had a pregnancy top exactly this colour. She'd been wearing it the last time I'd seen her, along with the jewelled cross.

'This could be my sister's,' I said, rubbing the cloth between my fingers.

'Was she wearing it earlier?' Wolf asked.

'I don't know,' I said. 'I didn't see her this morning.'

Wolf pointed to the hut door. 'Does anything strike you as odd about that?'

Holding the torn blue fabric in my hand, I stared again at the battered iron. The door had a normal keyhole which looked as rusty as the rest of it, but it was also fastened with an elec-tronic metal padlock that hung from a chain. Both padlock and chain glinted in the sunlight.

I had a sudden flashback to the empty beach hut in Norbourne where I'd been kidnapped when I was younger. I could remember the smell of the rotten wood and the tight grip of my captor's hand on my arm. That hut had been falling apart, but the lock on the door had been brand new. Just like here.

The memory sent a surge of panic shooting through my veins. I felt sick. 'Someone put the padlock on the door recently,' I whispered. My hands were shaking. I shoved them in my pockets so Wolf wouldn't see.

Wolf nodded. 'I think so too.' He pointed to a sealed panel on the wall near the ground that I hadn't noticed before. 'That looks like it contains controls – maybe lighting or heating or air con. He glanced at me. 'D'you want to see what's in the hut?'

I looked again at the scrap of cloth we'd found in the door. Had this torn off Lauren's top as Baxter's men forced her inside?

'Yes.' I breathed out slowly, trying to calm myself down.

'Come on, then.' Wolf held the padlock in his hand. It was square, with a small keypad in the centre. 'We need a code,' he said. 'It's probably four numbers.'

'Jeez, it could be anything,' I said.

Wolf nodded thoughtfully. 'The 3 looks a bit more worn than the rest . . . maybe that's used twice.' He paused. 'I'm going to try a few obvious dates. Things like significant holidays or . . . birthdays. Baxter's birthday . . . Esme's . . .'

'We don't even know if Baxter is involved . . . he doesn't own the property anymore,' I said.

'Well, do you have a better idea?'

As I shook my head, my phone rang. It was Jam.

'Madison?' He sounded really worried.

'Hi,' I said.

'Listen,' Jam went on. 'I've been thinking about what you said, ever since you called. And I'm . . . I'm starting to get worried.'

'Are you?' My heart skipped a beat.

'I can't get hold of Lauren. It's been hours since we last spoke. She said she was going swimming, but there's no way she'd be this long. I've told the hotel she's pregnant and asked them to page her and she hasn't answered and she still isn't in her room and then, about ten minutes ago, I got this weird text from her saying *darling can't wait to see you later . . .* It just doesn't feel right and—'

'Was she wearing her blue pregnancy top this morning?' I interrupted. 'And that vintage cross you gave her?'

'Er, yes, I think so,' Jam said. 'How did you know? Why—?'

'I think I found a bit of the top,' I said. 'I think she's here, at Appleton Cross.'

'*Where?*'

I explained how I'd worked out the clue Lauren had left, then tracked down Baxter's former house with Wolf's help.

I glanced over at Wolf as I spoke. He was still bent over the electronic keypad, trying out code numbers.

198

'Are you sure you can trust Wolf?' Jam said anxiously. 'Mo, I don't like you being there. You could get hurt.'

'I'll be fine,' I said. 'I mean, we don't know for sure Lauren's here, but this scrap from her top makes it likely, doesn't it?'

'Oh, man.' Jam's voice cracked. 'I can't believe someone's taken her.'

'Hey,' I said, trying to sound reassuring. 'You know Lauren. If there's anyone who can take care of herself . . .'

Jam blew out his breath. 'I'm leaving work now,' he said. 'Tell me exactly where you are. I'll pick up the car and meet you.'

I could almost feel the weight lift from my shoulders. Thank goodness for Jam. He had always been such a rock. And now he was coming here. He would take the lead and take care of me and Lauren. Just like he always had. I gave him the address. Jam repeated it back to me.

'OK,' he said. 'I'm on my way. Promise me you'll be careful around this Wolf guy. And above everything, promise me you'll wait – away from the house – until I get there. I'll bring bolt cutters from home – something to break the chain on the door of this hut you've found.'

I gazed over at Wolf, still hard at work on the keypad. There had to be millions of potential combinations. It was unthinkable that we'd crack the code and open the door. Jam was right to suggest we left. If we couldn't get into the hut, we should back off, wait for Jam nearby.

'I promise,' I said.

Jam rang off. I pocketed my phone and walked back to Wolf. The sun went behind a cloud. I checked the time. Nearly 5.30 pm. Jeez, it was hours since I had come downstairs at home intending to make a sandwich. I'd been hungry then, but food had gone out of my head after I received Baxter's call. I should be starving by now, but my stomach was tied in tight knots. I didn't feel hungry at all.

A metallic click made me look up. Wolf was staring at the padlock – now open – in his palm. He glanced at me, a grin spreading across his face.

'You did it,' I said.

'I used Esme's twin brothers' birth date,' Wolf said. '1212, 12th of December. It's cute because there are two of them and the number 12 twice, though it's strange there was no 3 in the mix. That number *definitely* looked more worn than the others.'

'Never mind.' I grinned. 'The point is you opened the door.' I took the padlock from his hands and ran the chain through the metal. It made a soft clinking sound as it released. Jam's warning repeated in my head.

I gulped. Should I still keep my promise? It was one thing to do so when we hadn't been able to get the door open. But now . . .

'What do you want to do?' Wolf said uncertainly.

I *had* to know if Lauren was here. We'd seen no sign of anyone in the grounds, and the fact the hut door was locked from the outside suggested that whoever was inside was a prisoner. Jam would surely understand the urgency . . .

'I have to find Lauren,' I said. 'I have to rescue her, if she's here.'

'Right.' Wolf gritted his teeth. 'Let's go.'

I turned the handle and gave the iron door a push. With a menacing creak, it opened.

27

Finding Lauren

I put my finger to my lips, to signal we shouldn't speak any further. After all, we didn't know who else might be in here. I crept past the door. The interior of the hut was bare concrete: dimly lit and cool. That was odd. Why would anyone line a garden shed with thick concrete walls? It was empty too. All I could see ahead of me was a flight of stone stairs, leading underground.

'Madison,' Wolf whispered. 'Wait a sec.'

I turned round. He was still at the door. He gestured at me to hold it open while he fetched a large stone from outside. He brought the stone back and placed it carefully between the door and its frame. 'We don't want this shutting and automatically locking us in,' he whispered.

I nodded to show my approval. Thank goodness he was here. I was so intent on finding Lauren I hadn't even thought about wedging the door open.

Wolf closed the door so that it rested against the stone. Inside the hut it was dark apart from the slim shaft of light that led from the door towards the stairs. I tiptoed over. There were seven or eight steep stone steps down. I couldn't make out any details of the room below. No lights. No sounds. Just gloom and shadows.

It was cold. The hairs on the back of my neck rose. If Lauren was here, then she must be unconscious, or tied up or . . . My guts twisted into a sickening knot as it struck me she might be dead, that this hut might simply be a place where Baxter had stored her body. He wanted revenge on me for taking away Natalia and her baby. What better payback than for him to permanently take away my sister and *her* unborn child? Was Baxter capable of murder? Natalia had thought so . . . she'd been convinced he had killed her friend Lana.

Trying to push these thoughts out of my head, I crept down the stairs. The stone was cold under the thin soles of my shoes and the steps themselves very steep. One. Two. Three. I paused on the bottom step. My eyes were adjusting to the gloom. I could just make out a row of shelves on the wall ahead, stocked with cardboard boxes. The room bent round to the right. What was there?

I took the final step, onto the concrete floor, and peered around the wall.

'AAAGGGH!!' A huge roar. A dark shadow loomed towards me.

I shrank away, arms outstretched, as Wolf leaped in front of me. He pushed the dark shadow away with a thud. It was solid. Not a shadow after all but a plank of wood.

The figure holding it stumbled back.

'Madison?' It was Lauren. A split second later, she flicked a wall switch and light flooded the room.

Lauren stood in front of me, a wooden slat from a packing crate still raised in her hand, her mouth open with shock.

203

'Oh, Mo.' Lauren's lips trembled. She dropped the wooden slat and pulled me into a hug. I squeezed her fiercely, feeling the swell of her belly between us. Lauren drew back. 'I thought you were the guard coming back. What the hell are you doing here?' She turned to Wolf. 'And who's this?'

'This is Wolf,' I said. Relief filled me – along with a new urgency. We had to get Lauren out of here before anyone came back. 'We followed the clue you left . . . the cross and the apple . . . We came to get you out. Come on.'

'They were clues for *Jam*,' Lauren said, looking appalled. 'Clues for him to call the *police* to help—'

'But you talked to Jam earlier,' I said. 'He wasn't *going* to the police.'

'No, but he would have once he got back from work and realised I wasn't answering my phone anymore.' Lauren stopped, her face screwed up in pain. She bent over, gasping.

'What is it?' I said. 'Are you OK?' I looked around for somewhere to sit her down.

The underground concrete room we were in was about three metres by ten metres in size. The floor and walls were plain and bare and contained nothing except a mattress at one end, some shelves stacked with boxes at the other. I started to lead Lauren over to the mattress, but Wolf put his hand on my arm to stop me.

'We should go,' Wolf said firmly. 'Lauren, it's nice to meet you and I'm sorry you're in pain, but if you can walk at all, we should get out of here.'

He was right. 'Lauren?' I said.

Lauren nodded, her face still drawn. 'It's just all the worry, I think,' she said as I led her carefully to the stairs. 'I've been having terrible shooting pains in my lower back for the past two hours.' She gave me a wry smile. 'Don't look so panicky, Mo. The baby isn't due for weeks.'

'Who kidnapped you this morning?' I asked.

'A guy with dark, cropped hair and a leather jacket. Late twenties,' Lauren said.

I nodded. That sounded like the same guy Baxter had sent after us when we rescued Natalia from the Burnside Road flat.

'He came to the flat, pretended to be delivering a package for Jam. Soon as I opened the door a crack, he barged in . . . forced me to call Jam and say I was going to some hotel then took my mobile.' Lauren paused, wincing as she stepped slowly onto the bottom stair. 'What I don't understand is *why*. The Leather Jacket guy wouldn't explain it at all.'

I looked away. *I* was the reason 'why'. Baxter had arranged for Lauren to be kidnapped in order to punish *me* for supposedly betraying him. It might have been Wolf who had actually talked, but I was responsible for Lauren being here.

'I heard him talking to someone else on his phone,' Lauren went on, not noticing my awkwardness. 'That's how I knew to leave the clue about Appleton Cross. I insisted I had to go to the bathroom. I knew he'd check to see if I left any message with lipstick or whatever, but I'd been eating an apple anyway, so it was easy to leave it in the bath with my cross. Then he put me in the back of a car and drove me here. But *why*?'

'We can explain everything when we're out.' I squeezed Lauren's arm as she climbed onto the next step. 'Let's just get out of here.'

I looked up. The hut above us was in total darkness. Where was the light from the door that Wolf had left wedged open? Anxiety clutched at my throat. Even allowing for the contrast with the bright electric light in the basement, making everything up there seem darker, there should be *some* light. There had been a shaft of sunlight earlier . . .

Heart pounding, I said nothing as I helped Lauren up the last step. Then I raced towards the door. I could barely make it out in the gloom. I reached it . . . found the handle. But the door was shut.

'What's happened?' Wolf had run up past Lauren and was right beside me. 'Why's the door closed?'

'The stone you left must have moved,' I said. 'Or . . . or else . . .' A shiver threaded down my spine. 'Or else someone has deliberately shut us in here.'

28

The Wait

I banged on the door. Wolf joined me. We pushed at the metal with all our strength, but the door didn't budge.

'What's happening?' Lauren asked. 'Why can't we get out?'

I turned to face her, desperation rising inside me. Lauren was standing at the top of the stairs, silhouetted against the bright light from downstairs. She was holding her belly – a tender, protective gesture – anxiety etched on her face.

'The door's been closed on us,' I said, trying to steady my voice. 'When was the last time anyone else was here?'

'I've only seen that one guy in the leather jacket,' Lauren said. 'He brought me here then left, but that was hours ago.'

'There's no way the rock I wedged the door with could have moved by itself,' Wolf insisted.

'Then who moved it?' I said. 'Why haven't they come in to see who's here?'

'Maybe someone was following us?' Wolf suggested. He turned and pushed at the door again. It was no good.

I shivered. It was terrifying to think we'd been watched.

'So now we're all trapped?' Lauren's voice had a flat finality.

'I'll call the police.' Wolf took out his phone. 'Now we know you're definit—' He stopped, staring down at his mobile. 'There's no signal.'

I checked my phone. 'Same here,' I said. Panic whirled inside me. I tried to focus. 'It's OK, Jam knows we're here. I described it exactly. He's on his way now, in the car.'

'Jam's coming? Oh, thank goodness.' Lauren's voice filled with relief. 'Because there isn't another way out – I've looked.'

The three of us went back down to the bunker basement. Wolf immediately explored the boxes on the shelves at the far end.

'They're mostly empty,' Lauren said. 'Though I couldn't reach the ones on the top.'

Wolf was already clambering up the shelves. Lauren winced with pain, bending over, her hand on her side.

'Are you OK?' I said.

'Apart from being thirty-seven and a half weeks pregnant and trapped in a basement?' Lauren raised her eyebrows.

I stared at her anxiously. 'Did the man who brought you leave you any food or drink?'

'Yes.' Lauren led me over to the far corner of the underground room. A small cupboard I hadn't noticed before was bolted against the wall. Lauren opened it up, revealing a row of small water bottles and a tray containing cellophane-wrapped sandwiches. I peered suspiciously at the sandwiches. Despite the fear still ploughing up my guts, I was starting to feel hungry. I hadn't eaten anything since a biscuit when I'd got up this morning.

'I think they're OK,' Lauren said with a sigh. 'I mean, I don't think they're poisoned or anything. If Leather Jacket wanted to kill me, I'd be dead already.'

She spoke in a matter-of-fact way, but I could hear the fear behind the bravado.

I glanced over at Wolf. He was back on the ground, busy examining the contents of the boxes from the top shelves. As I watched, he headed to a small door in the corner. I hadn't noticed it before: it was partly hidden by the shelves.

'It's a bathroom,' he said, disappearing inside.

'It's tiny,' Lauren grimaced. 'Just a sink and a toilet.' As Wolf shut the door, she turned to me, lowering her voice. 'Who is *he*, Mo?'

'I met him through—' I stopped, not wanting to mention Allan Faraday. Until this moment I'd forgotten all about my argument with Lauren over him. She had been right, of course, Allan *was* a loser. And in trying to impress him by following his lead on Miriam 21, I had got involved with Declan Baxter, rescued Natalia, and brought down Baxter's revenge on Lauren's own head.

'I guess you were right about Allan Faraday,' I said softly.

Lauren shook her head. 'I was too harsh,' she said. 'I've been thinking about it. When I was your age, I had Mum and Dad and they were basically great, but it still wasn't enough. You've just got Annie and a big hole where Sam used to be. I can totally understand why you went looking for your birth father.'

209

We looked at each other. A big wave of emotion swelled inside me. I flung my arms round her. 'I'm so sorry, Lauren. I'm so sorry I got you into—'

'Sssh.' Lauren drew me away from her and peered into my face. 'None of this is your fault, Mo.'

I swallowed hard, trying not to cry. Lauren was wrong. It *was* my fault. And now she was here in this incredibly vulnerable position and I couldn't bear it. She was the *brave* sister. I couldn't be strong without her.

I looked across the room. Wolf was still in the bathroom, but he'd already laid the contents of several boxes on the floor. I could see a row of small food tins, a couple of dog-eared paperback books and three toilet rolls.

'It's not exactly five-star accommodation.' Lauren made a face. 'The man told me not to drink the water from the tap.' She lowered her voice. 'So . . . how d'you feel about Wolf?'

I glanced at the bathroom door to make sure he couldn't hear me. 'I don't know,' I whispered. 'I'm all mixed up about it. He's nice, but . . .'

Lauren nodded. 'I remember when I realised how I felt about Jam,' she said softly. 'He'd been interested for ages and I just hadn't seen it. Then one day it hit me how much I felt . . .' She paused. 'We met when we were younger than you are. Sometimes it's hard to know what you want. Jam and I split up for nearly a year once, while we were at uni.'

My mouth gaped. 'You and Jam broke up?'

Lauren nodded. 'I thought we were too young to settle down, that we should go out and live a bit.' She gave me a

210

wry smile. 'I went to a lot of parties. Jam did too. But after a bit, I realised that it didn't matter how young we were, or what we had or hadn't done. All that counted was how much we loved each other.'

'Wow.' I couldn't believe it. Ever since I could remember, it had been Jam and Lauren. Together. I realised, with a jolt, that I couldn't conceive of a world in which they weren't a couple.

'I'm just saying, don't worry about feeling confused.' Lauren lowered her voice further. 'You'll work out how you feel about Wolf in time. But he obviously adores *you*.'

Did she really think so?

At that moment Wolf emerged from the bathroom, a hammer in his hand. He turned to face us, beaming with pride. 'Found this under the sink,' he said. 'It could *really* be useful.'

I nodded. 'That's great.'

'When do you think Jam should be here?' Lauren asked.

'A couple of hours, max,' I said. 'Hey, Wolf, are you hungry? There are sandwiches.'

'I'm starving.' Wolf came over, still clutching the hammer. We hid it under the mattress. Wolf seemed much more positive than before. He was confident that between us, the hammer and the plank of wood Lauren had ripped off one of the other boxes earlier, we'd stand a good chance against whoever next came into the bunker.

We sat in a row on the mattress and ate. Lauren said the pains she'd had earlier had passed. Her face did look less drawn.

'We're armed and we're fed,' Wolf said. 'We're going to get out of here.'

'We should wait upstairs for Jam to get here,' I said. 'He won't know that code you used. We'll have to tell him so he can open the padlock again.'

'We just have to hope there's no-one outside when he gets here,' Lauren said.

'Maybe we can escape before Jam arrives,' I suggested.

But there was no way out. The basement room and the hut above were completely sealed.

'All the air in here must be controlled via that panel on the wall outside the hut door,' Wolf said. He sounded calm and confident. I could see Lauren liked him.

I was starting to realise just how much I liked him myself.

Wolf and I agreed to take it in turns to wait upstairs for Jam to arrive. Wolf insisted on taking the first shift. I went up to relieve him later.

'Hi,' Wolf said as I reached the top of the stairs. I could barely make him out in the shadows by the door. 'How's Lauren?'

'She's fine, no more pains,' I said. 'And Jam should be here soon.' I let my eyes adjust to the gloom, then walked over to where Wolf was standing. 'Lauren likes you.'

'Well, she's pretty cool herself.' I couldn't see his face clearly, but I could hear in his voice that Wolf was smiling.

My heart skipped a beat. I stopped thinking about the danger we were in, and Lauren downstairs. I walked right over to Wolf. I touched his arm.

212

'Thanks for being here,' I said softly.

Wolf lowered his head. His eyes glistened in the dim light. 'I'd do anything for you, Madison.'

I lifted my face and he leaned closer until our lips touched in a soft, sweet kiss. Slowly, we drew apart. Neither of us spoke for a moment.

'You better get downstairs,' I said. 'Check on Lauren for me.'

'Of course.' But Wolf didn't move. Instead, he leaned closer again.

I closed my eyes, ready to give myself up to another kiss.

Bang. With a loud thud, something heavy landed against the door.

Wolf and I sprang apart, both turning instinctively towards the noise.

'Jam?' I hissed.

Silence. The door creaked. A crack of light appeared.

Wolf drew the hammer from his pocket. He held it high over his head. I braced myself as the door opened more fully.

A body was pushed through. With a moan it, landed on the concrete floor. The door slammed shut.

Darkness filled the room again. Wolf and I looked down at the figure on the ground. It was Jam. His wrists and ankles were bound with rope and a large scarf had been wound round his face. I dropped to my knees and pulled the scarf away.

'Who's there?' Jam's voice was a low groan. 'Is that you, Mo? Where's Lauren?'

'*No*,' I said, my whole body filling with despair.

'Oh, God,' Wolf said behind me.

I shook Jam's shoulder, but his eyes flickered shut.

'It's Mo, I'm here,' I said.

But it was no good. Jam was unconscious.

29

A New Life

'Jam?' I bent closer, shaking his shoulder. But Jam didn't respond. He was out cold.

'Has he been hit or shot?' Wolf said anxiously.

'I can't see any marks, but it's too dark to really tell.' I peered at Jam's face.

'Come on.' Wolf grabbed Jam's legs. 'Hold his head so it doesn't bump on the concrete.'

Together we moved Jam's limp body across the floor to the top of the stairs. There was more light here. Wolf laid Jam's legs gently on the ground and I examined his head properly. No bruises. No blood.

'I don't get it.' I looked up at Wolf. 'There isn't a scratch on him.'

'Maybe he was drugged.'

I nodded. That made sense. The same guy who'd seen us come in here must have been ordered to watch the entrance. When he saw Jam getting closer, it would have been easy enough to creep up behind him and slap a cloth containing something to knock him out over his face.

I shivered, remembering how I'd watched, years ago, as a man called Cooper Trent had done exactly that to Annie, then

215

gone on to set alight the building that Lauren and my other sister, Shelby, were trapped inside.

'D'you think we should try getting him downstairs?' Wolf asked.

I nodded. Lauren was going to be desperately worried when she saw Jam like this, but I was sure she'd want to try and make him as comfortable as possible while we worked out what on earth to do next. 'Lauren!' I called out.

There was no reply. I stood up. Why wasn't she calling back? In fact, how come she hadn't heard us already and come up to see what was happening?

'Wait here a sec,' I said to Wolf.

Filling with dread, I sped down the steps to the bunker basement. Lauren was sitting on the edge of the mattress. She was bent over, rocking backwards and forwards.

'Lauren?' I said.

She didn't look up, just carried on rocking. I scurried over. 'Jam's here and he's fine,' I said, though I really had no idea if he was going to be OK or not. 'He's unconscious, but he spoke a bit first and I'm sure he'll come round soon.' I squatted down beside her.

Lauren looked up – an unfocused gaze. 'Mo?' she said hoarsely.

I frowned. She didn't look like she'd even heard me speak, let alone clocked what I was saying.

'What's wrong?' I said.

Lauren put her hand over her belly. 'It hurts,' she said. 'More than before. Has done since you went upstairs.'

216

My throat tightened. 'Maybe you should lie down,' I suggested.

'No.' Lauren's voice was still hoarse with pain. She started rocking to and fro again. 'I need to move . . . keep moving.'

I stared at her, feeling helpless. 'Wolf!' I yelled up the stairs.

A moment later, he was by my side. We stared at Lauren together. It was almost as if she wasn't properly aware of our presence.

'Lauren?' I said. 'What can I do?'

She turned to me with wide, fearful eyes, focusing on me properly at last. 'It's the baby,' she gasped. 'It's coming. I can feel it.'

My stomach seemed to fall away inside me. 'No,' I said. 'It can't be coming. It's too soon.'

'I'm having contractions,' Lauren said. 'I think I might have been having them all day. But they're much worse now. Mo, I'm scared.'

I glanced at Wolf. He was white-faced. 'What should we do?' he said. 'In movies they always boil water, but we can't here and anyway, I don't . . .' He tailed off, looking as though he might be sick.

My heart thudded against my chest. I couldn't handle this. Not a baby. Not my big, brave sister in terrible pain. I needed someone to take charge – an adult . . . someone who knew what they were doing. I gulped, running through the options. Jam was unconscious. Wolf probably knew less than I did about people giving birth.

217

There was no-one else. It was down to me. I had to get Lauren through this. Nothing else mattered. I took a deep breath. 'May I have a look?' I said.

Lauren nodded. She turned around on the mattress. Wolf backed away, towards the little bathroom. He needed something to do.

'See if you can find any blankets,' I said. 'Anything to wrap the baby in. And one for Jam as well, while you're at it.'

'OK.' Wolf strode over to the shelving area.

'Jam?' Lauren glanced up at me. 'Is Jam here?'

I'd just told her he was, but she'd obviously been in so much pain she hadn't even heard me. I hesitated. Now I could see the state she was in there was no point making things worse. Lauren needed hope. Hope and faith. 'Jam will be with you soon. I meant *you*. A blanket for *you*.'

Lauren nodded as she peeled off her leggings. I peered down.

Jeez, was that the baby's head? Panic whirled through my body. What was I supposed to do now?

'Mo?'

'You're right, I think the baby is coming,' I said. 'What did they tell you at . . . at the classes you went to?'

'Breathing.' Lauren clutched at the word like a lifeline. 'We had to do special breathing.'

'Do that, then,' I said, though inside I was screaming. How on earth was breathing going to help?

'I've found a dusty old rug and a clean towel,' Wolf said from across the room.

218

'Take the rug upstairs,' I said, indicating with my expression he was to use it to keep Jam warm. 'I'll have the towel.'

Wolf handed me the towel then went upstairs. Lauren was squatting on the mattress now, taking deep breaths, then letting them out in long, low moans. She sounded like an animal. I peered down again. The top of the baby's head was clearly visible, a purplish dome between Lauren's legs. I put my hand on the very tip. The skin was warm. It thrilled through me that this was a life . . . literally, a life in my hands . . .

I felt a new strength. 'We're going to get through this,' I said.

'OK.' Lauren's eyes fixed on mine. The look of fear faded slightly from her face. 'OK, but it still really, really hurts.'

I felt the baby's head again. 'Come on, sweetheart,' I murmured. 'You can do it.' I looked up at Lauren, vaguely remembering a film we'd been shown at school years ago. 'Don't you have to push or something?'

Lauren nodded. 'It comes and goes,' she panted. 'The urge . . . to . . . push . . .'

'Well, next time it comes, just take a big breath and push, all right?' I said, hoping that was good advice.

'OK.' Lauren nodded, then let out another low groan.

I positioned myself, both hands now cradling the baby's head. 'Almost out.'

'OK, I'm . . . it's time . . .' Lauren's voice shook with pain. She gave a huge, agonised moan.

219

More of the baby's head appeared. I could see the eyes now. Tight shut. The skin was all purplish and covered in some sort of white wax. I had no idea if any of that was normal.

'Again,' I said. 'You're doing so great, Lauren, breathe.'

'I am breathing,' she panted. 'Oh, God, it hurts.'

'You're doing great,' I repeated. 'Come on, push again.'

'*Aaagh* . . .' Lauren took another breath. Another moan. Another push. Again.

Again.

With a burst of water and blood, the baby slithered out, into my hands. I held it, too shocked for a moment to speak.

'Oh, God,' Lauren whispered.

I stared down at the baby. A little girl. The umbilical cord was still inside Lauren. As I watched, the baby opened her tiny mouth.

'WAAH!' A thin wail filled the air.

Quickly, I reached for the towel and wrapped the baby in it. I couldn't take my eyes off her. She was tiny and wrinkled and . . . so old-looking. Nothing like the babies – or pictures of babies – I'd seen before. I lifted her up to Lauren. She reached down for her, scanning her furiously.

We held her together. 'Is she OK?' I said. 'What's all that white stuff?'

Lauren drew the towel over the baby and pressed her close against her chest. The wailing stopped. The baby stared up at Lauren with huge, unseeing eyes. I kept my hand on the baby's arm. Her five fingers were so small, so perfect.

'I think the white stuff is called vernix,' Lauren said. 'It's a protective thing . . .'

'Is she OK?' I asked again. 'She's so minute and . . . and . . . so crumpled.'

Lauren made a noise somewhere between a laugh and a sob. 'She's early, but I think they normally look like this . . .'

'*Too* early?' I was holding my breath. As the shock of the birth was wearing off, I could feel myself filling up with a new feeling. I didn't understand it, but it was powerful. I *had* to know the baby was all right.

Leaning against the wall, Lauren held her closer. I let go, sitting back and watching them.

'Anything between thirty-eight and forty-two weeks is supposed to be OK,' Lauren said, her voice soft. She still hadn't taken her eyes off the baby. 'I think she's fine, Mo.'

I gazed at them still, letting the reality of what I was seeing settle on me. My sister was a mother. I was an aunt. This baby was my blood.

The powerful feeling flooded through me, right to my fingertips. This was the fiercest love I'd ever known. Lauren looked up. Our eyes met. And I knew that all my former fears had been for nothing. This baby wasn't going to come between Lauren and me. We were going to love her together.

She was our family.

'Oh.' The word breathed out of me at the enormity and the power of what I had done and felt and understood.

'Yes.' Lauren nodded, knowing exactly what I meant.

221

Slam. Upstairs the door crashed open. A split second later, footsteps thundered down the stairs. Two men wearing surgical masks stormed into the basement. One carried a gun. He pointed it at me.

'Move away,' he ordered.

Terrified, I scrambled back. The second man crouched down in front of Lauren.

'What are you doing?' I glanced up the stairs. I could just make out Jam's body, still prostrate at the top. There was no sign of Wolf, but I could hear him talking to someone upstairs, demanding to know what was going on.

I looked back at Lauren. The second man was peering down at her.

'It's OK, I'm a doctor,' he was saying. He was murmuring something. I caught the word 'placenta'.

Lauren gave another groan. I held my breath. Was she OK? The doctor was still examining her. He cut the cord, then looked up.

'Let me check the baby,' he said.

'No.'

But he had already taken her. He was opening up the towel, eyes intent on the tiny bundle inside. 'She's fine.' He was speaking to the other man, whose gun was still pointing at my face. Both men strode to the staircase. The baby started crying again.

'Wait, what are you doing?' I said.

'Stay back.'

As they raced up the stairs, Lauren screamed out. 'No!' Her yell rose up, over the baby's thin wails.

And then the bunker door slammed shut and Lauren fell silent, her face the colour of ash, as the baby's cries died away, fading into the air as if they had never been.

30

The Wall

I couldn't move. Couldn't breathe. Wolf pounded down the stairs. He rushed over to me.

'Madison?' He grabbed my arm. 'Did they take the baby?'

I nodded. Lauren was still sitting, motionless, a picture of utter despair. I walked over and squatted down beside her. I had no idea what to say . . . how to comfort her . . .

'We'll get her back,' I said.

Lauren looked up at me. Misery was etched into her face. I'd never seen anyone look so completely devastated. A terrible blistering guilt bled through me. This was all my fault. If I hadn't tried so hard to impress Allan, I would never have found Natalia. And if I hadn't tried to help Natalia, then Baxter wouldn't have taken Lauren's baby.

I helped Lauren back into her leggings, then laid her down on the mattress. She let me help her as if she were a child, then closed her eyes and turned away to face the wall. Feeling helpless, I wandered across the room to the shelving area, where Wolf was rummaging through the contents of a cardboard box.

'What I don't understand is how Declan Baxter and his men knew the baby was coming,' Wolf said quietly as I joined him. 'I mean, Lauren wasn't due to give birth for a couple of weeks . . . there weren't any obvious signs it would happen when she was captured. And there aren't any cameras in here, either.' He glanced up the stairs to the hut above.

I followed his gaze. 'What happened upstairs?' I asked. 'There was a man guarding you, wasn't there? Did he hurt you?'

'No,' Wolf said. 'When they left, I could hear them outside, tinkering with that control panel by the door, but I don't know what they did.'

'What about Jam?'

'Did you say *Jam*?' Across the room, Lauren sat up. 'Is he *here*? Why didn't you say? Is he all right?'

I exchanged a look with Wolf. 'We think he's been drugged, but—'

'Oh, God.' Lauren got up from the mattress. She clutched at her side, leaning against the wall.

'Are you OK?' I asked anxiously, rushing over.

Lauren gave a fierce, sharp nod. 'I have to see him.' She staggered across the floor. I caught her arm.

'Wait,' I said. 'Wolf and I will bring him down.'

This took some doing. Wolf held Jam under the shoulders, taking the bulk of his weight, while I guided his legs down the steep stone steps.

It took at least fifteen minutes to get him down the stairs and onto the mattress. Lauren sat beside him. Tears were now streaming down her face. Again, I didn't know what to say. Jam moaned and shifted a little.

225

'I think he's going to be fine,' I said, trying to sound hopeful.

'How am I going to tell him about the baby?' Lauren sobbed.

I stared at her. I'd never seen Lauren in such a state before. She was always so strong and resourceful – I couldn't bear watching her break down like this.

'Do you have a name for . . . for her?' I said, hoping to give Lauren something else to focus on.

'Yes,' Lauren wept. 'Ellie.'

I smiled. 'That's pretty.'

'Jam and I decided last week.' Lauren looked up, wiping her eyes. 'Ellen Shelby Caldwell for a girl.' She paused. 'I wanted Shelby's name to be in there somewhere.'

She looked at me, tears welling up again. 'Oh, Mo.'

'We'll be fine.' I said the words with more conviction than I truly felt. 'We'll be OK and . . . and so will Ellie. We'll find her, I promise.'

Lauren sniffed. 'I'm going to see if I can wash in that bathroom,' she said.

Wolf and I helped her up. She seemed a little steadier on her feet as she walked to the room with the tiny sink. Then I went over to Jam. He was breathing deeply, as if he were asleep, but I had no idea if he were any closer to consciousness than he had been before.

I sat back against the wall. Wolf was pacing across the room, deep in thought. I suddenly realised I was sweating.

'Is it me or is it hotter in here than when we arrived?' I peeled off my long-sleeved top and bundled it into a ball.

'It is.' Wolf stared at me. '*That's* what the men were doing outside with the control panel. They were turning off the air conditioning.'

I placed my top under Jam's head as a pillow, then went over to Wolf. I lowered my voice so that Lauren wouldn't hear inside the bathroom.

'Doesn't that mean we'll suffocate?'

Wolf nodded, his eyes wide with fear. 'With four of us in here, I reckon we've got an hour – maybe two – before the air becomes unbreathable,' he whispered.

I gulped. So this was Baxter's plan . . . take the baby and leave the rest of us to die here.

'But Baxter knows your dad,' I said. 'Surely he won't let you die just because you helped me?'

'How would he know I'm here?' Wolf said miserably. 'Those men upstairs didn't look properly at me. Anyway, why would Baxter care if I got killed? He's never paid me any attention – and I'm sure he's going to do his best to make sure no-one finds out that he's responsible.'

We stood in silence for a moment, then Wolf pointed at the wall that led from the bathroom to the corner of the room where the shelving started.

'Does anything about that look strange to you?' he asked.

I stared at the wall. At first glance it appeared exactly the same as all the others in the room.

'I don't see—'

'Look at the paint, it's a slightly different colour.'

I moved closer. It was true: the wall Wolf was looking at

227

was a greyer shade of white than the rest. 'OK, but I don't get—'

Wolf tapped the wall. It made a light, hollow sound.

'It's not solid,' I breathed. 'But that doesn't make sense; all the other walls are reinforced with concrete.'

'Exactly,' Wolf said. 'The concrete was added *after* the hut and this basement area were built. I think it was originally designed as a storage area. And I don't think this is a proper wall at all.' He gave it another hollow tap. 'I think it's just a bit of plasterboard,' Wolf said. 'Which means there's got to be something on the other side.'

A bead of sweat trickled down my forehead. I wiped it away. 'Come on.' I picked up the hammer Wolf had found earlier and slammed it against the plasterboard. It made contact with a smack. A satisfying crack spread across the wall.

Wolf fetched the plank of wood Lauren had torn off a packing crate before. He thrust the end against the crack I'd made. The crack deepened. I hit the wall with the hammer again.

Lauren appeared from the bathroom. 'What's going on?'

I explained as Wolf took the hammer and rammed it repeatedly against the wall. He stopped, gleaming with sweat, after a few minutes. I took over. Then Wolf took over from me. In ten minutes we had created a hole big enough to crawl through.

Jam moaned from the mattress. 'Lauren?' he rasped.

Lauren went over to him as Wolf disappeared through the hole.

'What can you see?' I said, torn between wanting to help Wolf explore and concern for Jam.

'I was right,' Wolf said. 'This *is* a storage area. Come and have a look.'

I glanced over at Lauren and Jam. Jam was raised on his elbows now, his face pale, intent on what Lauren was telling him. A look of terrible pain twisted across his face. He reached out and held Lauren in a hug.

I decided to leave them to their private moment, and crawled through the gap in the wall after Wolf. Enough light shone through from the other room for me to make out that we were in an empty space roughly three metres square. The air smelled damp and fusty.

'If nothing else, this will buy us a little more time to breathe,' Wolf said.

'Why would anyone wall this area up?' I said.

'Maybe it's unsafe,' he suggested.

'Great,' I said. 'So we're now choosing death by suffocation or death by wall collapse.'

Wolf gave me a wry smile. 'I love how you always look on the bright side, Madison.'

In spite of everything, I smiled back. 'You can call me Mo, if you like.' As soon as the words were out of my mouth, I felt scared. It was a big thing, letting Wolf use my nickname. Only Jam and Lauren were allowed to call me Mo.

I busied myself exploring the far corner of the empty room.

'Thanks, Mo.' Wolf sounded sincere – pleased, but not over the top with it.

I relaxed slightly. Maybe it was OK admitting to myself I liked him.

Maybe it wasn't something to be so frightened of after all.

I felt my way across the wall. It was rougher here – and damp. My fingers hit a ridge. It was cold and metallic. I traced the outline as my eyes grew accustomed to the darkness. I'd found some sort of rusting metal flap. It was about a metre wide by half a metre high. I felt for the bottom edge and prised it up. A metal rail slid into place at the side, holding the flap open. I felt inside. It was a kind of chute – made of earth and sloping upwards.

'I found something,' I whispered.

Seconds later, Wolf was at my side.

'I'll climb up,' he said. 'Take a look.'

'Me first,' I said. 'I'm smaller.' I clambered into the chute. The earth was tightly packed under me, the darkness ahead deeply unnerving. I remembered Wolf's warning that the area might be unsafe and tried to push the thought to the back of my mind.

I kept going, clawing my way through the earth. Dirt fell on my hair and my face. I forced myself on.

'Are you OK?' Wolf's voice sounded much nearer than I expected. It felt like I'd moved miles, but I had only come a couple of metres through the chute so far.

'Fine,' I said. I clawed more earth under my fingers. Two fingernails broke as more dirt fell on my face. I spluttered, trying to blow the flecks off my mouth.

'Is it getting any lighter?' Wolf said.

'No.' My heart sank. The absence of light meant there was surely no access to the outside up ahead. Still, I had to know for sure.

'I think the chute must be for pouring coal, or maybe wood, down,' Wolf said.

'Right.' The ground ahead of me opened and flattened slightly. I reached out gingerly with my hand. A sloping sheet of iron met my touch, similar to the one I'd climbed through before. I felt around the rusty edges. It appeared to be a similar size. I gave it a push. It was stuck.

'There's an iron flap at the top,' I explained to Wolf, '. . . like the one at the bottom.'

'Can you open it?' Wolf said. I could hear the urgency in his voice.

I pushed again at the iron sheet, this time using both hands. Nothing happened. I gave it another shove. But it didn't budge.

We were as stuck as ever.

31
The Betrayal

'I can't get out,' I sobbed. 'I can't get us out.' Terrified misery soaked through me. I lay against the earthy wall of the tunnel in the pitch black, damp and dirty. Tears trickled down my face. When I'd found the chute, I'd really thought I'd found a way to free us all. And now I had to face the fact that we were going to die here. That Lauren and Jam's baby had been taken from them and that we were all going to lose our lives – it was just a matter of time.

'Mo!' I suddenly realised Wolf was talking to me. Something was tapping against my foot. 'Try this,' Wolf said. 'It's the hammer.'

I wiped my tears into the grime already on my face, then reached down with my hand. By flexing my foot and bending my knee through the few centimetres that the space allowed, I could just bring the hammer far enough up to touch my fingers. I edged it higher until I could hold it properly in my hand.

'Try freeing the earth around the metal flap,' Wolf urged.

I did as he suggested. Dirt fell on my head and my hands. I spat it out of my mouth, the earth mingling with the tears and snot already on my face. I felt the metal ridge of the flap. The rusty edge was definitely more prominent, which meant it was getting freer.

'D'you want me to have a go?' Wolf asked from below, in the bunker.

'No.' A new hope surged through me. 'It's working.' I hacked at the earth all around the metal, then pushed at the flap. It gave slightly. More hammer blows, dull thuds against the soil. More dirt fell, this time into my eyes. I brushed it away, ignoring how it stung.

I pushed the flap again. With a creak, it opened slowly, onto sweet, damp fresh air. *Yes.* I reached my hand through. A light drizzle was falling. I had no idea what time it was, but the fading light suggested early evening. Could so much time really have passed? I hauled myself half out of the hole. I was still in the woods, but closer to the house. The flap was set into a crumbling brick wall we hadn't noticed as we'd passed through the trees. A path led away, towards the back gate of the house. I couldn't see or hear anyone.

'I'm through,' I called softly down the chute.

'Awesome, well done,' Wolf called back. 'I'll fetch the others.'

I wriggled properly out of the flap onto the ground and stood up. The woods were silent – just the pattering rain and the soft breath of the wind in the trees. The house still looked dark and unoccupied. Still, I couldn't be totally sure I wasn't being watched. After all, someone must have seen us – and Jam – arrive earlier. That was how we'd been trapped in the first place. And I still had no idea how they'd known that Lauren had gone into labour.

As I looked around, my phone rang. The sound echoed through the trees. I jumped and delved into my pocket, desperate to shut the thing up.

Allan calling.

I put the phone to my ear in a panic. 'Hello?' I whispered.

'Madison, thank God. *Please* don't hang up.' Allan sounded desperate.

I looked around me again. The woods were still silent; the rain was drying up. No-one was coming running. No-one had heard the mobile ringing. It was OK.

'Listen, Madison,' Allan went on urgently. 'Baxter knows you're onto him. I've been making some calls and—'

'I *know*. He had my sister trapped underground,' I hissed. 'We're just getting away now.'

'What? Are you OK? Are you safe?' He sounded really concerned.

I looked around. Still no sign of Baxter or his men. I peered into the chute. I could hear Wolf and Jam talking in the distance, but not what they were saying. *Hurry up.*

'We're almost out,' I whispered. 'Why are you calling me?'

'To warn you. And careful what you say. Baxter's known for using hidden mikes to entrap people. He could have one planted on you right now.'

I gasped. A microphone on me?

'How do you know?' I said.

'I've been investigating – *honestly*. Look, it doesn't matter how I know. Just trust me on this. Baxter uses hidden mikes.'

My head spun. Was Allan right? Could I trust him? A hidden mike certainly explained how Baxter had known so speedily that Jam was coming and that Ellie was being born. I gazed down at my top and jeans. I was covered in dirt. Could Baxter really hear what I was saying right now? 'So if I *was* carrying a hidden mike,' I whispered into my mobile, 'what would it look like?'

'It could be tiny, like the size of a pinhead,' Allan said. 'Probably on something near your face – a strap or a collar.'

I felt the straps of my vest top. Nothing. I'd been wearing a long-sleeved top until just after Ellie was born, but I'd used that as a pillow for Jam so it was still inside with him.

'You need to get away from there, fast,' Allan urged.

I glanced back down the chute. I'd left the metal flap open, to make it easier for Wolf to get the others through. Their voices sounded closer, but there was still no sign of them. I gulped. I couldn't see either Jam or Lauren making it out of the bunker all that quickly. Lauren had just given birth and would only just fit through the chute while Jam had only recently regained consciousness.

'Madison? Are you there? I'm so sorry for getting you into this. Please get going . . . get to safety.'

'OK,' I said. 'I'm just waiting for the others.'

'Others? You mean your sister?'

'Yes, er . . .' I stopped, not wanting to reveal that Jam and Wolf were here too – or to tell Allan about the baby.

Allan drew in his breath. 'I understand you not trusting me,' he went on, 'but nothing I've ever done was about hurting

235

you. I'm devastated that Baxter has come after you and your sister. I'm trying to *help*. And right now you really need to leave.'

I looked at the chute. Now I could hear Wolf's voice clearly at the other end, helping Jam push his way through. Were either Jam or Lauren in a state to manage this?

'Hurry!' I hissed down the chute.

'On our way!' Wolf's whisper echoed up the tunnel towards me.

'There's something else,' Allan said. 'I've been investigating Baxter. He has various properties in the south-east of England which he could be using to keep pregnant girls in.'

'I think we're in one of his old places now – at Appleton Cross.' I hesitated, worrying I'd said too much.

'Let me take a look . . .' I could hear Allan tapping away at his keyboard. 'Have you got the others yet? Are you on the move?'

As he spoke, Jam's head appeared through the metal flap in the crumbling brick wall. He looked exhausted. His face was covered in earth, but his mouth was set in a determined line. He hauled himself through the hole, then reached back inside.

'Lauren?' Jam said. 'Feel for my hands.'

'OK, I've found the Appleton Cross place,' Allan said down the phone line. 'Baxter sold the house two months ago. The new owner is an Alexander Yates. He was at Baxter's party the other day. He's a businessman, a friend of Baxter. He owns lots of properties too. Must be in on the whole thing. Er . . .' I could hear him tapping away. 'I can't find a picture,

236

but his Bizznet profile says he's forty-seven, lives in north London, married with an only son about your age: Wolfgang William Yates.'

I froze. That was *Wolf.*

'You really need to be leaving, Madison,' Allan said. 'Find the mike. Destroy it. And dump your phones too. Baxter can track you through those as easy as anything. Just get out of there and get to the nearest police station. I'll meet you there.'

My head was spinning. *Wolf's father* owned Appleton Cross?

'OK, Madison?'

'Yes,' I said. 'Find mike. Dump phones. Get to nearest police station.'

'Good, I'm calling the police for you now.' Allan rang off.

Trying to pull myself together, I switched off my phone and turned to the chute opening. Jam was helping Lauren out. As soon as she was through, she collapsed onto the ground, holding her belly.

Jam squinted anxiously down at her.

'Are you all right?' I asked.

'I can't see properly,' Jam said, rubbing his eyes.

Wolf's hands clutched at the side of the chute opening. He'd be out in a few seconds.

'We need to dump our phones,' I said.

'Mine was taken earlier,' Jam said.

I nodded. I already knew Leather Jacket had removed Lauren's mobile. I chucked my own phone into the trees. It landed with a faint thud on the grass.

'Here.' Unsteadily, Jam untied my top from around his waist. He held it out to me. 'Thought you might want this back.'

I took the top. If Allan had been right about Baxter using mikes, maybe one was planted on this. I lifted the collar and ran my finger along the seam. Straight away I felt the bump of the hidden microphone. With shaking hands, I took it out and held it in my palm – it was tiny, no bigger than a pinhead, just like Allan had said.

This explained how Baxter and his men had found me – and known that Jam was coming and that Lauren was having her baby. But how did it get on my top? After leaving home earlier, I'd gone to Lauren's flat where I'd found the clue to Appleton Cross. The only person I'd seen since who'd been close enough to plant this on my clothing was Wolf . . . who had chosen to visit me just after I found out about Lauren. And whose father also owned the place where we'd been locked up and left for dead. Unless Allan had lied about that? Was him calling me part of some elaborate trick I didn't understand?

Confusion whirled like a tornado inside my head. I threw the tiny microphone onto the ground and stamped on it, then looked up to see Wolf emerging at last from the chute.

Jam was still busy, trying to get Lauren onto her feet. I strode over to Wolf. My feelings tumbled out of me.

'Why didn't you tell me your dad owns this house?' I said furiously.

Wolf blinked rapidly. 'What are you talking about?'

238

I stared into the bewildered blue-grey of his eyes. Was he faking that innocence? How could I be sure?

'I just spoke to Allan,' I said. 'He says your father bought this house from Baxter two months ago.'

A look of recognition crossed Wolf's face.

'You *knew.*' I backed away from him. 'How could you, Wolf? I thought you were my friend.'

32

Running and Driving

'I *am* your f . . . friend.' Wolf's face burned red – was that guilt or confusion? 'I told you when we got here that the house looked f . . . familiar. My dad buys and sells lots of properties. I must have seen a picture of it. Remember, I *said*?'

It was true. He had said that. Still . . . I pointed to the fragments of microphone on the ground. 'Someone put that on my top so Baxter could hear everything I said,' I hissed. 'It *must* have been you.'

'What's going on?' Jam stumbled over, rubbing his eyes. 'Lauren's ready to walk now.'

'It wasn't me.' Wolf took a step away from me. '*Please*, Madison.'

I shook my head. 'But your dad *owns* this house. He *must* be involved in what Baxter is doing – the girls, the babies . . . taking Lauren and Jam's baby.' My guts twisted with misery. 'I can't believe you'd help him do any of that.'

'I *didn't*,' Wolf insisted. 'And I don't believe my dad's involved, either.'

I turned away. I didn't know what to think. It was hard to mistrust Wolf, but something in Allan's voice had made me feel sure Allan himself wasn't lying. Anyway, the hidden mike was surely proof.

'Madison?' Jam caught my arm. 'We should get out of here.'

'Yes,' I said.

Lauren staggered over, still clutching her belly. She looked beyond exhausted. Jam and I put our arms round her – one on each side – and led her towards the edge of the woodland. Wolf walked behind us. I didn't look at him directly.

'Could you go any faster, Lauren?' I said, trying to keep my voice light and encouraging. But the truth was, I was scared. Jam was as unsteady on his feet – thanks to his blurred vision – as Lauren was slow. Panic rose up inside me. The mike had been on my top, so even if Jam lying on it in the underground room had muffled the noise of us breaking down the wall, the device would have definitely picked up Wolf, Jam and Lauren crawling out through the chute. I reckoned Baxter had been aware of our escape for about ten minutes, which was roughly as long as it had taken him to realise Ellie had been born and snatch her out of our hands.

'Guys, we really need to hurry,' I urged.

Both Jam and Lauren tried to walk faster. Would we get out in time? The far edge of the woodland and the gate out of the house were still several metres away.

Wolf strode up beside us. 'Please, think about it, Madison. What you're saying doesn't make sense. If I wanted to spy on you, why not wear a mike myself? I've been with you the whole time – why take the risk of you finding something I

241

could hide more easily on my own clothes? And remember I was going to die in that bunker just the same as you. Why would Baxter let that happen if I was secretly working for him?'

The low rumble of a car engine sounded up ahead. We all froze as the car stopped somewhere beyond the trees. Two doors opened, then slammed shut. A moment later, low male voices filled the air.

Wolf grabbed my arm. 'I'll distract them,' he whispered. 'You get Jam and Lauren out of here. Go!' He ran off.

'Come on, Mo,' Jam whispered.

A million conflicting emotions were swirling about my head, but there was no time to unravel any of them. Jam, Lauren and I crept on, to the edge of the trees. The car we'd heard was parked several metres along to our right – a large black estate. It was empty. Were the men who'd been inside now chasing after Wolf?

The gate leading out of the house – just a few metres across the grass to our left – was closing slowly.

'We can get out there,' I whispered.

I put my arm round Lauren again, helping her and Jam on to the gate. It was still shutting, the two sides just a couple of metres apart from each other. I had to get Jam and Lauren through that gap. There was no way either of them were in any fit state to climb over the gate.

'Hurry!' I pushed them on. I could feel both of them urging their bodies to move faster. It was working. We sped up.

We reached the gate. Jam squeezed through, pulling Lauren after him. I glanced over my shoulder. There was no sign of Wolf — or of the men chasing him through the woods.

'Come on, Mo,' Lauren urged.

I followed her through the gate. Jam had already turned left. He put his arm round Lauren's waist and hurried her along the country lane. He held one hand outstretched in front of him, as if wary of bumping into obstacles. His vision was obviously still really bad.

The light was fading fast from the sky. It seemed like days instead of hours that Wolf and I had walked down here. Jam's car was parked just before the end of the lane. He fumbled for his car key and opened the door as we approached.

'Can you drive?' Lauren asked anxiously.

Jam made a face 'Everything's still really blurry.'

My heart thudded. Jam *had* to be able to drive. Lauren wasn't up to it so how else were we going to get out of here? Jam opened the door to the back seat and helped Lauren inside. She lay back with a groan. I'd never seen her face so pale and drawn. Then Jam turned to me.

'Mo, we need to get away then call the police about the baby. And get Lauren to hospital.'

'Sure. Of course.' I looked around. Where was Wolf? There was neither sight nor sound of him through the trees. Was he doing what he'd said, and leading Baxter's men away from us? Or was this all, somehow, part of a bigger trap?

'So you'll have to drive,' Jam said.

'*What?*' I said, turning back to him. 'But I . . . I can't, I don't know how.'

Jam shrugged. He handed me the keys. 'I can't see further than a couple of metres in front of me, and that's all blurry. And Lauren's in no state to do anything. Just get us away from here. I'll help.'

Jam fumbled for the driver seat door. He held it open for me, then ran round to the other side. He got into the front passenger seat. I took the driver's place.

Up ahead, Leather Jacket appeared. He was running out of the trees with another of Baxter's men. No sign of Wolf. Was he OK?

'Oh, Jeez, it's two of Baxter's men,' I said.

'Go!' Jam urged. 'Put the key in the ignition and turn.'

'What about Wolf?'

'The police will find him. *Go!*'

With shaking fingers, I took the key Jam had given me and inserted it into the slot just under the steering wheel. I gave it a sharp turn. The engine revved.

Jam moved the stick between us. 'Is that in "D"?' he asked. 'It's an automatic so you don't have to worry about gears.'

'D' for *Drive*. 'Yes.'

'OK, now press down on the accelerator. That's the pedal on the right.'

I grabbed the steering wheel and pushed the pedal at my feet. With a roar, the car leaped into action. We were off.

33

The Attic

It was weird as well as terrifying. Of course I'd *seen* people driving all my life, but actually to be sitting in the driver's seat of Jam's car and making it move was totally surreal. My feet pressed the pedals. My hands gripped the wheel. My eyes peered into the early evening light. Thank goodness there was no traffic.

'D'you need the lights on?' Jam said beside me.

'No . . . er, not yet.' I was holding the wheel so tightly my knuckles were white.

'What can you see?' Jam asked. 'Are there any people? Any houses?'

'Not so far.' We were still on the small country road Wolf and I had walked up earlier.

Where *was* Wolf? Had he escaped from Baxter's men? Was he really in league with his father? Everything he'd said to convince me he was innocent made sense. But could I really trust him?

'Could you manage a bit faster, Mo?' Jam asked.

I pressed down on the accelerator. The car leaped forwards.

'Whoa!' Lauren let out a groan from the back seat.

'Steady,' Jam said.

'Sorry,' I muttered. I tried again, pressing more slowly this time. The car sped up. Faster and faster. The junction at the end of the road was zooming towards us. We were going too fast.

'How do I stop?' I yelled.

'Brake!' Jam shouted. 'Pedal on the left.'

I slammed my foot onto the floor of the car, pressing down on the pedal for all I was worth. The car skidded to a stop. Lauren gasped.

'Damn.' My confidence was evaporating, fast.

'It's OK, you're doing fine.' Jam said. 'Just press the accelerator again, but more carefully.'

I pushed down my foot and the car lurched forwards. I eased up and we slowed slightly.

'I think I can hear something behind us,' Lauren said. 'Is that a car?'

'Check the mirror, Mo,' Jam said. 'It's above your head.'

I looked up. I could just make out the reflection of the black estate car from the wood in the rear-view mirror. It was moving fast towards us. I pressed harder on the accelerator. The other car grew smaller, then larger again, as it sped up.

'It's chasing us!' I said, panic rising inside me.

'Faster!' Jam ordered.

I forced the accelerator down towards the ground. The car picked up speed. My heart was racing. Jam's hands were flat against the dashboard. It suddenly struck me that none of us were wearing seat belts and I thought of Annie. She would totally flip out if she could see us.

246

'Check the mirror,' Jam yelled.

I glanced up. The black estate car was gaining on us. I went faster. So did the other car. The hedgerows outside were speeding past. The junction at the village green was coming up at an alarming rate. At least there were shops there . . . the newsagent's Wolf and I had visited earlier . . . we could stop and . . .

I reached the village green and glanced out of the window. *No.* The newsagent's was dark, locked up for the night. I sped straight on at the crossroads. Now the road was wider. The other car was in the lane beside us.

'God, they're right here,' Lauren shrieked.

I could sense Leather Jacket in the driver's seat of the black estate car, but I didn't look directly over. My eyes were on the road ahead. I had to stop the other car going past us. With a furious roar, it zoomed ahead. A split second later, it spun around, blocking our way.

'Aaagh!' I screamed, slamming my foot on the brake. We stopped, just centimetres from the other car.

'Put it in "R",' Jam shouted.

But even as I reached for the stick, the door beside me opened. Large hands grabbed my shoulders and hauled me out, into the cold air. A cloth bag was rammed over my head. Plastic ties were bound tightly round my wrists. I screamed. Jam and Lauren yelled. It was all happening so fast. Then a voice hissed in my ear: 'Be quiet.' I felt the press of cold metal against my neck. Was that a gun?

I shut up. So did the others. A second later, I was bundled

247

into the back seat of Leather Jacket's car. I could feel Lauren next to me, shaking. I leaned against her.

'Mo?' she whispered.

'I'm here,' I said.

'Oh, God.' She was crying. 'What are they going to do with us? What's happened to Ellie?'

'We'll find her,' Jam said from Lauren's other side.

The car engine started up. 'Be quiet,' ordered a voice from the front, as we moved off. It was Leather Jacket.

My heart sank. We were captured, again.

I lost track of how long we drove for. Both Jam and Lauren demanded to know where we were being taken and what Baxter had done with baby Ellie. But every time one of us spoke, Leather Jacket told us to shut up. So the journey passed mostly in silence. At last the car slowed and turned. The wheels crunched over gravel for a while then came to a stop. The door beside me opened and rough hands pulled me out into the cold air. I shivered, breathing in the sharp tang of salt. Were we by the sea? I felt the familiar rise of panic I always experience by the ocean. Memories of nearly drowning when I was younger crowded into my head – that terrible sensation of not being able to breathe, imagining the water filling my lungs, dragging me down.

I forced these thoughts away and tried to work out which part of the coast we could possibly be on. My knowledge of geography wasn't very good – I knew Appleton Cross had been north-east of London, but I had no idea what direction we had driven in after that. It was dark outside now, but I had the sense of dim lights to my left. Were they coming from a building?

'Jam?' I said. 'Lauren?'

'We're here, Mo.' Jam's voice sounded close.

'Where's my baby?' Lauren's voice cracked as she spoke. 'Please just tell us she's all right.'

I had a sudden flashback to the way Ellie had slithered into my arms, how perfect she had been.

'Enough talking,' Leather Jacket's voice barked over our heads.

I felt the press of gun metal against my arm.

'Walk!' he ordered.

I stumbled forwards, unable to see where I was going. I took three or four small steps, my feet scrunching up the gravel. Leather Jacket ordered us to stop.

'Where are we?' Jam demanded.

'Shut up!'

Something sharp poked into my back. I inched forwards.

'Go up a small step!' Leather Jacket ordered.

I lifted my foot, feeling for the step.

'Now walk straight ahead.'

I did as I was told. All of a sudden the wind dropped and the floor under my feet was soft. We were indoors.

I could hear a door shutting behind me, then I was prodded again. Up one flight of stairs. Then another.

'Is our baby here?' Jam demanded.

I could hear the smack of a hand across his head and the muffled yelp of pain he let out. I gulped.

'Jam?' Lauren asked anxiously.

'I'm fine,' he said.

We climbed up a third, narrower, flight of stairs. A rough hand pushed me along a corridor, then shoved me through another door. The bag was whipped off my head. I blinked in the electric light as Jam and Lauren stumbled in beside me. Lauren immediately sank to the floor, weeping.

We were in an attic room – a tatty carpet on the floor, paint peeling off the walls, a sloping ceiling that came right down to the ground at the eaves. I glanced over. Jam couldn't stand fully upright even in the middle of the room. There was no furniture. No window. I took in all this in a split second.

'Madison?'

I spun round. Declan Baxter was standing in the door. He looked much as he had at the party: tall and in a smart suit with his thick grey hair brushed carefully off his face. Back then he had barely noticed me. This time, however, I was getting his full attention.

His dark eyes pierced through me. Several beats passed before he spoke.

'You've caused me a lot of trouble, Madison,' he said slowly.

I glared back at him. Inside I was terrified, but I didn't want him to see. I wondered if Wolf's dad was nearby . . . if Wolf himself knew where we were . . .

Across the room, Jam clenched his fists. He put his arm round Lauren. She was wiping her eyes, struggling to her feet.

So long as I had them with me I was strong. I met Baxter's gaze.

'What have you done with the baby?' I demanded.

Baxter raised his eyebrows. 'You heard me earlier – an eye for an eye. You took Natalia and her baby from me. So I'm taking your sister's baby from you.'

Lauren let out a soft, low moan. For a second my resolution faltered. And then I knew what I had to do.

'You can't keep a baby from its mother,' I said, keeping my sights fixed on Baxter's mean eyes. I took a deep breath. 'Let them go. Take me instead.'

34

Trapped

'No!' Lauren and Jam spoke together.

Baxter looked at me, a sardonic smile curling round his lips.

'You are of no use to me, Madison. As I already told you, you've caused me a great deal of trouble.'

'I'm just trying to protect my family,' I insisted. I could feel Jam and Lauren behind me. For a second I felt the weirdness of what I was saying – always, all my life it seemed, it had been Jam and Lauren looking after me. And now, here I was, desperate to save them. 'You can't take their baby,' I said. 'It's wrong. Just like it was wrong to take Natalia's baby – and all those other girls'.'

Baxter shook his head. 'I had a contract with those girls. They agreed. I was paying them money.'

From what Natalia had told me, I knew this was true. Then I thought about how Ellie hadn't seemed real to me until she was in my arms, and how desperately I had loved her as soon as she was. It didn't matter what people agreed before their child was born. It was just plain wrong to tear any baby away from its mother.

'OK, so they agreed to give up their babies for money,' I said. 'Money they desperately needed. But they changed their minds – at least some of them did. Natalia definitely did. And there was another girl.' I thought rapidly back to what Natalia had told me. 'A girl called Lana. But you wouldn't listen. You—'

'Oh, do be quiet,' Baxter interrupted. 'You don't know what you're talking about, Madison. Those girls entered into a straightforward and legal contract with me. OK, so a little extra money exchanged hands under the table. That's me *looking after* the girls, not exploiting them. Unlike *you* . . .' He glared at me. 'You came into my home under false pretences. You made my daughter think you wanted to be friends with her, when all along you were spying for that weasel, Allan Faraday.'

I could feel Jam and Lauren both staring at me, but I kept my eyes on Baxter. 'Allan was *investigating* you,' I said. 'I was just helping him.'

'Right.' Baxter snorted. 'You and Faraday were just *investigating* me – which justified stealing from me and lying to my daughter – but *I'm* somehow the bad guy? Don't you understand? I'm not any kind of villain in this.'

'Yes, you are,' Jam said, his voice shaking with fury. 'Whatever happened in the past, you still took our baby.'

Baxter turned his steely gaze on Jam. 'I had a customer – a childless woman – lined up for Natalia's baby. What d'you want me to tell her? That after months of waiting and hoping, there *is* no baby?'

'It's still not right to take ours,' Jam insisted. Beside him, Lauren's mouth trembled. Tears trickled down her face.

253

'You don't have a choice about it.' Baxter spoke with an air of finality. 'As I already told Madison, it's "an eye for an eye". She *owes* me. And don't think there's any way out of this – I've been one step ahead of you all the way.'

'You mean the hidden mike?' I said.

'And the door to the hut.' Baxter laughed – a dry, ironic chuckle. 'You and that stupid boy didn't think you'd actually worked out the code, did you? We were listening to everything the pair of you said. I opened the door remotely.'

I bit my lip, remembering Wolf trying out various Baxter family birthdates. Jeez, he'd pointed out the number 3 on the keypad had been more worn than the others, yet the number that apparently opened the door didn't feature a 3. I should have seen the whole thing was a trap right then.

'Anyway, I'm afraid I can't let any of you go now,' Baxter went on. 'It was just supposed to be your sister and her baby. I was planning that Lauren would meet with an accident . . .' Beside me, Jam clenched his fists. 'But now you've dragged the baby's father into it too, not to mention young Wolf.'

I stared at him. He was talking as if Wolf was part of the forces ranged against him. Did he really mean that? Or was everything he said about Wolf just a bluff? I couldn't be sure; I just knew that I desperately wanted Wolf to be on our side.

'Wolf will go to the police,' I said defiantly.

Baxter shook his head. 'My men will catch up with him long before he can do that.'

My heart leaped. If Baxter was telling the truth and Wolf was loyal to us, at least he hadn't been captured yet. I focused

254

on Baxter again. 'There are other people who know what you're doing,' I said.

'You mean Allan Faraday?' Baxter raised his eyebrows contemptuously. 'I don't know how you came into contact with that man, but whatever he thinks he knows about me, he has no proof. That's what you haven't yet realised, Madison. I don't leave a trail. And I always get what I want. You mentioned Lana earlier. She was Miriam 20. She tried to defy me too, but in the end she paid the ultimate price *and* I took her baby.'

I gasped. *The ultimate price.* Baxter meant that he had killed her. And now he was planning on killing us.

Baxter smiled nastily at the look of horror on my face. Then he turned and walked out, locking the door after him.

Lauren sank back to the floor. She put her head in her hands. 'He's really doing it . . . he's really taking Ellie away,' she breathed. She wasn't crying, but her agonised whisper was worse than tears.

'We're not going to let that happen,' Jam said, sitting down beside her. 'We're going to save ourselves so we can save her.'

'Yes,' I agreed. But as I looked around the bare attic room, I could see no way that we could prevent Baxter from selling Ellie to another family – or from killing the three of us whenever he chose. And from what he'd said about Lauren, I was sure he'd make our deaths look like an accident.

The next hour passed unbearably slowly. Lauren told Jam the whole story of Ellie's birth – how she'd had pains all day, but hadn't thought they were contractions until near the end, when the baby had come so suddenly.

'Like she knew it was time – and wasn't prepared to wait any longer,' Lauren said. She turned to me. Jam followed her gaze. 'Mo was amazing,' she said, explaining how I'd sat with her, encouraging her, helping . . . 'I honestly don't think I could have done it without her.'

'Thank you, Mo.' Jam looked up at me, his eyes glistening. 'I can't tell you how much that means to me . . . that Lauren wasn't totally alone . . .'

I shrugged, feeling embarrassed. 'I didn't have a clue what I was doing,' I said.

'But you did it anyway,' Jam said firmly. '*That's* the point.' He pulled me and Lauren into a hug then the two of them sat back, talking in low voices for a while.

I wandered across the room. Had I been brave? It hadn't felt like it. I'd just done what, surely, anyone would have done in the circumstances. Anyway, it had all ended in disaster. If I hadn't got involved with Allan Faraday and tried to help Natalia, Lauren and Jam and their baby would be safe right now.

My mind drifted to Wolf. Now I had time to think, I couldn't believe he had really betrayed us. Baxter had referred to him as 'that stupid boy' earlier and said his men would soon catch up with him. Surely that couldn't be part of a cover story? No. It didn't add up. Wolf had helped get me to Appleton Cross. That couldn't have been in Baxter's plan. If Baxter had wanted me down in that basement prison, he'd have kidnapped me along with Lauren, wouldn't he?

My thoughts skittered about, one minute convinced of Wolf's innocence, the next wondering if he was guilty after all. His dad did own the Appleton Cross house. And then there was the hidden microphone. In the time between Baxter finding out I was responsible for rescuing Natalia and her baby and my arrival at Appleton Cross, the only people who could possibly have placed a tiny pin microphone on my top were Annie – who clearly hadn't done it, and who was probably worried sick about where I was right now – and Wolf. He'd come to my house with Esme, pretending to want to make up with me and . . .

Esme.

Wolf wasn't the only person who'd been close enough to me earlier to hide a microphone on my clothing. Esme had been there too. She'd been the one, in fact, who'd insisted on coming round in person to visit. I remembered the goodbye hug she had given me. Plenty of opportunity for her to put the mike on my collar.

Of course. Her father must have got her to plant the microphone on me after he'd made that threatening phone call. In fact, Esme could easily have given him my phone number *and* told him that I had a sister.

Would she really have done all that?

I thought of how I had lied to her, taking advantage of our newfound friendship to find out about Baxter's illegal operations. I hadn't *meant* to use Esme, but Baxter would, no doubt, have said that I had, making me out to be calculating, cruel and manipulative, presenting my actions in the worst possible light.

In which case it was no wonder Esme had betrayed me.

I groaned, letting my head sink into my hands.

'What's the matter, Mo?' Lauren asked. I looked up. Her face was drained of all colour and there were dark shadows under her eyes. I had never seen her look so pale or so drawn.

Jam was gazing at her, his face creased with concern.

I shook my head. 'Nothing.' They didn't need to hear my anxieties about Wolf and Esme.

'How's your eyesight?' I asked Jam. 'Less blurry?'

'Much better, thanks,' he said. He looked around the bleak attic room. 'Any thoughts on how we get out of here?'

'D'you think Wolf will have gone to the police?' Lauren asked anxiously.

'I don't know,' I said. 'But Allan must have called them by now so—'

'Allan Faraday?' Lauren's head shot up.

I nodded. 'He called me while you were climbing out of that chute,' I explained. 'He said he wanted to help.'

Lauren rolled her eyes.

'I'm not saying he's any kind of superhero,' I said. 'You were right about him being a bit of a loser. But he knew . . . useful stuff about Baxter . . .' I told Jam and Lauren about the hidden mike then said, 'Allan *promised* he would call the police.'

'Do you think we can trust him?' Lauren asked.

'Even if we can, he doesn't know where Baxter has taken us,' Jam said. '*We* don't know.'

'I think we're by the sea,' I said. 'I could smell it earlier.'

'Me too,' Jam said.

'Sssh.' Lauren put her finger to her lips. 'What was that noise?'

Jam and I fell silent.

'I don't—' Jam stopped as a faint shuffling sound rose from outside the door.

I rushed over and tried to peer through the keyhole. It was an old-fashioned lock, nothing state-of-the-art like the electronic lock from the hut door. I couldn't make out anything on the other side. Was that because it was dark? Or because someone was standing there?

As I opened my mouth to speak, the distinct sound of a key sliding into the lock met my ears.

I took a step back away from the door. 'Someone's there,' I hissed.

Jam leaped to his feet. He balled his hands into fists. 'If there's only one, I'm taking him, gun or no gun.'

Lauren's eyes widened. The door opened . . . slowly, carefully . . .

A face peered into the room. It was Wolf.

He looked right at me – a powerful, meaningful look full of emotion that said better than words that he had not betrayed me.

Would *never* betray me.

My heart flipped over in my chest.

'Mo,' he said. 'Are you all right? Did they hurt you?'

I shook my head, too overwhelmed to speak. He was here. For us. For me.

Wolf glanced at Jam and Lauren, then back to me. 'Let's go,' he said. 'There's not much time.'

35

Fire Escape

I scurried to the door. Wolf pointed to the top of the narrow steps we had climbed up earlier.

'Down there,' he mouthed. 'Follow me.'

'Wait a sec,' Jam whispered suspiciously, pulling him back into the attic room. 'How do we know this isn't another trap? Why didn't you just call the police?'

Wolf put his finger to his lips. 'Sssh, my phone fell out of my pocket when I was running through the woods so I couldn't call anyone, but I knew that even if I got through to the police, they wouldn't know where Baxter's men were going to take you so I got into the boot of their car.'

'You were already inside the car that they made *us* get into?' I asked.

'Yes,' Wolf whispered. 'Come on, let's go.'

'Wait.' Jam grabbed his arm again. 'So why didn't you fetch the police when you got here?'

'We're in the middle of nowhere,' Wolf hissed. 'There aren't any phones. Plus, I overheard Baxter talking to that Leather Jacket guy. They're going to kill you and dump your bodies way out to sea. They're just waiting for the boat. I heard them say it was almost here so I crept into the hall and

261

stole the key to this room from where they'd left it on a table. They could see that it's missing any second.'

Jam's face blanched. Lauren and I both gasped.

'Now come on, we have to hurry,' Wolf said.

Jam still looked sceptical.

'I trust Wolf,' I said, absolutely sure now that he was totally loyal. 'We should do what he says.'

'All right,' Jam said. 'If you trust him, Madison.'

Wolf squeezed my hand.

'What about the baby?' Lauren asked. 'D'you know where she is?'

Wolf shook his head. He led us down the narrow steps. We crept, single file, into a small corridor. Voices drifted up from the stairs at one end. Wolf turned and led us the other way, past a series of closed doors, to the fire door at the far end.

He pressed down on the bar, then lifted it gently up. It released with a metallic click. The four of us froze. I held my breath, listening to see if anyone had heard us. No, the voices downstairs rumbled on.

Wolf carefully pushed open the door. It scraped along the floor. Cold, sea air swept over us. Again, we all stood stock-still, listening hard in case anyone had heard. This time the voices stopped. A beat passed. My heart thudded loudly against my ribs.

Footsteps sounded across the hall below us. Then a male voice – not Baxter – called out.

'Boat will be here in five.' It was Leather Jacket. 'Tell Mr Baxter.'

262

There wasn't much time. I caught Wolf's eye. He pointed outside. It was totally dark beyond the house, the electric lights casting a murky glow just a few metres into the surrounding grass. I could hear the swish and sway of the sea in the near distance and a shiver of terror shot down my spine. I focused on the sight immediately in front of me: an iron fire escape that led down to the ground floor.

'Turn right when you get to the bottom of the steps,' Wolf whispered. 'Run away from the house as fast as you can. There's a shed about ten metres away. I saw it when I was sneaking in. The main road must be along from that.'

We crept down the fire escape, single file. Jam led the way, followed by Lauren, then me, with Wolf bringing up the rear. The wind whistled in my ears. None of us made a sound. As Jam reached the bottom step, a light went on at the ground-floor window right next to where he was standing. A yellow glow stretched out across the grass around us.

I shrank back into the shadows. Behind me, Wolf swore under his breath. If anyone looked out of the window, they'd be able to see us as soon as we stepped into the light. Despite the chill night air, sweat trickled down the back of my neck.

Jam came back up the steps. 'We'll be too easy to spot if we all go at the same time,' he whispered. 'Let's head for the shed, one by one. I'll go first and check it's safe.'

I peered into the gloom. I could just make out the outline of the shed Wolf had mentioned. It looked a long way away.

'Follow right after me.' Jam gave Lauren a quick squeeze of the hand, then raced off.

263

I held my breath. Was anyone watching from the window? Surely, any second, someone would realise we were gone. Then all hell would break loose. Lights would come on everywhere. Men would start shouting. I shivered as Jam disappeared out of sight and into the gloom behind the shed.

'He made it,' Lauren breathed. She turned to me. 'You run *right* behind me, Mo, OK?'

I nodded. Lauren set off. She didn't move as quickly as Jam. My heart was in my mouth as she ran past the window. Anyone looking out would definitely see her. She pushed herself on, into the darkness. She was safe.

'You next,' Wolf urged.

I nodded, bracing myself, ready to run.

And then two men appeared in the distance. It was Leather Jacket and the other man and they were heading in our direction.

I froze. We were hidden here, in the shadows, but if we stepped into the light, we would definitely be seen.

'Hurry up!' Baxter's distant shout filled the air. The two men broke into a jog. 'Get the jetty lights on!' Baxter yelled. 'I have to go in a few minutes and I want to know those kids are on board and away from here before I leave. Nothing's going to go wrong this time.'

I gasped. Wolf had been right: Baxter was planning on killing us and dumping our bodies at sea. Leather Jacket and the other man sped up. They were heading straight for us.

Wolf drew me back so we were pressed right against the

rough, cold brick wall behind. I prayed the shadows from the house were dark enough to swallow us up. Wolf pulled me closer. His heart beat wildly against my back.

The two men charged past. We stood like statues, waiting to make sure no-one else was coming. Silence. The sea wind roared around us. I peered into the darkness opposite. At least Jam and Lauren had made it to the shed.

'Come on.' Wolf took my hand, ready to lead me across the grass so we could join them.

And then a thin wail emerged from the house. Faint but instantly recognisable. I turned towards the sound. It came again.

'That's Ellie,' I said. 'That's the baby.'

Wolf met my eyes. I gritted my teeth.

'I have to go back,' I said. 'I have to save her.'

36

Into the Woods

'What?' A look of desperation crossed Wolf's face.

'I *have* to find her,' I said. 'You heard Baxter. He's leaving in a minute, once he's made sure we're on the boat. He'll be taking Ellie with him.'

Wolf's eyes hardened with determination. 'OK,' he said. 'OK.'

We crept up the fire escape. Lauren and Jam would be waiting for us by the shed, wondering why we didn't come. I was sure they couldn't have heard the baby's cry from where they were hiding – it had sounded faint even to me. We reached the fire door leading back to the first-floor corridor. The house felt quiet and still. It was furnished in a really old-fashioned style, with carpets everywhere and patterned wallpaper. Completely different from Baxter's home in London and the Appleton Cross house.

I strained my ears, wondering where Ellie's cry had come from. It was impossible to tell. My thoughts darted back to Jam and Lauren. Hopefully they would find the main road, get to a phone and call the police. Help would come soon, wouldn't it? And I *must* find the baby. I *had* to stop Baxter from leaving with her.

But where was she?

Wolf beckoned me down the corridor. We tiptoed along, pausing outside every door to see if we could hear Ellie's cry again, but there was no sound other than the distant *whoosh* of the wind and the sea. We reached the stairs. I tried to work out how many men Baxter had with him. We'd seen Leather Jacket and one other man running down to the jetty. Who else was left in the house? Maybe it was just Baxter himself.

Another faint cry echoed up towards us. It sounded like the baby was on the ground floor. We crept on, down the stairs. I was trying to make as little sound as possible, taking small, shallow breaths and staying as light on my feet as I could. We reached the ground floor hallway. Lights seeped out from under the doors on both sides. I hesitated. Wolf leaned forward and whispered in my ear.

'Which way?'

I shook my head. I had no idea. My heart was racing and my palms sweating. We were totally exposed, standing in this hall-way. Baxter or one of his men could come through any second. It was impossible to tell which direction the baby's cry had come from – or where she was now. A shiver wriggled down my spine. *Come on, Madison.* We had to move . . . do something . . .

'That way.' I pointed to the door to our left.

Wolf crept to the door. He leaned his head against the wood, listening for sounds from inside. 'I can't hear anything,' he mouthed.

Nodding, I twisted the handle. It felt cold in my clammy hands. I pushed open the door. The room inside was a living

267

room complete with sofas, a large-screen TV and a big brick fireplace. It was empty, though there were signs that people had been in here not long ago – smoke wreathed into the air from the cigarette stub in the ashtray on the coffee table. Several empty glasses were scattered around it.

A set of glass French doors opened out onto a patio. I'd lost all sense of where we were in the building. The fire escape had definitely led down to the side of the house. Where did the doors from this room open out?

Wolf rushed silently over to the doors. The key was in the lock. He turned it and opened it slightly.

'We can get out of the house through here, if we have to,' he whispered.

'OK,' I mouthed.

We crept back to the living-room door. The door to the room across the hall was still shut. There was no sign of anyone about and no sound either.

'Maybe they've gone already,' Wolf whispered.

I shook my head. Baxter had said he was about to leave – but also that he wanted to make sure we were loaded onto the boat at the jetty first. He was surely still in the house – which meant Ellie was too.

I reached for the door. The light was on inside. Footsteps sounded across the room. They stopped. We could hear drawers being opened and shut, then a door closing with a bang. Silence.

What was going on in there now? Had whoever was inside left the room? There was no way of knowing. I took a deep breath and opened the door. It was a kitchen. Declan Baxter was standing behind a large table on the other side of the room. And there, on the countertop just to our right, was Ellie. Tiny and crumpled inside a baby car seat, I could see at a glance she was sleeping and covered with a blanket.

Baxter's jaw dropped as he saw us.

'You!' he shouted.

For a second, we stared at each other. Then Baxter took a step forwards. *Wham.* In his haste to reach me, he'd barged into the table in front of him. As he let out a yell of pain, I darted to the counter, grabbed the car seat by its handle and raced out of the room. Wolf was ahead of me. He pounded across the hall and through the living room.

'Come back here!' Baxter shouted after us.

Wolf flung open the French doors. I rushed outside after him, still holding the car seat by the handle. The cold wind slapped at my face. The sea sounded louder than ever. Wolf charged across the patio, onto the grass beyond.

I could hear Baxter running after us. 'Stop them!' He was yelling for his men. They would surely hear him and come straight up from the jetty, wherever that was.

My arm ached from the effort of holding the car seat steady. Panting for breath, I ran on, peering into the darkness ahead. Where was the hut Lauren and Jam had hidden behind? We had obviously exited the building at a completely different place.

Were those trees ahead? *Yes.* Wolf had reached them. He darted into the darkness, his outline swallowed up by the shadows of the swaying branches. I glanced over my shoulder. Baxter was still charging after us, just a few metres behind. I reached the trees. As I thundered onto the soft, damp earth, the wind roared furiously around my head. Wolf appeared from nowhere. He grabbed my free arm.

'Come on,' he rasped, his voice hoarse from the wind and the running.

I tore after him, still trying to keep the car seat from swinging too wildly. Wolf darted between the trees, pulling me behind him. The branches above our heads swayed violently, almost drowning out the terrifying roar of the sea. We ran deeper into the undergrowth. The night air was cold. It smelled of damp earth.

We reached the far edge of the trees. Wolf stopped. He glanced anxiously around, panting for breath. I set Ellie down in her car seat, then squatted down to check she was OK. She was still, miraculously, fast asleep. I touched her cheek gently. It was cold. I felt lower. The part of her face under the blanket was relatively warm, but she was only a few hours old – she shouldn't be exposed to this wind at all.

As I fiddled with the car seat harness, Wolf squatted down beside me.

'Is she all right?' he asked.

'I think so.' I released the harness and took Ellie out. 'Did we lose Baxter?'

'Dunno.' Wolf stood up and peered into the trees.

I wrapped Ellie tightly in the blanket. She was still asleep, her tiny body all floppy. I held her close to my chest, as Lauren had earlier, and she nuzzled into me.

'Sssh,' I murmured, though she wasn't making any noise. 'It's going to be OK.'

As I stood up, footsteps sounded close by. It was impossible to tell what direction they were coming from. Wolf laid his hand on my arm. I looked up, into his eyes.

'Madison?' Baxter's voice echoed through the trees. He sounded close. 'You're being stupid. You can't stop me taking the baby. You're just putting your sister and her boyfriend at risk.'

I gulped. Had Baxter found Jam and Lauren? Were they OK? Wolf bent his head down. His lips brushed my ear.

'Look after the baby, I'll distract him,' he whispered.

'Madison?' Baxter called again. The wind was carrying his voice so strongly it seemed to sweep through the trees from all directions. I looked around, desperate to work out where the sound was coming from.

'The hut and the road beyond are over there.' Wolf pointed through the trees to the left.

I stared at him. How on earth did he know that? I had lost all sense of where I was in relation to the house, let alone the hut.

'Straight through the trees?' I whispered.

'No.' Wolf made a zigzag motion with his hand. 'You have to head left at first, then more to the right when you reach the edge of the trees.'

'Madison?' Baxter yelled again. 'There's no way out of here. Come back, be sensible. You're putting the baby at risk being out in this cold air.'

I looked at Wolf again. I badly wanted to hand everything over to him, to let him be responsible for dealing with Baxter. But that wasn't right. I had got us into this situation, it was up to me to get us out of it.

'It's me Baxter wants; he doesn't even know you're here,' I whispered. '*I'll* cause the distraction. You get the baby over to the hut. Find the others. Fetch the police.'

'No—'

But before Wolf could say any more, I pushed Ellie into his arms.

'You know the way,' I whispered. I reached over and tucked a stray scrap of blanket over her fragile body. 'Keep her warm. Keep her safe.'

And without looking at him again, I turned, picked up the empty baby car seat and ran out of the woods.

37

Deep Water

I raced hard across the grass. It sloped sharply down, the momentum making me run faster until I was almost flying downhill into the darkness. Wind whipped through my hair, chilling my skin. The empty car seat banged against my legs. I wanted to drop it, but then Baxter would know Ellie wasn't inside. The sea roared angrily in the distance.

I tried to slow myself. No point me running if Baxter wasn't following. The whole point was to draw his attention . . . to make sure Wolf had plenty of time to get away with little Ellie.

I glanced over my shoulder. Was Baxter there? Yes. He was running down the hill towards me. I could just make out his outline in the dim light from the house. I turned round and raced on. The slope was levelling out, but the land beyond was pitch black. Surely, if there were houses or other buildings there would be some light. I glanced to the left and the right. The same total darkness.

It suddenly hit me. That blanket of dark was the sea. And it surrounded me on all sides. I slowed right down. The wind was even fiercer here than it had been up in the woods. Another few steps and I saw the water.

Jeez, I'd run in absolutely the worst direction possible. I scanned the horizon. I was on a cliff top that jutted out over the sea. Baxter was heading straight for me, effectively cutting me off from the land on either side that led back to the wooded area on my left and the house on my right.

I glanced down at the waves, feeling my old terror of the ocean rise inside me. Yells echoed faintly up from the jetty far below. It was about fifty metres away, a short wooden platform lit by a string of lights jutting several metres into the sea. Leather Jacket and the other man were down there, watching a boat approaching fast, its front light flickering above the choppy waves. Immediately beneath me, the rock face ran sheer, straight down to the sea beneath. Powerful waves slapped against the side of the cliff. I watched, mesmerised, as the suck and drag of the tide pulled them back before hurling them at the rock again.

I looked up. Baxter was almost here. There was no way in the world I'd be able to dodge round him. He ran closer . . . closer . . . I froze, paralysed with fear. The car seat was still in my hand. I looked down, checking the back was facing Baxter. He mustn't realise Ellie wasn't inside. I *had* to give Wolf every chance to keep her safe.

Baxter stopped, two metres in front of me. He bent over, clutching his side and panting for breath. I couldn't move. I gripped the car seat.

Think, Madison. Wolf only needs a bit more time. All you have to do is delay Baxter – just for a few minutes.

Baxter straightened up. 'Give me the baby, Madison,' he said sharply. 'This has gone on long enough.'

'No.' I moved the car seat slightly behind me, checking again to make sure that Baxter couldn't see it was empty.

'A newborn baby should *not* be out in this wind,' Baxter snapped. 'Tiny infants can't control their body temperature very well. You're putting her at risk.'

'*You* put her at risk by taking her away from her mother.'

Baxter growled with impatience. Down below us, far to our right, the boat was drawing closer to the jetty.

'Give me the baby,' Baxter repeated. 'Give her up and I'll let you go.'

I shook my head. No way did Baxter have any intention of letting me go.

'You're going to kill me,' I said. '*And* the others. That's what the boat is for. You're going to take us out to sea and kill us and dump the bodies in the water.'

Baxter said nothing, but he took a step towards me. I took a step back. I glanced over my shoulder. I was really near the edge now. One more step and I'd be over the cliff.

'I'm not letting you take her,' I said.

Baxter raised his arm. I caught the faint metallic glint of the gun in his hand. My legs trembled.

'I'm not giving you a choice,' Baxter said.

I took a small step backwards. The earth at my feet crumbled, giving way under my heels. My head spun at the thought of the dark, cold water below.

Baxter was going to shoot me. He was going to take the car seat, realise the baby wasn't inside, and put all his efforts into finding her.

I had no proper idea how much time had passed since I'd left her with Wolf, but it was certainly no more than a minute or so. Not nearly enough time for Wolf to get Ellie to Jam and Lauren and make sure they were all safely away from here.

'Madison, *now*.' Baxter cocked his gun. 'Put the car seat down.'

I gulped. A light spray rose up from the water below, salty and damp against my face. And I knew what I had to do.

Baxter pointed the gun straight at me. 'I'm going to count to three.'

I looked down at the curling crests of the waves. Blood thundered in my ears, louder than the sea. If there were rocks down there, the waves would be whiter, wouldn't they? Unless the rocks were lurking just underneath the water.

'One,' Baxter spat.

My whole body tensed. If I didn't risk the rocks and the sea, I would die up here anyway. And Baxter would discover immediately that Ellie wasn't with me.

'Two.'

I steadied myself, trying to psych myself up for what I had to do. A memory flashed into my mind's eye from when I was eight and Jam and Lauren had saved me from drowning.

They weren't here to save me now.

'Three.'

I was out of time. It was jump or die.

I turned and, still gripping hold of the car seat, I hurled myself off the cliff top.

38

Finding Me

For a few seconds, time seemed to slow down. I was aware of the cold air slicing at my face and arms as I fell, of the salt sea smell, of the sound of Baxter's roar above me and of the slap of the sea against the rock face below.

The car seat I'd been holding on to so tightly was ripped out of my hand by the wind. I opened my mouth to scream. And then the icy water hit me. The shock of it took my breath away. All my senses seemed to dissolve into the feel of the sea on my skin – so cold it burned. I sank like a stone, the water rushing over my head. I couldn't breathe. Panicking, I flailed in the darkness. My hand hit something hard. A rock. It stung, but I wasn't connected to the pain. I was fighting, fighting the water, fighting the fear that consumed me, clawing, desperate to find air. I had no idea which way was up. Currents pulled at my arms and legs. In my mind I was a little girl again, struggling to keep my head above the water, losing all feeling in my body, hearing the terror in Lauren's voice. Knowing I was drowning . . . that I was going to die . . .

My head burst through the waves. I sucked in the salty air, gasping for breath. My eyes strained into the darkness. I could just make out the rock face in front of me – sheer and high and dark. The jetty lights twinkled an impossible distance away. I could see the boat moored there too, the boat Baxter had brought to take us and kill us in. I pulled desperately at the water, trying to head towards the beach between the jetty and the cliff, but the current was too powerful. Panic spiralled up inside me. Why did it have to be the sea? It was the monster that had always lurked in my dreams. While other kids feared the shadows under their bed, I would close my eyes and hear the creaking of a boat, the suffocating water closing over my head. Not being able to breathe. My worst nightmare.

I clawed at the water again. My hands were numb with cold. I forced my head above the waves. I had to swim to the beach. But I wasn't strong enough. The current was more powerful. As I pulled at the water, trying to head for the shore, the tide sucked me out again. The sea all around was dark and vast. I shrivelled inside myself, suddenly aware of how tiny I was, how helpless against this force of nature. Waves crashed inside my head. Always before there had been Lauren. Strong and fearless, her voice had given me hope. And Jam . . . Jam had saved us both.

But now I was totally alone. The current was too strong: it was pulling me away from them, from Annie, from my whole life.

From Wolf.

As I thought his name, I heard his voice.

'Madison!' Was I imagining it? I turned my head, spitting seawater from my lips, shivering with cold and fear. Where was the sound coming from?

There. He was running towards me from the jetty, along the rocky beach. The jetty lights were just bright enough to show his outline, dark against the stones on the beach. How far away was the shore? Ten metres at least.

Wolf reached the bottom of the high cliff from which I'd jumped. He stopped running and waved his arms. 'Madison!'

I tried to raise my arm out of the water, but I was too weak.

'Madison! Swim!' His yell was faint over the waves.

I wanted to shout back that I could barely move. That I'd never been a strong swimmer. That the sea was beating me. But no sound came from my mouth. I tried to do what he said. I pulled with my arms and kicked with my legs. Wolf was still on the beach, as close to me as he could get. He called my name again.

I fought to get nearer. But every pull of my arms seemed to take me back out to sea. It was hopeless. I looked towards Wolf again, hoping the sight of him would help, that I would find I was closer to shore than I thought, but Wolf was no longer there. I looked all along the beach. He had vanished.

Where had he gone? Crushing misery threatened to overwhelm me. Had I imagined him? Or had he gone to get help? It didn't matter. Without his voice urging me on, I wasn't going to make it to the shore.

Except I *had* to. For him. For Lauren. For Annie. For my beautiful new baby niece. I kicked and pulled. I wouldn't give up. My movements grew slower. Weaker. I was exhausted. I lost all sense of time and place. The water was rising, covering most of my face. I swallowed a gulp of brine. Spat it out. I wanted to cry, but I didn't have the energy. My limbs felt like they were made of cotton wool.

Something grabbed my arm. A hand. Strong and warm, I felt the power behind it. Wolf was in the water beside me.

'Come *on!*' he yelled over the wind. '*Swim!*'

He was here. Hope surged inside me. I kicked with my legs, trying to force myself on. Wolf pulled me after him, strong in the water. One stroke. Two.

'Put your feet down,' he ordered.

I did as he said. To my amazement, my feet touched the rocky seabed straight away. I stood. The water was only up to my chest. Wolf pushed me forwards, holding me round the waist with one hand, clawing through the waves with the other. The rocky beach he had called to me from was in sight. Closer and closer.

The water was up to my waist, then my thighs. A second later, Wolf stood too. He held me tight, propelling me on. The water was only at my knees. My legs were shaking. I couldn't walk. Wolf drew me even closer.

'Nearly there,' he gasped.

We reached the beach. Over the rocks. I staggered on, leaning against him. We stumbled across the slippery rock to the shingle beyond. The wind dropped slightly as we reached the shore. I sank to my knees, unable to stand any longer. Wolf fell beside me. We held each other.

And then Wolf drew back. He pushed my wet hair off my face. I was shivering uncontrollably. He stood, ran across the beach. A moment later, he was back, his jacket in his hands. It was dry.

'Put this on,' he said, draping the jacket over my shoulders.

I sank into it, grateful for its warmth. 'Thank you,' I breathed.

'You were almost here,' Wolf said, fastening the jacket round me at the front. 'You'd almost made it. I just came in to help you with the final bit.' His teeth were chattering.

'Where's the baby?' I said.

'Safe,' he said. 'With Lauren and Jam.'

I glanced over at the jetty. Men were charging over the wooden boards. I peered more closely. I could see at least five of them. Surely there had only been two before.

'Did those men come off the boat?' I said, tensing again. 'Shouldn't we hide?'

Wolf followed my gaze. Under the jetty lights I could just make out the word 'police' on the men's dark jackets. One of the policemen handcuffed Leather Jacket. He marched him off the jetty and out of sight, up towards the house.

Relief flooded through me.

'N . . . no need to hide,' Wolf said, his voice all jerky from the cold. 'That's the police.'

'You called them?' I asked.

'Not me.' Wolf shook his head. 'I just gave the baby to Lauren then came to find you.'

We stood up and made our way to the jetty. The wind still whistled around us and the sea still roared, but I was warmer now, inside Wolf's jacket and with his arm round me.

281

'What happened to Baxter?' I asked.

'I saw him running to the house as I was coming down here,' Wolf said. 'How did you end up in the water? Did he push you over the cliff?'

'Not exactly.' I told Wolf what had happened. As I finished, we reached the jetty. I could hear Lauren before I saw her.

'She's my *sister*,' she was shrieking. 'If she wasn't with Baxter, she *must* be here.'

'Lauren!' I tried to call out, but all that came out was a soft croak. Wolf helped me up, onto the jetty. My legs still felt weak and I was suddenly aware of a throbbing pain in my hand, where it had banged against the rock under the water. I caught sight of Lauren further along the jetty, just past a couple of uniformed officers. She was gesticulating wildly as she spoke, though the wind was carrying her actual words away from me. I stumbled across the jetty towards her. She saw me and broke into a hobbling run, clutching her belly.

We reached each other. Lauren threw her arms round me. 'Oh,' she wept. 'Mo, I thought you were dead.'

We hugged. Lauren was holding me so tightly I could hardly breathe.

'I couldn't bear to lose you,' she whispered. 'You know that, Mo. Don't you? You know how much I love you? You're as precious to me as Jam and Ellie.'

'I know,' I said. 'I love you too.'

Despite the chill of the night air pressing my wet clothes

282

against my skin, a warmth spread through me. A memory of how jealous I'd once felt about the baby flashed through my head. I'd been so wrong about that. Ellie's arrival didn't push me out of the picture at all. If anything, Jam and Lauren and I were closer than ever.

One of the police officers ran over to us. He gently prised me away from Lauren.

'Are you all right?' he asked me.

I nodded. 'Where's the baby?'

'She's fine. She's up by the house with Jam.' Lauren looked down at my hand. 'Oh, you're hurt, Mo.'

I held it up. Even in the dim jetty lights it was clearly red and swollen.

'We have ambulances on their way for Lauren here and the baby,' the office explained. 'I'll take you up to the house. As soon as the paramedics arrive, we'll have them check you out and get you warmed up.'

I looked around for Wolf. He was hanging back, watching us and shivering with cold.

'Wolf too,' I said. 'He came into the water to help get me out. I wouldn't have made it without him.'

Lauren reached out and touched his arm. 'Thank you,' she said.

The police officer helped us up the hill to the house. As we walked, I learned that Declan Baxter had been arrested as he tried to leave the premises, and so had the men on the jetty and in the boat.

'Who called you?' I asked.

'The call came through a 999 alert,' the police officer said. 'An Allan Faraday. How do you know him?'

I met Lauren's gaze. She squeezed my arm.

'He's our birth father,' she said. 'Our dad.'

39

The Future

The next hour or two passed in a blur. Two ambulances arrived and Lauren, baby Ellie and I travelled in one of them to a nearby hospital. We were all examined and pronounced remarkably healthy considering the ordeal we'd just been through. My hand was badly bruised, but no bones were broken. After my X-ray, I was taken into a separate cubicle where a nurse bandaged me up. Moments later, Annie arrived. She wept as we hugged.

'I'm fine,' I said, pulling away and squeezing her arm. 'Seriously.'

Annie nodded, her hands fluttering to her chest. To my surprise, the gesture no longer annoyed me. I was just glad to see her.

'But what happened?' she kept saying.

I explained everything, then we wandered along the ward to Lauren's cubicle. She was lying on the bed, Ellie nestling against her chest. Jam sat on one side of her bed, Lauren's adoptive mum and dad stood on the other. As Annie and I walked in, everyone started talking and crying – and then cooing over the baby. I picked her up properly. It was a bit scary at first, holding her in my arms with everyone watching. But after a few minutes, it felt totally natural.

After an hour or so, Allan Faraday turned up. He hung back, until I rushed over and hugged him and drew him into the room. It was weird seeing him shaking hands with Annie and weirder still watching as he and Lauren introduced themselves to each other.

'Wow, I can't believe I'm a grandfather,' Allan kept saying.

I laughed at the look of shock on his face. It was funny. I knew now that Allan was never going to feel like a proper dad – or be the hero I'd wanted him to be. It didn't matter. I would still rather he was in my life than not in it. For all his failings, he'd been loyal when it counted. And he had, effectively, saved our lives: it was his call to the police, urging them to investigate Declan Baxter's properties, that led them to the cliff top house. He told us that the police had not only arrested Baxter himself, but were in the process of raiding his London home. 'They're going to find details on all the *Miriam Project* girls,' Allan said.

I nodded. That was good. It was right that Baxter should be held to account for everything he had done. Not just kidnapping Lauren and the rest of us, but also manipulating the *Miriam* girls, and killing Natalia's friend Lana. I felt sorry for Esme, caught up in the whole thing. But there was nothing I could do for her. Sometimes life just doesn't allow for a totally happy ending.

After a while, I took Allan to one side.

'We need to talk,' I said.

'I know.' Allan's face reddened. 'I'm so sorry I didn't

explain properly about my work,' he stammered. 'You must think I'm such an idiot.'

I shook my head. 'It's not that,' I said. 'I was wondering if we could offer *The Examiner* an exclusive article on Baxter's attempt to take Lauren's baby. Matthew Flint gave me his card and said I should call if I got a good lead. And . . .' I hesitated, trying to work out exactly how I felt. 'It's important someone tells the truth,' I said.

'I think that's a wonderful idea,' Allan said. 'But it should be your story, Madison. I'll help, but it's your story.'

'Thank you.'

At that moment Annie came over and I found myself explaining the whole history of how I tracked Allan down. I'd expected she would be angry with me about that, but she wasn't.

'I'm just so glad you're safe,' she kept saying.

The nurse was warning us that all Lauren's visitors would have to leave in a few minutes, when Wolf came in with his parents. His father was grim-faced and seemed to exude annoyance, but his mum, who had the same hair and eyes as her son, smiled as they came over.

Wolf's dad ignored everyone else and held out his hand to me. 'Madison?' he said. 'I want you to know I had no idea Declan Baxter was still using the Appleton Cross property he sold me.'

'It's true,' Wolf said. 'He didn't.'

I shook his dad's hand, feeling awkward. I was aware of Annie and Lauren and everyone else watching us. Wolf was waiting and watching too, standing beside his parents. I glanced from him to his father. I believed Wolf's dad hadn't known about Baxter's illegal operation . . . but had he apologised to Wolf for ridiculing his suspicions earlier? Somehow I suspected not.

I caught Wolf's eye. He smiled – a soft, crooked smile.

My stomach cartwheeled. Oh, jeez. I suddenly realised just how awful it would be if I couldn't see him again . . . how much I wanted to . . .

'Are you all right?' Wolf's mum asked timidly. She seemed as shy as his dad was ferocious.

'Yes, I'm fine.' We smiled at each other and I knew that I was going to like her very much.

'No thanks to my son, I suppose,' his dad said. There was a sneering tone to his voice, which I recognised from when I'd met him before.

Annoyance flickered through me. 'Actually, your son saved my life,' I said. 'He swam out to get me when I was drowning. *And* he came into the house to set us free earlier. He could have just run off, saved himself. He was brave and you should be congratulating him, not acting like he's some stupid loser. I wouldn't be here without him. None of us would.'

I stopped, realising that I was now standing with my hands on my hips and that everyone in the room was staring at me. I shrank back slightly. Goodness, how had I dared to speak like that to Wolf's father? He peered down at me, his gaze at once puzzled and severe. I was guessing people didn't often stand up to him. I wished the ground would swallow me up.

Wolf's dad turned to his son. Wolf stared defiantly back at him.

'My son a hero?' I could still hear the sneer in Wolf's dad's voice, but this time it was edged with uncertainty. 'What d'you say to that, Wolf?'

Wolf cleared his throat and, when he spoke, it was without stammering. 'I guess it is true, all except the last bit. Madison didn't need me to save her. She's the bravest, strongest person I've ever met.'

I stared at him. How on earth could he think that?

'Madison helped Natalia, the girl whose baby Baxter was going to take,' Wolf went on. 'Even though she was in danger a lot of the time.'

'I just wanted to make sure she was OK,' I said. Surely Wolf could see I'd only done what anyone would do. 'I don't think that was brave.'

'Yes, it was,' Jam said. '*And* you went after Lauren all by yourself when no-one else believed she'd been kidnapped, even though I told you not to.'

'*And* you helped me give birth.' Lauren squeezed my hand. 'Which is a different kind of brave.'

'And you jumped off a cliff to give me time to get away with the baby,' Wolf added. 'So you see, Mo, we all think you're brave. Crazy, for sure . . .' he grinned, '. . . but definitely brave.'

I bit my lip. I was so used to seeing myself as Lauren's little sister and Annie's overprotected daughter, it was hard to accept what they were saying.

Jam smiled. He caught Lauren's eye. She nodded.

'Hey, Mo,' she said. 'There's one more thing you can do for us.'

'What's that?' I said.

'Be my bridesmaid when Jam and I get married.'

My eyes widened. I squealed. Annie and Lydia gasped.

'You're getting married?' I said.

'Jam just asked me,' Lauren said, beaming. She peered down at Ellie who was wrapped tightly in a blanket. 'And I said yes.'

'Wow,' I said. 'That's brilliant.'

'So will you do it, Mo?' Lauren asked.

I grinned. 'Try and stop me,' I said. 'Just don't make me wear a hideous dress.'

I glanced at Wolf and he smiled at me and I suddenly knew we were going to be together – at Lauren's wedding and beyond.

As the others all crowded round, wishing Jam and Lauren all the best for their marriage, it struck me that maybe what they said was true. In the past few days I had faced down my fears and taken risks.

Maybe I was braver than I thought I was.

Maybe I was ready at last to come out from behind Lauren's shadow, rise above my fears and take a risk on getting close to someone.

Maybe I was ready to be me.

SOPHIE McKENZIE

Sometimes the truth
can be dangerous . . .

SOPHIE McKENZIE

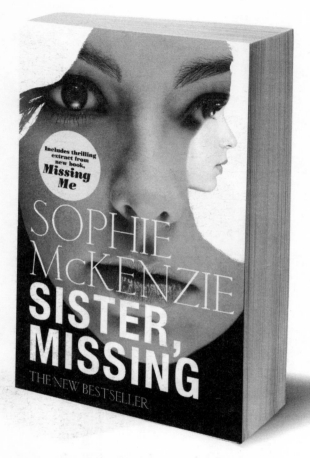

Can Lauren stop the nightmare
happening all over again?

SOPHIE McKENZIE

Could *you* be a clone?

"gripping, thought-provoking
and compulsive" *The Bookseller*

@ **sophiemckenzie_**
www.facebook.com/sophiemckenzieauthor
www.sophiemckenziebooks.com

SOPHIE McKENZIE

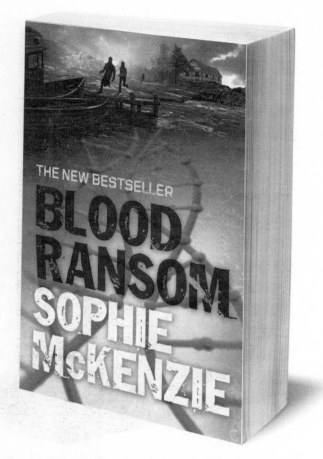

The sinister Aphrodite Experiment
is underway – will Rachel have to pay
the ultimate price?

SOPHIE McKENZIE

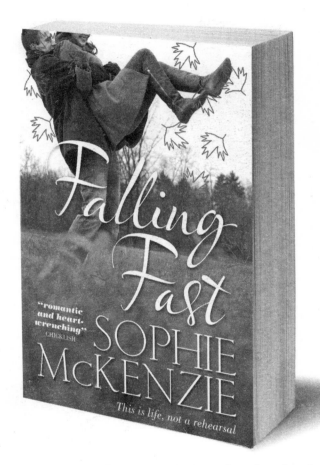

River is smitten by Flynn, who is playing
Romeo in the school play – but will he be
her romantic hero off-stage too?

@ sophiemckenzie_

www.facebook.com/sophiemckenzieauthor

www.sophiemckenziebooks.com

SOPHIE McKENZIE

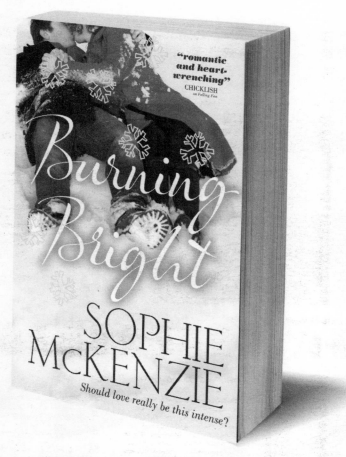

Will River and Flynn find
their happily-ever-after?